L. J. Black

Fear & Sand

L. J. Black

Fear & Sand

Copyright 2024 by L. J. Black
ISBN: 978-1-953240-24-8
All rights reserved.

The story, all names, characters, and incidents portrayed in this production are fictitious. No identification with actual persons (living or deceased), places, buildings, and products is intended or should be inferred.

Excerpt of "Frozen" by Breska Liotson used with permission.

Book Cover by Amanda Babcock using Canva

WORKS BY L. J. BLACK

Linguist
Plague of the Lost Ones

THE ANCHOR TRILOGY
Hope & Fire
Fear & Sand

THE POWERHOUSE SERIES
Altair
Lucy

ACKNOWLEDGEMENTS

A big thank you to my fellow BookTokers who have supported this journey in ways I never expected.

For J

For those who believe in spirits

THE WILDLANDS
THE DENT
UMBRA
THE WASTE
MATRAIZE
MATRAIZE
MATRAIZE
EGRARIA
LOEQUA
ATRUS
RESKAL
FALGAR SEA
AIROCK SEA
EGRIUM
EGRIUM
EPLYA
EGRIUM
EGRIUM
REBLUINIA
NAMORE
APRANA
GAEPIS
PLEASSAU

N
XATHEN DESERT
SMAUDAL
IOSNIA
PEPLEONA
SHIONIA
VERHILL
HUMSEA
NOTRIUM
FALGAR SEA
GLIUDOR
NOTRIUM
ASCAIN
OSTREIN
PLOU
PRIJA
THE SOUTHERN WASTE
LECRAIT
LECRAIT

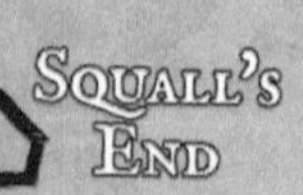

EGRARIA
SQUALL'S END
SHEPPORT
PORT NALRANG
KURRICH
KYNIS BEACH
RESKAL
TARNESTON
MUDLAND
BEACHMARSH
PROPORT
BOLTRIE BAY
ECRIUM

ESATON COVE
N
FALGAR SEA
BLACKEDGE
VROBRIDGE
INASLAND
BLACKGUARD
PRATERGARDE
REBLUINIA
MELGARDE

PORT NALRANG
TO SHEPPORT
UPPER EAST HERRON
TO ESATON COVE
SHEOCAG BAZAAR
FAWIALD YARD
WEST PREKROL
TROMMOL POINT
UPPER SOUTH SCAIHIAT
NALRANG BAY
NALRANG VILLAGE
PENSHAW
N
TO SNUSSAT POINT
FALGAR SEA

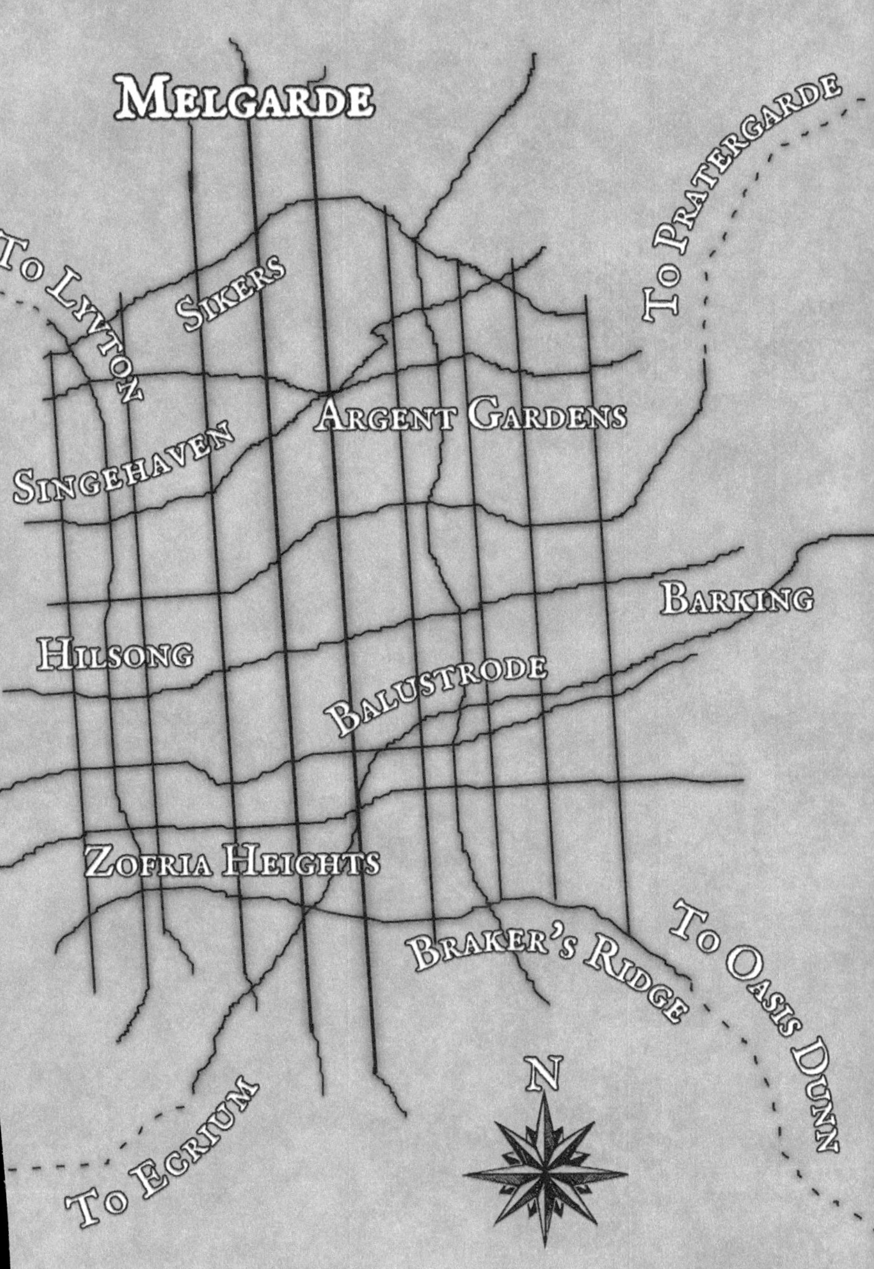

MELGARDE
TO LYYTON
SIKERS
TO PRATERGARDE
SINGEHAVEN
ARGENT GARDENS
BARKING
HILSONG
BALUSTRODE
ZOFRIA HEIGHTS
BRAKER'S RIDGE
TO OASIS DUNN
TO ECRIUM
N
NO MAN'S LAND

Fear & Sand

I don't connect anymore
With the things that used to awaken in me
The emotional response of tears or fears
Or love from which I fight to survive
The scars of memories still trace my mind
Lines of red across the dark sky
Fears that I'll never get back to who I was
Live in me and eat away at my peace of mind

— Breska Liotson, "Frozen"

Prologue

The fire consumes everything in its path. The buildings begin to buckle and crumble as the bricks turn to ash. Even the metal twists and breaks from the heat of the flames. Aidan Montgomery can do nothing more than watch in horror.

He did this. He is responsible for the fire.

The screams coming from the building fill his ears even over the sound of the flames and those fighting to put them out. Dread fills him as the sounds begin to diminish. He knows there will be casualties on this night. And he knows there is nothing he can do.

He is paralyzed with guilt.

Aidan wakes in a cold sweat, a sheen of moisture that evaporates almost immediately from his skin. He lays breathing heavily on his makeshift bed and stares at the stone ceiling of his cave dwelling. By now, Aidan has memorized the lines in the rock. He swallows, his mouth dry as usual, and rolls onto one side to stare outside. The opening of the mini cave he lives in shows the dim twilight of morning. The sun is starting to come up over the horizon.

He sits up on the slab of rock he uses to sleep. He has long since gotten used to sleeping on the hard surface and feels no discomfort anymore. In fact, he doubts he would be able to sleep comfortably on a mattress again. Sometimes he wonders if he will ever be able to rejoin society.

Outside the cave, a clump of holyoak tubers grows along the cliff face, providing Aidan with his main food source out here in the Waste. He gathers half a dozen tubers leaving a large growth behind. Holding the handful of plants, he looks east, in the direction of the Wastewalk. He is so far from it that he can't even make out a smudge on the horizon. He lets out a sigh that comes out as a wisp of smoke.

To the north, the wide expanse of sand fills his view. Somewhere over the dunes is the Dent in the planet, the deep ravine caused long ago by the passing planetoid that nearly destroyed all life before there were creatures to be called creatures. Some scientists speculate that the planetoid dragged along some microscopic life and seeded Yddril, the similarities in humans and Yddrilin too close to be coincidental. He is beyond wondering about academic problems like that though. Out here in this expanse of sand and loneliness, he finds himself focused only on the depths of his own predicament.

He heads to his cave.

Along the back wall, a small spring carves the alcove out of the cliff's greater rock. He takes the odd random pot he has and fills it with water. He relights the fire from the previous night and places the pot over the flames. After a few minutes, it begins to boil, and he adds the tubers to the pot. He has eaten the white starchy vegetables raw but prefers them boiled at least. He adds the tops of the plants to the water for seasoning. Aidan sits next to the fire and watches the Waste as he waits for the tubers to cook.

After an appropriate amount of time has passed, he lifts the pot from the fire and drinks down the boiling liquid. At one point, that would have bothered him, but now he drinks boiling water as if it is filled with ice.

As he eats the hot tubers, he reflects on how different he is as a person now. His elemental nature overtakes his humanity more often than he would like. And he wonders how long he has before he disappears to his power.

"Not long probably," he mumbles aloud.

His voice comes out in a croak, whether from the scalding water he just drank or just simple disuse he doesn't know. He doesn't feel pain from it but he suspects his voice will continue to worsen the more often he drinks like that. It's a bad habit he's developed since living alone has eroded all his manners.

Months have passed since he came here. He left the girls behind to find a way to calm the power within him. He loves them too much to put them in danger. A week before he left, he lost control and burned Elise pretty badly. They are fortunate to always be surrounded by healers, but it was enough to send him over the edge. A week later, he walked away from civilization. He took a horse and headed north, making his way to the Wastewalk where he left the horse and headed into the wild.

Now, here, on his own, he lives away from the dangers of people and spends his days using his powers to gain control. He knows he can't stay away from them forever. He knows he is not solitary enough to live like this forever. He knows he will eventually crave the company of his friends.

The tubers long gone, he cleans out the pot in the hot spring and sets it aside with the few belongings he has with him. He brought practically nothing into the Waste, just a change of clothes. He chose to live like this, in extreme poverty, avoiding the trappings of civilization for a time.

Done with breakfast, the sun coming up in full, he straightens up and walks out into the desert to train. He found a place when he first came here that has a slab of rock close to the surface of the sand. The more stable footing helps him focus more on what he is doing than where he is standing. He walks out into the middle of the scorched earth and begins to call up his power. Today, he is focusing on precision work, a single line of concentrated flames weaving into a complex loop. He discovered the deep concentration on something this precise helps his concentration on the bigger things. Today though, he would try something he had been thinking about but never dared to try. He was going to make glass.

Rather than stand and tire himself out, he sits cross-legged on the ground. The sand kicks up around him, the faint breeze starting this early in the morning. By noon, he would be huddled in his cave to avoid the potential dust storm. For now, the air is clear enough to endure.

Hours pass. His concentration improves, but he is fatigued. The energy pulled out of him to make fire is considerable. It fatigues his mind and soul.

He lays back in the sand, baking in the rising sun. He sighs to himself and grumbles aloud, "Maybe this is just impossible."

Frustration wells up inside him. His power feels so uncontrolled all the time that he wonders if it's even possible for elementals to be controlled. At least for fire elementals. He had met enough water elementals to know they could control their power enough to be among regular society. He fears being around people and wonders what would happen if he tried.

A thought comes unbidden to him from a deep memory of his time as a witch. He feels so disconnected from his previous life. But now, here in the Waste, a memory of sitting in the parlor at Nadia's house talking to Elise surfaces. Her voice feels foreign now, like she speaks another dialect or language.

"It's not a matter of working through it," Elise's voice rings in his head. "It's a matter of accepting the instincts the element gives you."

He had thought about those words since then before forgetting about them when he moved into the Waste. He still doesn't understand how Hydris is able to live among humans seemingly easily. Maybe it just has to do with the more temperate nature of water versus the tempestuous power of fire. How can he give into the fire and still be safe around others?

Aidan sits back up and draws a figure eight in the sand. He sighs and focuses again on the thin line of fire. He concentrates on the figure eight and pours the power into the tiny symbol. Before long, the sand begins to melt. He pauses, letting go of the power as he is exhausted. A perfect figure eight of glass sits glowing molten in the sand in front of him.

He picks it up, feeling the heat but not feeling a burn. He has a thought and gets up to walk the piece of glass back to the cave. In the cave, he dunks the piece of glass into the spring, producing a fizzle and steam. He looks at the piece of glass, inspecting it. The glass is cloudy, a milky white color. The figure eight sits in his hand, cool to his touch now, though it might burn anyone who isn't a fire elemental. He smiles at it and pictures the piece on a necklace around Elise's neck. Yes, he would keep it for her. When he finally makes it back to civilization, he would bring it to her.

His fist closes around the glass piece. He puts it with his few belongings.

Outside his alcove, a dust storm has kicked up. He squints into the dense cloud but sees nothing beyond the dust. The sky is blotted out by the thick sand.

Impulsively, he reaches into the sack containing his few belongings and pulls out the last letter he had from Nadia. The page is turning ragged at the edges, the paper beginning to fall apart. He reads again the words that comforted him in the hospital in Umbra when he first woke up with his elemental powers.

I know you might be trying to understand and settle into your new abilities. I know how that feels and how you must be struggling. But now that things are "as they are" I feel that things are as they are meant to be. I feel like you and I and Elise are exactly as we all should be. We have each taken a strange path to get here. We have each stumbled along the way. But I think now we are where we must be. And now we can move forward and find the paths we were meant to be on all along.

Aidan lets out a sigh. A wave of loneliness washes over him. He puts the letter away and stands at the mouth of the cave, watching the sand blow past. Perhaps it is time to leave this place. Perhaps he can finally rejoin humanity.

He looks down at his hands, slowly pooling fire in his palms. Can he finally learn to control this enough to leave this place? Or does he really belong out here?

He doesn't have answers.

One

Nadia Oswald sits perched on a rickety wooden stool. The thing keeps teetering every time she shifts forward to peer through the looking piece of the telescope. The stool is ancient even by regular standards. It was a gift to the professor sitting across the room from her, a gift given to a predecessor long ago, when trees were still cut down for furniture in the south. These days, wood is a luxury and a taboo.

"What do you see?" the professor asks.

"Just the usual. I can make out the greenery of Yddril. And some of the terrain," Nadia answers, peering through the scope again. The circle of Yddril fills the view of this powerful telescope built in the middle of the Egragrian-Mosnian plateau. It is second only in visual strength to the one in Umbra that she had the privilege of touring back before things changed.

A piece of chalk clicks and scrapes on the board to the left side of the circular room. Elise Chulyin stands there, writing out some equation or other on the optics of telescopy. Her mathematics prowess has only increased with the writer witch power, and she had been putting it to good use.

Elise catches Nadia staring at her and smiles over her shoulder as she triumphantly puts down the chalk.

Nadia gets up from her stool and stretches her back out as Elise heads over. She had been sitting on that stool for so long she had gotten stiff in the cool night air.

"We should call it there for the night," the professor says. "It'll be dawn soon and both of you look run down."

Footsteps on the stairs herald the arrival of the professor's assistant. "Professor Gordon," the assistant Jackson Cox says. "Are we wrapping up for the night?"

"Yes," Jay Gordon says as he stands up from his metal stool. The legs scrape on the floor, producing a shriek in the night. "Ladies, I will see you tomorrow evening at the usual time."

"Good night, professor," Nadia says, wrapping an arm around Elise. "Jackson, see you tomorrow."

The pair of them begin to shut down the electric cameras that capture the telescope's view. Jackson flicks on the ambient lights, illuminating the circular room. The yellow lights cast more shadows around the room than they do illuminate them. Papers line the tables along one curving wall, two chalkboards bear Elise's handwriting, and a smattering of stools and chairs pepper the room. An old school desk sits in an odd place that has been used by a revolving door of assistants. Nadia and Elise head down the curving staircase that recedes into the lower floors of the observatory.

"I'm exhausted," Elise says with a yawn.

"We'll have to sleep late," Nadia answers, giving Elise a gentle kiss.

They head down the stairs and through the lower floor of the observatory to the main door. They shut it softly behind them and walk through the dark night to the cottages where they are staying. The whole of the observatory staff stays in these cottages and walks back and forth to the observatory at all hours as needed. During the day, a radio telescope makes observing possible when the sun is up. So, there is always activity in the building.

Elise unlocks their cottage door, and they step

through, flicking on the light as they go. Nadia goes to the fireplace and starts a fire with her power, casting gentle glowing flamelight on the walls. Together, they get ready for bed and settle under the old patchwork quilt and blankets in the night. The stone cottage is somewhat chilly in the night air, even with the fire going.

Nadia wraps her arms around Elise, and they snuggle closely.

"How much longer do you think we'll be up here?" Elise whispers.

"At the observatory?"

"Yes."

"Another couple weeks, I think," Nadia says. "Did you want to go back?" They had been at the observatory for two weeks already. Nadia wondered if the trip was getting tiresome for Elise who isn't working on her magic but rather on her mathematics.

"Not exactly," she says. "I'm missing my parents tonight I think."

Nadia squeezes Elise and kisses her gently. "I understand." There is a pause. "Perhaps we can go north for our time off next month?"

"As long as we get the time off." Under her words are the strain and stress of the war effort down south.

How they convinced the Conscription Authority to let them go north for a month to the observatory, Nadia would never know. They are due to return to Port Nalrang when they finish their tour at the observatory. No doubt the war effort would suck them in again.

"Do you ever wonder about Aidan?" Elise whispers.

"Sometimes. I wonder where he is."

Elise smiles in the dim room. "Sometimes I catch glimpses of him. I get visions of him in his cave."

Nadia runs her fingers on Elise's cheek. "I hope he's ok."

"Me too."

They lapse into silence then, the crackle of the fire the only sound in the room. Slowly, they each drift off to sleep.

When Nadia awakens some hours later, Elise is still asleep, and the fire has nearly burned itself out. Rather than try to light it from the bed, she slowly and gently extracts herself from the bed to relight it. Even after noon as it is now, the room is chilly from the coming winter. The fire going again, Nadia turns back to the bed to see Elise awake. She climbs back into the bed with her.

"Should we get up yet?"

"Why?" Elise says. "We don't have to be anywhere until sunset."

Nadia chuckles and snuggles closer to Elise. "So, what do we do today?"

"Well, it's Sammday. We should go into the village for tea."

The village of Willowbend is not much on the map. The only thing going for it is the observatory built on the nearby hill. The whole village goes full blackout at night to stop the light from interfering with the observatory. Despite being a tiny dot on a map, there is one cute tea shop in town that the pair have started to frequent.

"I guess that means we have to get up," Nadia grumbles.

"Probably," Elise says.

A few minutes pass before Nadia pulls the covers off and climbs out of bed. She goes about what would be her morning routine had they been sleeping on a normal schedule. Elise is not far behind her. The pair get dressed in utilitarian day suits that are nothing fancy but not unfashionable either. Nadia pulls on her walking boots and lets Elise fix her hair. She does the same for Elise, styling her curly dark hair into a tidy coif.

"Shall we?"

Elise smiles and takes her hand. They extinguish the fire and are about to leave when the witchwire on the wall buzzes. Curious at who could be contacting them, Nadia lets go of Elise and goes to the contraption. She picks up the audible receiver and answers it.

"Hello?"

"Miss Oswald?"

"This is she."

"This is Major Moore with the Conscription Authority in Port Nalrang."

"Yes?" Nadia says, waving Elise over to listen in as well.

"We need you and Miss Chulyin to return to Port Nalrang by the end of the week," Major Moore says.

"Understood. Can you give us a clue as to why?"

"Not over the witchwire," the Major answers.

"We'll have to make arrangements with the observatory, but I think we can be back by Epday," Nadia says with as much confidence as she can.

"We'll expect you then. Come straight to us at the end of your journey." The tone of the order brooks no refusal.

"Yes sir," Nadia says.

They hung up then, Nadia replacing the audible back

in its carriage. She looks at Elise grimly, neither of them having high hopes for why they are being recalled early.

"Should we skip tea?' Elise asks.

"No," Nadia says. "We'll stop at the observatory on the way back and get everything arranged for our trip."

Though they were both barely fifteen, their status with the Conscription Authority has given them some independence. Not to mention the commitment ceremony giving them standing as an established couple. They were both still technically wards of their respective parents, and they traveled with Kaye and Hughes, respectively. However, they were free to travel and work now without parental permission.

"Let's go," Elise says. "Tea won't wait forever."

They lock the door to their cottage behind them and begin the walk down the lane and down the hill towards the village. Elise opens her parasol, and they share it on the way to Sammday tea the way they used to in Coreton.

Part of Nadia wishes they were back at Fernsby and going to Sheffield's for tea. She misses meeting with Atley Bishop and the hibiscus tea she made so deliciously.

Someday they will return there.

Someday they will be able to revisit their past selves.

Sadly, that day would not be today. They will one day. But not today.

Two

Morvath ap Gwynedd wakes up early every day. He drinks coffee in the morning, a preferred expensive drink from the southern hemisphere. He drinks it straight black and dark, thick as mud and rich in taste. He savors the drink one sip at a time. His butler, Regnor, serves him a light breakfast of eggs and toast before he goes to his study to work. It is on this Vriday in Larandy that he is working for his cause.

A pile of paperwork and a couple maps line his desk in a cluttered manner. His desk is the only space the staff is not allowed to clean. His housekeeper disapproves of the mess, but he doubts even a hospital would be clean enough for Mrs. Winston. She lives in the attic with the rest of the small staff that runs his Port Nalrang home.

The house is tastefully situated in the affluent neighborhood of Trommol Point, nestled on the eastern side of the great metropolis, but not so far out that it is inconvenient. Morvath works in the Egrarian Parliament, as a Human Minister of People serving on several committees. He takes his work seriously, but no one knows it is not his priority. His priority is the stack of work occupying his desk.

For two decades, he has been chasing the rumors around the globe. He has traveled on the pretense of diplomatic business as far north as Umbra and as far south as Lecrait. He has even sailed along the Falgar to Verhill and seen many other small countries in his time. In his younger years, he gained a reputation as an explorer, writing memoirs of his time abroad. About five years ago he ran for office with Parliament to legitimize the travel to foreign lands. But all this has been just a disguise for his real purpose.

Everyone knows the Central Dogma of magic. And everyone knows the Three Laws of witchcraft that govern the magic of their world, and likely all the worlds in the solar system. On a piece of paper he has the three laws written out, a scribbling of absent-minded thinking:

1. *Energy is the root of Magic. Magic is the root of*

Power. (The Root Law)

2. *All species have Energy. Only humans do not have Magic. (The Law of the Human Constant)*

3. *All magic is conserved. (The Conservation Law)*

It is the third law that interests him the most. The basis for the Vacancy Principle, the method by which witchcraft can be transferred, the Conservation Law proves to be difficult to truly understand. Some years ago, he started noticing a pattern: some magic was not conserved.

Impossible. It seemed impossible. Conservation is a law of natural philosophy as much as it is of magic. Nothing can be created nor destroyed, only transformed. So, what happens in those cases where conservation doesn't appear to happen?

Morvath pours over an account from almost a hundred years ago. He has read the story over and over again, probably hundreds of times in the past two decades. It is the story that made him curious and got him started on this journey of philosophical discovery. So why doesn't he communicate his research in his memoirs? Why does no one know what he is pursuing? He found out a truth that has been hidden from the human population for millennia.

There is a fourth type of witchcraft.

By definition, the fourth type would have to be higher in the hierarchy than writer witchcraft. By definition, if the Conservation Law holds firm, it would be the witchcraft that prevails over the lower form. This got him wondering what kind of craft would be so powerful as to be the best kept secret on Terra. How many *witches* even knew the craft existed? He immediately knew he wanted to find the answers to his many questions. He immediately knew he would find resistance everywhere.

So began his quest for knowledge. As a human, he never *had* to take the Central Dogma courses in school. He had, on a whim, opted to take them in his misspent youth. By some miracle, he remembered what he had studied. He had spent some time revisiting that knowledge and digging through textbooks and history books, and eventually through primary sources like memoirs and journals, to find any reference to the failed Conservation Law.

He found nothing.

He was not deterred. He continued searching. And finally, on a trip to Mosnia, his quest bore fruit. He learned of an incident in a tiny rural town where a writer witch died and their power did not displace the caster witch's present. The writer witch had been struck by a horse cart and died before making it to any medical care or healer. The caster witch, one of the first on the scene, was unable to save him, but had tried the whole time to work. Despite being inordinately powerful, he did not gain the writer witch's power. The power seemingly dissipated completely, never to be seen again. Which begged the question, what happened to the power?

Morvath determinedly visited the town and poured through their archives to find any reference to either the man or the incident. For something so unusual, there was surprisingly little. The last reference he found to the caster witch was when he was exiled on accusation of unethical magical practices. The charge was vague enough to cover just about anything he could have done. And who knows? It might have just been a cover-up for something else.

He wondered if the caster witch was considered a traitor to witchkind because of his interaction with the dying witch. Morvath doesn't know witches' motives though. He doesn't pretend to understand their choices.

The world turned on its head again a few years later. He heard about a Matraize writer witch, a common type of witch there, who was killed by an Ecrium soldier for his power. The power didn't displace into the Ecrium soldier but displaced into the community. The soldier was arrested for the murder, but the mystery of the power went unmentioned throughout the rest of the accounts. Why would the power not displace into the soldier who had no power and was human as far as the accounts went?

Morvath dove into the research with a renewed gusto, realizing that these events still happen in the contemporary era. There is no way of knowing when or where one would happen, but he wondered if he could track down one of these witches with the secret fourth power.

Jealousy swelled in him. Jealousy and anger at the deviousness of witchkind. How dare they hide this most powerful form of witchcraft from humans? How long had this master secret been kept? And for how much longer could they hide this power from all humanity? It isn't right. It shouldn't be kept by witches who don't put the benefits of all humans over their own selfish natures. They shouldn't have exclusive access to it. They shouldn't hoard it for themselves. That's when he made the decision.

Morvath wanted the power for himself.

Why shouldn't he get the power that has been coveted and keep the power for himself? Why shouldn't he reveal its existence to humankind? It really isn't right.

Regnor jogs him out of his thoughts with a knock on the door. The butler lets him know lunch is served. Determined to return to his work afterward, Morvath gets up and follows Regnor down the hall to the dining room. He sits down to eat a simple lunch of cold roast chicken salad and fresh vegetables, something he requests regularly for his lunches. After another cup of coffee, the expense meaningless to him, he returns to his study to get back to work.

One a sheaf of paper he writes:

Possible 4th Power Candidates:

And stares at the paper. On his witchglass, his personal witchwire device, he pulls up the roster of current high-power witches, some of which are mere seers. He studies their incident reports over the past decade and filters for high power moments. He begins to write down names.

Thorryn Creer

Erik Satterthwait

Saknor Howells

Dalia Ekinor

Euphemia Goliyant

After another half hour of searching and reading the recent incident reports from the past six months, he adds another two names to his list.

Nadia Oswald

Aidan Montgomery — former?

Of all the people on the list, two of them seem the most likely to be fourth power witches. The incident with Oswald and Montgomery caught his attention because Oswald was a writer witch before. It was recorded as a higher-order writer witch displacement, but he doubts that could happen. He stars Oswald's name.

The second name he stars is Goliyant's. Her prowess with magic has earned her a reputation. He doubts she is just a writer witch. Her involvement with some of the witch conventions makes him wonder why they would even host one where she is housed, if not for an unusual ability. It seems likely anyway.

Morvath sets his pen down, satisfied with his options. Now to figure out how to get close to one of them without alerting suspicion. Now to find a way to capture their power.

Three

Vriday Nadia and Elise find themselves riding horses provided by the local Conscription Authority, Kaye and Hughes following close behind. They were two day's ride from Port Nalrang. They would stop in another village for the night, a little hamlet called Doving. It is not bigger than Willowbend, and doesn't have the attraction of the observatory, but they stayed at a tiny public house there last time they came through.

Near sunset the village comes into view, a smattering of houses and a market space surrounding a village well. Without the well, there would be no village. Without water, it's impossible to survive the plateau.

After crossing into the village, they head to the south side of town where the Anxious Tulip pub is situated. The town curves around the edge of a desert hill, the slope providing some protection from the plateau's vicious night winds. The pub sits facing south at the wide vista of open plain between the village and Port Nalrang. The curving line of road cuts the view, disappearing into the haze.

The girls dismount their horses, Kaye taking the reins. Hughes accompanies them inside the pub where they are greeted genially by the proprietor.

"Will you be staying the night?" she asks.

"Yes, we'll need two rooms," Elise says.

"Very good," the stout woman answers. She is portly, with her hair tied up in a handkerchief and an apron covering her practical blue dress. She walks around the bar and pulls keys from a lock box for the upstairs rooms.

Kaye comes in behind them with their bags. Together, they follow the proprietor up the creaky back stairs and down a narrow hallway to two doors of heavy metal. She unlocks the first door and lets them in. Kaye steps through and sets down the girls' bags in one room and brings his and Hughes's bags into the other room. Nadia and Elise enter their room and the proprietor leaves them, mentioning that dinner would be served in thirty minutes in the pub.

The room is not glamorous. A cast iron bed occupies the far end with a medium-thick mattress and a couple of feather pillows. Two quilts layer over the linen sheets, an extra blanket draped over the end of the footboard. Elise shuts the door and turns the lock.

"Should we nap before dinner?"

Nadia looks mischievous as she says, "If you want to *nap*."

Elise pulls her close and they kiss as passionately as ever.

An hour passes. They are pulled out of their lover's passion by a rap on the door. Nadia pulls herself out of bed and makes herself presentable. She opens the door to find Kaye waiting.

"You're going to miss dinner," he says matter-of-factly.

"Sorry," Nadia says. "We're coming now." She shuts the door for privacy.

Elise straightens herself out and puts her shoes back on. Nadia does the same, and they head out the door. Down the creaky stairs, they find Hughes holding a table in a bustling pub. The place is surprisingly packed, given the small village. Then again, this is the only watering hole in town.

The girls take seats and the four of them have plates of stew put down in front of them, laden with meat and veggies and a hearty brown sauce. Crusty bread occupies a basket on the table, butter in a dish next to it. There is also a side dish of fresh greens dressed with lemon and vinegar. The group eats their dinner quietly, listening to the village bustle around them.

A man at the bar who has clearly had something to drink is loudly complaining about the country's involvement with the war. Nadia tries to ignore him, but the voice pierces even the noisy pub atmosphere.

"We shouldn't get involved in a war on the other side of the Falgar."

"It won't stay on the other side of the Falgar for long."

Nadia exchanges a look with Elise and tries to tune out the words the man says. She continues to tear pieces of bread and dunk it in her stew. She willfully tunes out the words of those around them. Elise, somehow intuiting the distress in Nadia, reaches over and squeezes her hand. They are constantly reminded of the war in their daily work. They are constantly on the precipice of involvement.

"I don't understand why we must rely on witches for

all this," a voice cuts into her thoughts.

She looks up, startled and on edge now, exchanging looks with Kaye and Hughes and Elise. It takes great discipline to keep her from looking over her shoulder to see who the speaker is.

"What do you mean?"

"We rely so much on witches for our defense. We shouldn't have to rely on their kind."

Nadia bristles but does her best not to show it. She takes a couple breaths to calm down. Elise squeezes her hand. Nadia should be used to prejudice by now, but the truth is she never got used to it with her mother. How could she be used to it with strangers?

"I don't trust them."

"Who cares? As long as we're protected. Would you rather humans be put out there? I'd rather send witches."

Nadia exchanges a glance with Kaye. He very subtly shakes his head. They need to get out of there and lay low for the night. She didn't expect to find such prejudice in a hamlet like Doving. They hadn't heard talk like this last time they went through here.

"Can I get you anything else?" the proprietor asks. She clears their empty bowls from the table. "I can bring you a sweet or a savory."

"Can we take it upstairs?" Nadia asks. She's still hungry.

The proprietor glances to the right, in the direction of the group at the bar. "I'll get you a basket to take up to your room," she says. She goes back to the kitchen and returns a few minutes later with a medium-sized basket. Kaye takes it and the four of them get up from the table. Nadia and Elise lead them upstairs.

Voices float up the stairs behind them. An argument is breaking out below. It seems there's a witch in the crowd taking umbrage to the prejudice of that man. Nadia's jaw clenches, glad they thought to get out of there. Kaye opens the girl's room and the four crowd in there, setting the basket down on the desk.

"Unbelievable," Nadia mutters.

"I believe it," Elise says. "With everything going on lately, I'm not surprised to find this kind of prejudice even here."

The small town feels so far removed from the big cities of the south that it shouldn't be infected by the bigotry growing there. Nadia shakes her head, feeling some kind of disappointment and sadness at discovering it here. There is nothing that could be done.

The voices escalate downstairs. They can't make out

the words. Kaye goes to the door and locks it. Hughes shakes his head as he opens the basket and brings out the savory and the sweet.

"She gave us egg and cheese tarts and flan," Hughes says.

"I'll take both," Nadia says, the stress getting to her. Her power also tends to make her hungry. She's discovered that anchor power draws more energy latently than the writer power ever did. She would have to actively be using the writer power to lose energy to it. Anchor power relies on her mere existence. So, she always finds herself losing energy to it.

Eventually, the noise downstairs dies down. It seems the proprietor got control of the situation. Nadia munches on bites of egg and cheese and uses the tiny spoon provided to eat the flan. When they're done with everything, Kaye repacks the basket.

"We'll leave you two for the evening," he says. "Be sure to lock the door."

Hughes pokes his head out the door. A low murmur of conversation comes from downstairs, but no more than that. So, he and Kaye head out, Kaye taking the basket downstairs and Hughes heading for their shared room.

Elise gets up and locks the door behind them. She rejoins Nadia on the bed, both of them laying back exhausted from the day of travel.

"Are you tired?"

"Yeah. I'm going to fall asleep soon."

"Me too."

They lapse into silence, listening to the murmur of voices from downstairs and through the window behind their bed. Nadia kisses Elise and wraps an arm around her. Elise lets out a contented sigh.

"I wonder how Aidan is," Elise says.

"Me too. I wonder where he is."

"I wish he had taken a witchwire with him," she says. "I wish he had decided to stay in civilization."

"I think he felt it safer to be on his own for a while," Nadia says. "I think he felt like he was going to hurt someone."

Elise snuggles closer and doesn't answer. They hear the door slam shut from downstairs, and the noise dies down as well. The sun has set by this point and only the gas lamps produce a yellow glow in the street outside. Nadia leans up and peeks out, spying the last people from the pub heading down the street. The village has gone quiet with the coming of night. The houses are all shuttered against the wicked wind blowing through the streets.

"Looks like the night might be quiet after all," Nadia says. From her vantage point, she can't see the desert. She can only see the brick buildings lining the main street and the well a little ways down that serves the houses of this neighborhood.

"We need a quiet night."

Nadia lays back down and snuggles with her partner. Elise flicks a finger in the direction of the lights and snuffs them out. Together they doze off still in their clothes from the day.

Four

Port Nalrang comes into view around lunchtime on Epday, the last day of the week. They will have to go directly to the Conscription Authority as soon as they cross into town, so they dress accordingly for it. Both Nadia and Elise wear their everyday uniforms of slacks, button down jackets, boots, and hats. They also wear goggles, and both have cloth scarves covering their noses and mouths to protect against the sand of the plateau desert.

Around teatime they make it to the edges of the metropolis, heading down the northern road through Upper East Herren to Sheocag Bazaar. The streets of Sheocag Bazaar bustle with the Epday market. People move out of the way of the four of them when they see the military uniforms and their witch markings. Nadia doubts anyone knows what to make of her special marking. She resents having a marker showing that she's an anchor witch, though it's not widely broadcast what the patch means. Most people would probably assume she is a writer witch specialist of some kind. Either way, the patch makes her more of a target and she resents that.

They take the turn through the outlying parts of town toward the tall building that houses the Conscription Authority. The metal and glass structure fits in with downtown Port Nalrang, a utilitarian facade flanked by pristine lawns where military exercises take place. The four of them ride up to the east side of the building where they can leave their horses while they head inside.

Kaye and Hughes are ushered to a waiting area while Nadia and Elise follow a lieutenant through the maze of hallways to the central lift. He takes them up to the fourteenth floor and leads them down the hallway to a suite of offices. He indicates that they should sit and wait for Major Moore to call them into the Colonel's office. The lieutenant heads back out and down the hallway.

Nadia and Elise sit uneasily in metal chairs that aren't the most comfortable things in the world. Neither of them fidgets, disciplined as they are from their deportment training back at Fernsby. Nadia's mind wanders back to that time, marveling at how long ago Fernsby feels.

The inner door to the office opens and a person who could only be Major Moore steps out. "The Colonel will see you now."

Nadia and Elise get up and follow him into the inner office space. They both salute Colonel Ergamenes who salutes them back and asks them to take a seat.

"Miss Chulyin, this doesn't necessarily apply to you. You are not officially a member of the Egragian Conscription Authority and thus not subject to deployment orders," the Colonel begins. Elise exchanges a glance with Nadia. Knots are forming in Nadia's stomach. "That being said, I expect you will want to stay with your partner."

"Yes, sir," Elise answers.

"Then it is important for you both to know that Nadia is being deployed to Rebluinia."

"What?" Nadia says, completely forgetting her manners.

The Colonel looks somewhat annoyed. "You don't have a say in the matter. I understand you won't create killing spells or anything of the sort," he continues, "but you will use your magic to help the war effort."

"What exactly are you going to have us do?" Nadia asks.

Colonel Ergamenes straightens up and leans on his desk. "I will not go into specifics, but suffice it to say we will not be having you join weapons. You'll be working with the strategists across the Falgar to get Ecrium back to their sovereign land."

Elise asks, "Similar to what we did before?"

"Yes."

"We don't have Aidan," Nadia says.

"No," the Colonel says in annoyance. "But I believe you can do enough without him."

"I doubt it. But we can try."

"Yes, you *will* try," Colonel Ergamenes says definitively.

All Nadia can do is just acquiesce and grumble internally. It's not bad enough they got pulled off the observatory detail. They were being sent even further south.

"When are we going?"

"Tisday."

"That's only three days from now!"

"And you best use those three days to prepare."

Nadia exchanges a look with Elise. "We need to return home to inform my father and make the necessary arrangements." She pauses, then asks, "Will my father's man be able to come with us?"

"No," Colonel Ergamenes says. "You will not travel with anyone not military."

"My family won't like that," Elise says.

"I cannot bar your family's man from coming. You are a diplomat," the Colonel says.

That eases Nadia's mind somewhat that she will have a familiar protector around. But she has to ask. "Who will be my protection?"

"We have someone in mind. You will meet them at the port on Tisday." With that, Colonel Ergamenes dismisses them.

Nadia leaves the room feeling absolutely deflated over what just happened. She walks down the hall with Elise by her side, following the Major through the building and back downstairs. They don't say anything until they get to Kaye and Hughes and make their way to their horses.

"What did they want?"

"Nothing good," Nadia grumbled.

"They're sending Nadia to Rebluinia," Elise says.

"I'm going with. But they barred Kaye from coming."

"Your father won't like that," Kaye says to Nadia.

"No, he won't." She shakes her head in annoyance. "Let's go home and break the news. We have to get ready to leave. They want us at the port on Tisday."

"Fast," Kaye says. "Is Hughes able to go?" he asks, hailing a taxi, the horses having belonged to the Conscription Authority.

"Yes, but only because Elise is technically a diplomat."

"Ugh," Elise says. "Let's get home."

A taxi pulls up to where they wait outside the Conscription Authority. Nadia sighs heavily, already weary at the daunting prospect of going that far south. She climbs in the cab with Elise next to her. Kaye sits up front with the driver and Hughes takes the last seat next to them. The cab, a steam carriage, turns down the street and begins to weave through the busy thoroughfares of Port Nalrang to Nadia's neighborhood.

Some twenty minutes later, they pull up to her building, a building she hadn't seen in a few weeks. They extract themselves from the cramped cab and make their way inside. Kaye had gathered their bags and was carrying them in ahead of Nadia and Elise. The doorman greets Nadia pleasantly. They climb into the lift and make their way to Nadia's floor. A few minutes later, she is breathing in the smell of home.

Kaye goes ahead of Nadia and Elise and brings their bags to Nadia's bedroom. Needing to change out of her uniform, Nadia pulls out an afternoon dress and begins to take off the dusty clothes. The blue linen dress feels safe and comfortable on her skin. She wonders how much longer she'll get to wear clothes like this.

Elise comes over to her, sensing her mood, and puts her arms around her. "I'm sorry this is happening to you," she says. "You will always have me with you."

"I know," Nadia says softly. "I'm glad you're by my side." She kisses Elise gently, feeling the electric connection between them that has nothing to do with their powers.

"We should have tea," Elise says.

"Yes, because that will solve everything," Nadia answers with a laugh.

They head for the parlor. Apparently, Salter has anticipated their need for tea and is laying it out for them as they come in. Nadia and Elise take seats next to each other and Salter serves them tea. He lays a tower of treats and sandwiches on the table in front of them.

"Will you need anything else?" Salter asks.

"No, thank you," Nadia answers. "I think we're good for now." Salter leaves them to their tea. Nadia immediately picks up an egg tea sandwich and devours it in an unladylike manner.

"Mrs. Winthrop wouldn't approve," Elise says in amusement. Mrs. Winthrop was their deportment teacher back at Fernsby.

"I don't care, I'm starving."

Elise picks up a sandwich and eats it in a more sedate manner. "It's late for tea, but I'm glad we're eating."

"I doubt we'll be eating dinner before eight tonight," Nadia says. She takes another sandwich, cucumber and smoked salmon this time, and takes a bite of the luxury she hasn't had in weeks. The cream cheese and dill weed provide a nice complement to the fish. Salmon is only found along the banks of the Falgar, where the water creeps into tiny rivulets along the shores.

The door to the parlor opens and Salter lets Nadia's father through.

"I see you have started on tea without me," he says.

Nadia sets her cup down and stands to greet her father. He kisses her on the cheek and makes his way to the settee opposite them. Nadia retakes her seat, Elise patting her knee. Her father accepts a cup of tea from Salter, and he also picks up an egg sandwich from the tower. Salter ducks out of the room again.

"What did the Conscription Authority want this time?" her father asks.

Elise looks at Nadia who lets out a sigh. "They're sending me to Rebluinia to help with the war effort."

"Excuse me?" her father says, putting his cup down with a clank.

"Colonel Ergamenes informed us this afternoon. We're to leave on Tisday," Nadia continues.

"That's not the worst of it," Elise says.

"Then please tell me the worst," he answers.

"They won't let Kaye come with us."

"Well, that is unacceptable." Her father sets his cup on the table without the usual finesse. "They just keep taking advantage of you both. But they fail to realize you are both fifteen. You should not be going anywhere unaccompanied."

"Is it worth the fight? And do we have time to fight it?"

"I'm not sure," her father admits. "I will raise the issue with them though. You will likely have to leave in either case."

"I'm going with her," Elise says. "Hughes is able to come with me."

"Well, that's something," he mutters.

Nadia picks up a tiny cake, one with lemon filling. She is rueful about her whole situation and the sourness of the lemon matches her mood.

They finish their tea and Nadia's father gets up to leave. "I'll make arrangements to speak to Colonel Ergamenes tomorrow."

Nadia has her doubts, but there's no stopping her father from doing what he wants to do. She knows he's too stubborn to be reasoned with sometimes. He leaves the parlor, Nadia and Elise just staring after him.

"Well, I doubt that will go well," Nadia says.

"Probably not," Elise answers. "But at least we'll have Hughes with us."

Nadia sighs. "I need to study up on my geography," she grumbles. "I barely know where Pratergarde is."

"I think I'm going to take a nap," Elise says, getting up.

"I'll join you later," Nadia says. She gets up as well.

Salter begins to clear the tea. She and Elise go down the hall, Nadia to her father's study and Elise to their bedroom. Nadia shuts the door softly and makes her way to where her father keeps the atlases. She pulls one down that focuses on the Falgar and the surrounding countries and sits down at her father's desk to page through it. She loses herself to the study of maps showing far-off lands she would soon be visiting.

Five

More than a month had passed since Aidan first made the glass pendant for Elise. He had since made several others, one for Nadia and the rest just for practice. He thought about his family and especially his mother and giving one to her. He thought about his life before he became an elemental. Everything before felt pale in comparison.

"Why are you leaving?" Elise had asked him the day before he headed to the Waste. "You're making so much progress."

But Aidan didn't feel like he had made progress. He felt like he was regressing and the fire, as it strengthened within him, was becoming more uncontrollable.

Fire burns.

That universal truth is the fact that terrifies him every

night in his ruddy little cave. Fire burns everything unstoppably. He is down to two pieces of clothing because of his fire. The first couple weeks here he burned through half his clothes and soon after had only one shirt and one pair of pants left. He never felt cold anymore, so that didn't worry him. But the fact that even the flame-retardant clothing burned worried him immensely.

He had made progress though. He had to admit that. His ability to hold on to the fire and calm it at night made a huge difference. Gone are the days when he would wake up naked with ash around him.

Aidan takes the time to wash himself in the water of the hot spring at the back of the cave. He is ready now. He knows it's time for him to return to civilization and find the girls again. He knows better than to think he'll have a choice about where to work, given the Conscription Authority's likely hold over his life. But he wants to see them again. And his soul is tired of the time in the Waste.

He might not be an extrovert, but he does miss the people he used to have in his life. He misses John Belstone, the partner he had learned to rely on all those years. He wonders how John and all the rest of his friends are doing.

The morning dawned in full as he pulled on his boots. He hadn't worn them much since he settled into the Waste, but he wore them now that he was planning on leaving. It would take him the better part of the day to reach the base of the Wastewalk. It would take time for him to go home, but he was ready to make that journey. He was ready to rejoin humanity.

Aidan makes his plan and begins to pack up his remaining belongings. He would walk the distance to the base of the Wastewalk where he would use their witchwire to forewarn everyone of his return. Then he would climb the plateau and head south. He will stop in Avita Spring and Courtthostur to see family and friends before continuing to Port Narlang. He would have to hire a horse in Northpass to make the journey take less time. Perhaps the Conscription Authority would have one he could borrow. They do owe him for his service after all.

An hour after dawn, he begins his long walk. He shoulders a linen bag that he made of the remnants of his clothing. The strap is leather from an old belt, and he used a prickly plant needle to sew the bag together. He will forever be grateful for the sewing skills his mother and aunt bestowed upon him.

Once outside, he takes a long hard look at the place that has been his home for several months now. He lived alone out here. That ruddy cave was his home. He felt solitude in spades. He woke up every morning to the expanse of desert that came right up to his little cave. He knew he would miss it. He knew, deep inside, he would one day return. But for now, he needed to return to people again. He would have his whole life to spend as a fiery hermit in the Waste.

Around noon, he sighted the Wastewalk for the first time as he walked around a bend along the plateau. The cut of road formed a hazy line along the horizon. A plume of smoke from the Inn Below rises in the distance. Then he turns another bend, and the Wastewalk disappears from view for a while.

By late afternoon, his legs were beginning to deeply tire. He had gotten used to walking on the sand out here, but even with that training he wouldn't be used to the long distance he is walking now. Fortunately, he could see the inn again, a stone building constructed of the darker rock common on the lower plateau face. The dark building seemingly springs closer to him as he approaches.

The sun is setting behind him as he walks across the wide flat area around the inn. A stable and many mules and horses stand off to the left, a safe distance from the cliff face. Beyond the stable, the curve of the Wastewalk disappears into the distance, the first bend around a particularly tall dune in the distance. Several people roam about, ignoring Aidan as they go about their business. He is happy to be ignored, his unique status drawing more attention than he would ever be comfortable with.

He opens the door to the inn and is immediately greeted by stares of those in the main gathering area. He looks around, spots the bar where a bartender looks like they might be the proprietor. Aidan approaches, his normal movement of approaching a bar seemingly making him less interesting.

"What can I do for you?" the bartender asks.

"I'm looking to use your witchwire if you have one. And possibly get some more clothes," he says, knowing he looks ragged in appearance.

The bartender studies him for a moment, eyeing his state. The man is a witch, no doubt about that, but can't be more than a caster at most and possibly is just a seer. His power feels miniscule next to Aidan's. No doubt the bartender feels Aidan's immense energy from his elemental power.

"Did you come from the Waste?" the bartender asks cautiously. An eerie silence falls over the room as he waits for Aidan's reply.

"Yes," he says with no explanation. They will ascertain that he is an elemental and not a spirit. He just did not feel he owed anyone an explanation.

"The witchwire is in the back, I'll take you," the bartender says. He calls over his assistant and leaves the bar to be tended by the younger man. He comes around the bar and waves Aidan over. He follows the bartender down a skinny hallway. The walls are all stone brick and the floors a terracotta tile, a fact which makes Aidan more comfortable. Nothing super flammable around him.

The room in the back is a different story. The desk at the center of the room is clearly made of Umbrian cedar. And there are wooden shelves lining the walls filled with books. Aidan pauses at the door and then heads in. The witchwire is on the table.

The bartender steps aside to let Aidan past. "Do you need help?"

"No," Aidan says. "I've used one before."

"Alright, take your time with the witchwire," he says. "I can dig out some clothes from the lost and found for you. Do you have an account to pay with?"

"My family's account," Aidan answers. "I can pull it up through the witchwire."

The bartender nods and steps out of the room.

Aidan begins by pulling up his personal communications account. His percom has clearly been inundated with messages since he left civilization several months ago. He doesn't have time or the patience to look at the messages now. He sees that many of them are from the girls, but he doesn't open them. Instead, he opens a new message and writes a note.

> *I'm on my way south. Visiting family and friends first. Then I'll be in Port Nalrang.*
>
> *See you soon —*
>
> *Aidan*

The message is short. He sends it without any further details. He'll get there when he gets there. Then he sends a similar message to his family and to John. Then he links into the central banking system and pulls up his family's account. He uses it to link with the bar account and deposits what he hopes will be enough to cover his expenses at the bar.

A few minutes after the deposit goes through, the bartender pokes his head back in. "I have a room for you if you want it,," he says. He is carrying a pile of clothes presumably from the lost and found. "This is everything that I thought might fit you. I can show you to your room where you can clean up and change."

"Do you have a bag I could keep?" Aidan asks, lofting his makeshift bag.

"I'll dig something out of storage," he says.

Aidan closes out of his percom and signs out of his connection to the witchwire. Then he follows the bartender out of the room and up the stairs. He catches stares from those in the main pub again. But there is nothing he could do about that.

The bartender opens the door for him and hands him the key. They both step into the room and the bartender places the pile of clothes on the bed. "Take whatever you need. Some of that has been in storage for years."

Aidan nods.

The bartender tells him where the communal bathroom is and where the towels are stored. Then he is about to leave when he pauses in the doorway.

"Are you a spirit?" he asks suddenly.

Aidan is taken aback at the question. He doesn't think he comes off as a spirit, but he must seem very wild to the average person. "No," he says. "I'm an elemental."

"Ah, I knew you weren't a witch," the bartender says. "May I ask what kind of elemental?"

"Fire."

This gives the bartender pause. He thought any of the other elements would not cause such an immediate fear response in the man. The bartender immediately begins to sweat.

"Well, don't burn the place down," the bartender says.

"I won't."

"Do you eat?"

"Yes," Aidan says, thinking wistfully of the tubers he had been eating for months.

"Dinner is served in an hour. Feel free to come down anytime."

"Thank you," Aidan says. He doesn't know how to completely express his gratitude. The fact is this first encounter with humans could have gone much worse.

The bartender closes the door.

Aidan is alone again, but the sounds of the pub below trickle in through the closed door. He sits on the bed for a moment just staring at the stone walls. The bed

is metal thankfully, but the linens make him nervous. He
would have to get used to it though. He would have to
get used to being surrounded by things and by people he
could so easily destroy.

He gets up and goes to take a bath.

Six

The sun set on Anday with some news. They had heard from Aidan for the first time in months. He would be coming down to Port Nalrang after meeting with his family and friends. They would miss him this time, but at least he has come back to civilization. Elise messaged him back and let him know they would be heading across the Falgar, but there was no response. He must have signed off immediately after sending the message.

The other bit of news was not so exciting. Nadia's father's request to send Kaye with her was denied twice. The last time they were told the decision was final and Nadia would have a guard of the military variety. Annoyed at not having her usual ally with her, Nadia had been admittedly sulking for the whole afternoon. She had holed herself up in her father's study, he still being out, and kept poring over the maps and ignoring everyone except Elise who sat in the room with her.

A knock on the door preceded Salter.

"Your father is home," he says. "And you will leave for dinner in an hour."

Nadia lets out a spectacular sigh. "I suppose we should go change."

Elise closes her book and sets it aside. She had been perusing Nadia's father's law collection, specifically some of the texts on the governance of both witches and humans. There are laws separate for witches and humans, especially where magic is concerned. But there are, of course, laws that govern both. Elise had taken an interest, given the state of their current affairs.

Nadia and Elise both change into evening clothes, the kind that they would wear with fancy company. Her father decided that they should go out for dinner tonight on their last night in the city for a while. So, he is taking them to the Sapphire Room, a swanky restaurant that overlooks the harbor below the cliff face and features a beautiful sapphire in a small art gallery within. Nadia admitted to Elise that she is looking forward to the evening.

Dressed appropriately and with hair pulled up and

jewelry donned, Nadia looks over at Elise, her beautiful partner, and can't help but smile.

"What is it?"

"I just can't think of when we'll get to do this again, so I'm enjoying the moment."

Elise makes a final adjustment to the tiara she is wearing—she is technically a princess, after all—and approaches her girlfriend. They kiss delicately and smile at each other. A contented sigh escapes Nadia, a far cry from the annoyed one she let out earlier.

"Let's go. We shouldn't keep your father waiting."

They head down the hallway of the apartment, Nadia musing that she had never expected to be living in Port Nalrang quite so much. She is a native of Avita Spring, after all, and her family originated from there. But her father's position in Parliament, a position he handily won once Nadia's power became known, guaranteed they would live in Port Nalrang at least half the year. Despite missing the dusty streets of Avita Spring, she was beginning to think of Port Nalrang as home.

Salter helps both girls and Edgar Oswald into their coats for the evening. Kaye would be driving them, as usual. They make their way down to the garage and all climb in the back seats of the steam carriage. Her father had really begun to exclusively use it, accustomed as he had become to the speed and efficiency of the vehicle. Kaye turns it out of the garage and down the main street towards the downtown area of Port Nalrang. They head towards the coast and head through the neighborhood of Trommol Point on the east end of the city. There, close to the coast, they find themselves parking at the glittering Golden Citadel, the hotel that hosts the Sapphire Room.

Kaye helps them out of the carriage and then turns the vehicle down the side street to park while the three are inside. A feeling of regret goes through Nadia that her companion and confidant can't join them tonight.

Inside the Golden Citadel, they cross the gorgeous lobby with tastefully appointed chairs and chaise lounges and small side tables and thick rugs on the marble tile floor. Together the group makes their way through the marble pillars on one side of the room through the double doors, made of solid wood, that lead into the Sapphire Room. Large blue gems—these ones fake— glitter on each of the doors.

Edgar Oswald heads up to the host who greets him genially. There they speak for a few seconds and then the host leads them to the interior dining room right through the gallery with the enormous sapphire the place is named for. For a moment Nadia and Elise pause to study it but are soon shooed along by her father.

Chandeliers of crystal and glass hang over the large dining room with electric light bulbs instead of gas flames. The whole place is a mix of modern and traditional. Traditional tables with white tablecloths and silverware and linens on each. Modern chairs of wrought iron with thick cushions on them for comfort. The thick carpet underfoot muffles the sounds of their heels as they cross the space. The host leads them to a table at the far end of the dining room by the large windows overlooking the bay.

Nadia takes in the view for a moment before taking her seat. Elise does the same, not having seen such a view of the Falgar in her time down in Egraria. Edgar Oswald looks amused at the girls' gawking, something her mother would have scolded them over.

A smartly dressed waiter comes over to their table and inquires about their drink choices. Surprisingly, her father orders a bottle of chilled champagne and three glasses. It's not like there was a law against them drinking champagne. Nadia had just never been given champagne by her father before. It was odd.

The waiter leaves and comes back a few minutes later

with the chilled bottle and the glasses. When they all have glasses half filled with champagne, her father raises his glass in their direction. They toast without saying a word and Nadia takes a sip of the champagne. It's not her first time drinking it. They had stolen a bottle from a professor back at Fernsby. This was a far superior bottle though.

Edgar Oswald sets his glass down. "You have a long journey ahead of you and I want you both to be safe," he says. "Look after each other."

"We will," Elise says. She reaches over and takes Nadia's hand.

"You're both in deep danger, more so than the Conscription Authority is willing to admit," he continues.

Nadia nods. "I feel it sometimes. The creep of something coming after us."

Elise looks at her, a concerned look on her face.

To her surprise, her father asks, "How is your seer ability?"

Nadia's eyebrows go up. "Not sure. I catch glimpses sometimes, but it's not a priority at the moment."

Edgar Oswald nods in understanding, as if he has been talking about witch powers his entire adult life. "Is that common?"

"Aidan talked about his difficulty with getting the hang of the lower powers, but he struggled with his *actual* power though," she explains. "I think every witch is different and requires some time to figure it all out."

"Have you heard from him?"

Nadia realizes that they hadn't told her father about the note from Aidan. "Yes, we just got a note from him that he's heading south again. But we'll be gone before he gets here."

"That's too bad."

"Edgar!" a voice calls out. They all turn to see a man approaching the table. He is lanky and tall, his auburn hair offsetting his lightly tanned skin. His demeanor suggests you shouldn't take the suit seriously, though he is dressed as formally as Nadia's father is. The brown eyes are darker than Elise's and look penetratingly around at the three of them. Despite the sharpness of his looks, a smile tames the face as he comes up to Edgar Oswald.

"Morvath," Edgar Oswald greets his fellow minister.

"How are you? And this is your daughter and her partner?" Morvath prompts.

"Yes," Edgar says. "My daughter Nadia Oswald and her partner, Elise Chulyin." Morvath shakes each of their hands in turn. "Girls, this is Morvath ap Gwynedd, Human Minister of People."

Nadia didn't need to be told he is human. She knew he was one the moment he walked up to the table. But his position is of interest. Her father must serve with him on several human law committees.

"It's a pleasure to meet the famous Nadia Oswald," Morvath says teasingly.

Nadia's eyebrows go up. "Am I famous?" she asks with a chuckle.

"Famous enough. We all tease your father that without you, he wouldn't have been elected."

Nadia's father rolls his eyes at the comment.

"But I tease," Morvath says. "I just came over to say hello and pay my respects."

"It's good of you to come by," Nadia's father says.

"I'll leave you to your dinner." Morvath turns to Nadia and Elise and says warmly, "It's a pleasure to meet you both." He shakes their hands again.

Nadia studies the beanpole of a man as he walks away to his own table.

"He's a good man," Edgar Oswald says. "He's very focused on his work though. I'm amazed he has time to socialize."

"He seemed nice to me," Nadia says.

"Oh, he's nice. Just don't get into an argument with him on human law." He spoke as one who had made that mistake in the past.

Their waiter approaches just then with menus for all three of them. Nadia reads through the four-course meal options, and they all make selections. Then she sits back in her chair, her hand in Elise's hand, and enjoys the view of the Falgar. Soon she would be on those waters, traveling to foreign lands.

The idea of traveling abroad doesn't bother her. She had been to Umbra a few times now after all. This is different. This is travel to a war zone. She doesn't know what to make of it. She doesn't know what to expect.

Their waiter approaches and sets their first course down in front of each of them. Nadia looks at the sphere of cheese over a light salad. The portion is modest, as she would expect from a four-course meal. She takes her knife and breaks open the cheese to reveal the creamy center. The cheese is called eppirel and is made from buffalo milk cheese and a thick cow's cream. The outside is hardened cheese, and the inside is made of the soft buffalo cheese and cream. The flavor is unmatched with the salad on the side.

Nadia muses she is like the eppirel in some sense: tough on the outside and soft on the inside. But like the eppirel she is made of another's power, another's strength. And she fears she could easily be pulled apart despite her natural inner strength.

She eats the eppirel and tries to set her thoughts aside. It is only a matter of hours before they board the ship bound for Rebluinia. She wants to savor this meal and the time she has left in Port Nalrang. Because she suspects that when she comes back here, she won't be the same person as she is in this moment. She suspects her time down there may change her drastically.

Elise is studying her as she eats her own first course. Nadia gives a wan smile. Then they continue their meal, and the night moves on.

Seven

The ECAS *Scylla* is a massive new steel ship powered by steam engines and the occasional rowing crew. It sits imposingly at the end of the Port Nalrang Pier, the engines quiet for the moment. The ship is formidable, designed for war at sea.

Nadia takes in the hulking mass as their steam carriage rolls up to the port at dawn on Tisday. Elise sits next to her, hand in hand as they approach the great machine that is the army. Hughes sits wedged next to Kaye up front who is driving. Nadia's father is next to her. They pull up to the port authority. Nadia's father gets out and helps Nadia and Elise out of the steam carriage.

Nadia's boots hit gravel. She takes a few steps forward and they produce a satisfying *thunk* on the steel pier. She turns around and looks back up at Port Nalrang, her home for all intents and purposes. She misses Avita Spring right then. She feels the loss of her childhood home.

Elise comes up to her and takes her hand, following her gaze. The hulking city on the cliff looks down at them like it is some kind of creature from myth. Nadia squeezes Elise's hand and turns away from the city. Her father chats with Hughes as Kaye sets their bags down on the pier.

"Kaye," she says, coming up to him. "Thank you." She doesn't say for what. He fully knows what he is being thanked for. Instead, she embraces her father's man, again feeling the slipping away of her childhood. She is only fifteen, and it still feels eons behind them.

The sound of boots on the pier heralds the arrival of Colonel Ergamenes and an unknown captain. Both Nadia and Elise turn and salute the Colonel and the Captain. They salute back.

"This is Captain Arjun Wood," Colonel Ergamenes introduces the Captain. "He will show you around the ship."

Nadia surveys the Captain. He is a caster witch by the markings on his uniform. She extends a hand to him, and he takes it. A jolt goes through her at the contact. The power he carries is considerable. Nevertheless, the Captain's eyes narrow at contact with Nadia. No doubt her power seems enormous to him. Even with all the power he carries. She lets go of his hand.

"Pleased to meet you," Nadia says.

"Likewise," the Captain says.

"You're from . . . ?"

"Esaton Cove," he says.

Nadia nods. With a surname like "Wood," he could only be from the coastal region that has trees. Esaton Cove sits east of Port Nalrang, almost on the border with Mosnia. It is known for the small woods along the coastal cliff that produce the small amount of timber still used in Egraria. Nadia has never been, but always wanted to see it. She's never seen the green spaces along the coast, just the dusty desert city that is Port Nalrang.

"Let's get you on board," Captain Wood says. "Say your goodbyes."

Nadia, irritated at the somewhat dismissive attitude of the Captain, turns back to her father. He surprises her by embracing her. The embrace is not exactly warm and fluffy, but it is an embrace, nonetheless. Perhaps the fact that she is leaving for a war zone had sunk in.

"Take care of yourself," he says sternly. "And watch your back," he says with a glance in the direction of the Colonel and the Captain. She wonders then if her father really doesn't trust the military after all.

Elise accepts a hug from Nadia's father as well. He whispers something to her that Nadia can't make out, but perhaps doesn't need to. She can surmise what he is telling his almost daughter-in-law. Then Nadia's father lets her go.

With one last look at her family, Nadia and Elise and Hughes walk down the pier, following Captain Wood and Colonel Ergamenes to the massive ship. Nadia spares a look back at her father and Kaye before heading up the gangplank to the ship itself.

They enter through a side hatch into the near bowels of the ship, the massive door drawn to the side waiting to be closed again. Inside, the dim light comes from the new electricity, the yellow bulbs providing just enough illumination to prevent one from tripping. They walk down the corridor to a narrow, steep stair. It's here that Colonel Ergamenes leaves them and heads to do who knows what.

Every step took them deeper into the steel beast of a ship. Eventually, the Captain led them to their cabin, a hole in the wall with two bunks designed for sailors. Hughes would be staying in the cabin next door. Nadia sets her bag down on the lower bunk and looks around. She could hold out her arms and touch both walls, the bunks on one side and a built-in series of lockers on the other.

"I'll leave you to settle in. You're expected on the bridge in an hour," Captain Wood says. He turned and headed down the hall, leaving them to wonder where exactly the bridge is.

"I guess we'll find them," Elise says with a laugh. She shuts their cabin door.

They spend the next half hour unpacking their belongings. The journey across the Falgar would take over a week, giving them ample time to get accustomed to sea life. They would dock in Rebluinia at Blackguard, the port city closest to Rebluinia's western capital Pratergarde. The city is so named for the dark cliffs that flank the cove. There's only two ways to get to the city, by sea or by a single road that zigzags up the cliff face. It is a well-fortified metropolis. Nadia looks forward to seeing those dark cliffs.

"Which bunk do you want?" Elise asks.

"The lower, I think. I don't want to fall out," Nadia

says with a laugh.

Elise laughs. "We should probably go find the bridge."

"Probably."

A knock on the door precedes the person who comes through. The familiar face of Arnaldo Sala. "I heard you two were on board," he says genially.

"What are you doing here?!" Nadia asks in surprise. A familiar face on this voyage abroad feels like a huge luxury.

Sala smiles at them both, leaving the door open to the hall beyond. "I am being commissioned to train a small group of Rebluinian casters," he explains. "And to see to it you two keep training on our voyage."

Nadia considers this, nodding as she does. "I guess that's wise. What can we do at sea?"

He smiles mischievously. "Oh, a great many things, Miss Oswald," he says. "Or should I say Lieutenant?"

Nadia shakes her head. "I haven't completed my training yet."

"You will," he says confidently.

"Do you know where the bridge is?" Elise asks suddenly. "We're supposed to report there."

"Of course," Sala says. "I'll show you the way."

He leads them out the door, shutting it behind them, and through a maze of corridors and up several rickety stairs. They make their way down a final corridor to a set of doors propped open. Behind the doors, they find the bridge and the huge vista that is the open Falgar sea. For a moment, Nadia is left speechless at the sight of so much water all around her. For a moment, she forgets where she is and what she is doing.

"Oswald, Chulyin," Colonel Ergamenes says, "I take it you've settled in?"

"Yes, sir," Nadia answers for both of them.

"Good," he says, surveying both them and Sala. "I see Sala has found you. You are aware you are to keep working with him?"

"Yes, sir."

"I expect a complete report of all training activities," he says.

A sinking feeling fills the pit of Nadia's stomach. No doubt he is just looking for a way to circumvent her convictions. No doubt he is searching for a way to prove she could be used as a weapon. She wonders why Colonel Cunningham wasn't assigned to this duty. She wonders about the machinations that lead to her being under Colonel Ergamenes's authority again.

"Carry on then."

The dismissal is definitive. Sala leads them off the bridge and back down through the bowels of the ship.

"Hungry?" Sala asks.

"Famished," Elise says.

Sala smiles and leads them to the mess hall. Nadia and Elise sit down next to each other, one squeezing the hand of the other, and eat the lunch provided to the officers there. Nadia needs the comfort today. She has a sinking feeling that things are not going to go according to plan. It's a feeling she can't seem to shake.

Eight

The road to Courtthostur is long for a loan traveler to take. Luckily, Morvath is not alone. He is never alone. His valet is traveling with him, a human loyal to Morvath. All Morvath's staff have signed non-disclosure agreements that protect Morvath from prying eyes. He must maintain a semblance of human mundanity to the public eye. He cannot for one second appear to be obsessed with witches like he actually is.

His trip to Courtthostur has been kept incognito. To his colleagues and compatriots in Parliament, his trip is that of a vacation to Mosnia. And he had left town headed in that direction. Parliament is on break right now, so he can take a long trip. He just didn't see the point in a vacation when he has work to do.

Meeting Nadia Oswald and her cohort Elise Chulyin

only motivated him to move forward with his plans. In his pocket, he always carries a pair of clockwork trinkets. They are designed with magic by a former writer witch, something he picked up along his travels years ago.

One is a sensor of sorts. It tells the levels of witches nearby and what their power strength is. The scale is arbitrary, but he has used it and carried it enough to know how to read the scale. The reading on the two witches proved that Nadia is indeed a witch of the fourth kind. Her power rating was off the scale compared to Elise's. While most witches wouldn't pick up on the difference without the precision of a sensor like the one he carries, he has no doubt that most witches would pick up that she is a powerful writer, as Elise is. The confirmation was enough for him to be grateful he has a cordial relationship with Edgar Oswald. The only disappointment stems from the fact that Nadia and Elise were being deployed to Rebluinia.

The second trinket is a shield of the power kind. Had Morvath carried any power in him whatsoever, he would be shielded from any witches' sensing of him. Even the sensor he carries in his pocket wouldn't be able to pick up on that power. He carries it constantly with him knowing that, one day, when he finally acquires the power of the fourth kind, he would need his power blocked. He would need his power concealed to protect himself.

One last clockwork item he carries with him is an eyepiece of the most clever design. It had also been acquired along his travels, this one from the shore towns of Matraize. When worn, the eyepiece shows the user the power output of any witch. It was crafted by a writer witch who had suffered several attacks from lower-level witches. It served as an early-warning system to attacks. He could not very well wear it all the time, but he did think it would be useful to have it with him when facing Goliyant.

And face Goliyant he will.

He knows she is a powerful witch. At the very least, a powerful writer witch. His contact with her would prove if she was a powerful witch of the fourth kind. At least he hopes so. He knows from previous experience that there are powerful witches of all kinds, and that the sensor is not able to differentiate between the types as well as he would like. A particularly powerful caster witch could read like a writer witch. He fears catching the wrong kind of witch, but not enough to stop him from taking this journey.

So, on the last day of his journey to the central plateau, Morvath and his valet travel into the outskirts of Courtthostur, heading for the rundown inn at the southern end of the city. When Morvath has checked into the inn, his valet sharing a room with him and unpacking their belongings, he takes his trinkets and a particularly strong knife and leaves the valet alone.

Night is beginning to fall in Courtthostur. He is dressed in dark colors, deep browns and blacks to protect him from being seen easily. The gas lamps of Courtthostur only occupy the central rings of the city, the places where the farms and markets need them. He sticks to the dark neighborhoods along the exterior and circles his way to Courrthostur Academy. He knows Goliyant lives near the academy and he has her address written down. Most of the side streets lack names, but the lanes near the school are marked to make finding the school easier.

So, it is just about nightfall when he finds himself in an alleyway between the school and a house of modest size. He hides in the shadows and waits patiently for Goliyant to pass by. As he waits, he puts on the eye piece and pulls out the sensor. He knows his presence is masked from her witch senses, so he is not worried about that.

Then he spots her.

A woman dressed in a white academic robe with a veil over her hair passes by on the main lane. One look at her and he knows he found the right person: in the eyepiece he sees a nearly blinding glow of magic about her. The sense registers her power and goes nearly off the charts. She *must* be of the fourth kind. She is too strong to just be a writer witch.

So Morvath follows her down the lane at a distance. He keeps to the shadows, but he can sense her intuition must pick up on the follower. She stops and turns around, staring penetratingly into the shadows. When her eyes land on Morvath, she squints and then relaxes an inch. Clearly, she can sense that he is human.

Morvath picks his moment to slowly approach her.

"What do you want?" Goliyant asks.

A smile comes across Morvath's face, a smile hidden by the shadows. "I want to know what kind of witch you really are."

Goliyant immediately tenses. She is carrying some books, but shifts them so a hand is free, likely for spellcasting. "I don't answer to you."

The non-answer is enough for Morvath. She would

have said if she was just a writer witch. But she must be more. She must be hiding her nature like all of them seem to hide their nature.

By now, Morvath is within ten feet of Goliyant. The knife is heavy in his hand and hidden by his side. Goliyant lifts her free hand to project a spell outward. This is his moment.

He throws the knife.

Whether she was caught off-guard or the magic in the knife did its job, the blade runs right through and past her spell and finds its home in her chest. She drops the books and flings another spell in Morvath's direction. This one hits him, but is so weakened by her injury that he barely stumbles.

Witches are surprisingly easy to kill.

He walks up to Goliyant as she falls to the ground, red staining the white of her academic robes. Her veil has fallen back, revealing graying brown hair. Her eyes look fearfully up at Morvath. She tries to pull away from him as he places a hand on her forehead. But even as she fights, the life is draining out of her. The knife has done its job. Spelled to kill witches, the knife had killed many more before Morvath acquired it. Goliyant would not be able to survive this.

Morvath stays by her side as she dies. He feels the Vacancy Principle enact, the magic within Goliyant coming loose and finding the vacuum in Morvath's humanity. The power seeps from Goliyant to him.

He lets go of the dead body.

The turmoil within him continues. He looks at his hands and feels the power waiting below the surface. For years, he had studied witchcraft with the desire to get it for himself. Now it sits and waits below the surface for him. And tonight, he would need it.

Morvath removes the knife from Goliyant's chest. He uses a few words and some intention to clean it and tucks it back in the sheath at his side. He can't just leave Goliyant's body lying there in the street. He must make this look like a robbery gone wrong. So, he uses his second act of magic to move her body into a space between two houses. He raids her body for anything valuable and takes it from them. He would bury it in the desert later to keep it from tracing back to him. And then finally he takes her books and scatters them along the alleyway, making it seem as if she were pulled into the alley unaware.

He takes a moment to cast one last spell, a spell he had long since memorized, knowing he would need it when he got the power. He cast a spell for any prying eyes nearby to unsee what they saw. To unsee the magic and the murder. Satisfied, he headed down the alleyway and towards the inn. His mission accomplished so quickly and so efficiently, he would even have time to circle through Mosnia and make it seem as if he were there the whole time.

His valet says nothing as Morvath returns to their shared room. Morvath takes a leisurely bath, using his new power at one point to warm the waters to his liking. Then he returns to the room where his valet has turned down his bed and prepares for a comfortable and deep sleep. For the first time in years, he finds himself calm and at ease. He feels more himself than he has ever been before. He feels he is finally who he should be.

Morvath sinks to sleep, dreaming of the magic he now carries and the ways he can use it in the future. For the first time in his life, he feels perfectly safe.

Nine

Aidan arrives in Courtthostur after spending nearly a week with his family in Avita Spring. He had given his mother one of the glass pendants he made in the Waste, still reserving a few of them for the other women in his life. His mother had accepted the pendant gratefully and immediately put it on. The supportive nature of his mother touched him even as he is less human now.

The first person to greet him at Courtthostur Academy is, of course, John Blestone. He has barely gotten his horse into the stable yard when John comes running up to him. One look at John tells him there is something wrong.

Absently, John hugs his old casting partner and then steps back, looking Aidan over. "Are you alright?" he asks.

"I am," Aidan answers. "But what's wrong?"

John shakes his head in disbelief. "Goliyant is dead."

"*What?*"

"She was found this morning in an alleyway near her house. Looks like a robbery," John says.

Aidan clenches his jaw. "Are we sure? What happened to her magic?"

John's brow furrows. "That's the thing. They're on the lookout for someone with her power. It wasn't conserved by the community."

Aidan removes his saddlebags from the horse and begins walking to the main academy building with John. He shakes his head. "So, it was a robbery of sorts," he mutters.

"You think they *meant* to take her power?"

"It wouldn't be the first time that happened."

As they walk up to the main entrance of the school, Dean Jaran Watters exits the building with patrol officers next to him. When he sees Aidan, he pauses and changes his path to intercept him. To Aidan's surprise, Dean Watters extends a hand and Aidan shifts the saddlebags to shake it.

"Aidan, I'm sorry you're here on such a sad day," he says. With a glance at John, he adds, "I take it Mr.

Blestone has informed you of our news."

"He has," Aidan says. "And I'm stunned. I don't know what to say. I was coming here in part to see her."

Dean Watters nods his head and says, "I figured as much." One of the patrol officers calls Dean Watters's attention for a moment. "If you'll excuse me," the Dean says, "I believe Mr. Blestone can show you to your room."

"Thank you," Aidan says. "If there's anything I can do while I'm here, please let me know."

John walks him inside and they head down the corridors to the residential hall at the back. As they pass Goliyant's office, he is hit with a wave of nostalgia and grief that the place sits empty except for the officers going through her multitude of belongings. The writer witch's death would be felt.

They get to the guest quarters assigned to Aidan. He is relieved to find very few flammable things inside. No doubt they made preparations to that effect.

"How long are you staying?" John asks.

"As long as needed," Aidan says. He sets his bags down on the bed and turns back to John. "You should think about coming with me." He had thought about this for a long time. In the Waste, he wanted nothing but to be alone. Here, among humans and witches again, he felt the need for company. He felt the need to have a partner again.

John seems taken aback by the idea. "I'm not quite done with school yet," he says. They are both, after all, only sixteen.

"That doesn't matter to the Conscription Authority," Aidan answers.

John's eyebrows go up. "They haven't conscripted me yet. Probably because I'm a low-level seer. But would they let me work with you?"

Aidan shrugs. "I stopped thinking about obstacles a while ago. I think we can just shape our future however we want. And this might mean telling them what we want to do."

John just shakes his head. "After what happened here today, I'm not sure of anything anymore," he says. "Goliyant was so powerful. I never thought she would get attacked, much less killed."

"I know," Aidan says soberly. "I feel that too."

John looks away for a moment, seemingly deep in thought. Aidan just watches John's back, the noise from the hallway filtering in and providing background to the silence. His old partner turns back to him and says, "I'll have to talk to my parents and teachers, but I would like to go."

The answer is so sudden it startles Aidan. He calms himself down immediately. "We have time to make arrangements," he says. "I'll be here as long as needed."

He wasn't in a rush anymore. With the girls getting deployed to Rebluinia, and the murder of Goliyant being here, he finds himself suddenly motivated to stay in Courtthostur. To be involved with all of this somehow. Though he knows the Conscription Authority would soon be calling him to work. Maybe sending him to Rebluinia as well.

John nods again and smiles at Aidan. "I'm glad you're back, friend. It's been too long."

And at that moment, Aidan realizes it's been almost a year since he and John last stood together in the halls of this building. Between his time in Umbra and his time in the Waste, he hadn't been home in so long Avita Spring was foreign to him. Here, though, with his former partner, he finds himself at home again.

"We should go downstairs," John says. "We can get some tea."

Aidan leaves his belongings and locks the door to his room. He doesn't have many valuables, but it's still wise to lock the door in the face of a recent murder. Though somehow, he doubts the murderer is still in town. If they're smart, they would have moved on to someplace no one knows them and can tell if they're a writer witch or not.

John pours them steaming cups of poisonously strong tea and they take some snacks from the sideboard to a seat near the middle of the dining hall. They are just taking their first sips when a voice calls out to them.

"Aidan!"

The voice belongs to Chloe Armstrong. She walks in accompanied by her sister Marnie and Alex Fowler. The trio of humans he hadn't seen since before he left for Umbra. Aidan sets his cup down and stands to greet them, giving each of them a heartfelt hug.

"How are you doing?" Chloe asks, looking Aidan over critically.

Aidan shrugs. "I'm alright, a little shocked by what happened."

She nods, a gesture mirrored by the other two. "I know, it's appalling," she says. "I can't believe it. Someone so strong . . ."

The three of them get tea and they all sit back down. "Where's Ethan?" Aidan asks suddenly.

"He's in Saphlaw with his family," Alex answers. "He'll be back tomorrow."

"Has anyone heard anything about who did it?" Marnie asks. No one has to ask what she's talking about.

John shakes his head. "No, not yet," he says. "I mean who would be crazy enough to attack such a powerful writer witch?"

"Someone who wants her power," Marnie says matter-of-factly.

"Or someone just flat out stupid." They all look at Chloe. "Well, it's true."

No one argues with her. She has a point, but the opposite could also be true. It could be someone extremely smart who did this, who hunted her down and killed her for her power. And Goliyant is not here to counsel him on his thoughts.

Aidan shakes his head. "When is the memorial service?"

"They don't know yet," Alex says. "Are you going to stay?"

"I'll stay as long as we need to be here," Aidan says, glancing at John.

"What do you mean?" Chloe asks, her gaze going back and forth between Aidan and John.

"I'm going with Aidan when he leaves," John says.

The statement is met with silence. The three humans are clearly stunned.

"Did you get conscripted?" Marnie asks John.

"No," John says, "but we'll work that out."

At that point, they are all distracted by the crowd going to the witchwire screen to watch the incoming report. Aidan gets up and John follows him as they join the crowd in the main common area. Jane Sherhand comes up on the screen to do the report.

"This afternoon's headline is the landing of Egrarian forces on the shores of Rebluinia," the woman's voice carries over the hushed crowd. Aidan realizes that all his friends are gathered around him. "Winslow Wilson is embedded with the first forces to make the landing in Blackguard."

The feed cuts over to Winslow on a boat off the coast of Blackguard. The distinctive black cliffs surround the bay, and the city sits in the distance. "The energy is high here today as the military arrives in Rebluinia. The battle between Rebluinian and Ecrian forces rages on just south of the city. These troops will be sent to reinforce Rebluinian forces."

The screen pans to include a colonel standing next to

Winslow. "I have with me Colonel Ergamenes." Aidan is startled to see the man on the screen. "Colonel, thank you for speaking with us. The people back home want to know what the plan is for the forces heading south," Winslow asks.

"I cannot divulge the full military plan," Colonel Ergamenes says. "However, we have a few weapons up our sleeves that I'm looking forward to deploying at the front."

Aidan briefly wonders if he means Nadia.

"What kind of weapons, Colonel?" Winslow asks.

"Witch kind," Colonel Ergamenes says. "We have a few particularly strong witches with us on board that should prove useful to the war effort."

"Well, we'd like to meet them, if possible," Winslow says.

The Colonel smiles coyly and says, "We'll have to see about that."

"Do you have a message for the people back home?"

Colonel Ergamenes turns to face the camera and says, "Do your duty. If the call comes for you, we can use all the help we can get. Join the effort and support the Rebluinian war."

A knot forms in Aidan's stomach. Somehow, he

feels like the Colonel's words are directed right at him. He feels like he's being called out directly for being absent for so many months.

He heads out of the common room, tuning out the rest of the news. Today has been too much already. Between Goliyant's murder and the forces landing in Rebluinia, likely the girls landing in Rebluinia as well, he has a feeling in the pit of his stomach that has nothing to do with hunger.

Aidan heads outside. He breathes the free air, for a moment feeling as if he is back in the Waste. Then he looks over and sees the patrol officers on the other side of the school gate still doing their investigation. He knows what he has to do, and he doesn't feel good about it.

Ten

Goliyant's funeral was planned for four days after her death. According to her wishes, she would be cremated, and her ashes would be scattered on the open plateau. Aidan thinks the tribute is fitting, given how much time Goliyant spent on the open plateau. It doesn't change the sad fact that she is dead and gone.

The funeral took place at sunset. The gathered students, colleagues, friends, and family all watched as Dean Watters expertly cast a spell to send her ashes far and wide on the plateau. It was beautiful, in a way, watching them go. And it was sad that the ashes were all that was left of her. Of her physical form at least.

After the funeral concluded, Aidan headed back inside the school. The Dean had opened up the dining and common rooms to allow for mingling. The kitchens laid out an overwhelming spread for the gathered mourners to snack on as needed.

It is during this mixing that Aidan finds himself wandering away from the crowds again. He finds a quiet corner and tucks himself away with a plate of hot snacks he can handle eating. As he is often reminded, he must keep the human parts of him going, no matter how much in the minority those human parts are, these days.

"There you are," John says, finding Aidan in his little corner. "Are you hiding?"

Aidan smiles a half-smile at John. "I don't do well in crowds these days."

John takes a seat in the cushy chair next to him and nods in understanding. "They still have no clue who killed her," he says. "Or why."

"I really do think we all know why." Aidan shakes his head. "She was too powerful. I don't understand how she got caught off guard."

"She might have let her guard down if it was a human," John says.

Aidan takes a drink of scalding hot tea before saying, "I don't feel like talking about this right now. I think we should let her rest for a while."

John nods in agreement. There would be plenty of

time for speculation later on. Instead, John asks, "Do you know when you want to leave yet?"

"I don't know," Aidan answers. "Have you spoken to your family?"

John leans back in his chair. "I haven't heard from them yet. I sent them updates on everything, including the update on Goliyant. I don't think they're going to object to me leaving school," he says. With a smile, he adds, "I think they're more surprised that I've been staying in place this long."

Aidan smiles at the thought. John comes from the nomadic people of the central plateau. "Where are they at these days?" Aidan asks.

"Somewhere near Bexley," he says. "Down close to Esaton Cove."

Aidan nods and smiles at the thought of them near a metropolis. They do sometimes camp in the outskirts of major cities to get some of the benefit of being close to those places. John had once told Aidan that they would go to magic displays when he was a child and that helped him develop his seer abilities. John comes from a family of witches, all seers and all proficient at their abilities. None of them is particularly powerful, but they all make do with what they have.

The dichotomy between him and John always made him wonder why they were paired up. He loves working with John, but he always wondered why Goliyant paired him with such a low-power witch. But there was wisdom behind it. Aidan had learned more from John than he ever could have imagined. Perhaps there was still more to learn from his casting partner.

"We're going to visit them before we go to Port Nalrang," John says suddenly.

"Are we?"

"Yeah," John says. "I just saw it."

"Where do we visit them?"

"I'm not sure," he says truthfully. "But it's a small town."

They would be passing through several small towns on their way to Port Nalrang, so Aidan doesn't doubt the truth to John's vision. John's family likely saw the same vision and would make it happen.

At that moment, Dean Watters comes around the corner, spots the pair, and walks up. He is alone, which is unusual for the Dean who is constantly surrounded by teachers and administrators.

"Mr. Montgomery, would you and Mr. Blestone please accompany me to my office briefly?"

Surprised, Aidan assents and he and John get up from their seats to follow Dean Watters upstairs. They head down the hall to the Dean's office, passing the other administrators' offices along the way. Dean Watters unlocks the heavy wooden door, an artifact from the founding of the school, and lets them in. The Dean circles the metal and glass desk and takes a seat, indicating the pair should do the same.

Aidan glances around the office, noting to himself the tidy nature of the Dean's surroundings. It is a far cry from Goliyant's cluttered office downstairs. He wonders briefly who will take over that office now that Goliyant is dead.

"I just received word from the Conscription Authority about you," the Dean says, nodding at Aidan. "They are calling you south as soon as possible. I know you wished to stay a few more days, but the urgency of their message cannot be overstated."

"What about John?"

"I relayed to the Conscription Authority your desire to join Aidan in his work," the Dean says to John. "They denied the application." Here the Dean smiles mischievously. "But I believe the workaround is quite simple. You need to enlist."

"What?"

"Yes, just enlist as a regular soldier and then you—" he indicates Aidan— "simply refuse to work with them unless John is by your side."

Aidan and John exchange a look.

"I'd outrank you by a bit," Aidan says. "More than if you completed school and enlisted then."

John shrugs. "That doesn't matter to me," he says. "So, I'll have to salute a lot. Oh, well."

The Dean hands John a green witchwire note. "From your parents I believe."

He takes the note and tears open the envelope from the witchwire office. John reads the contents before looking up with a smile. "They give their permission to enlist and say they support my decision to go with Aidan," he says. "My mom must be having a good seeing day."

"Must be."

The Dean nods as if everything is in place. "Go to the Conscription Authority office in town and enlist at your earliest convenience," he says. "I would go first thing tomorrow. Then report with Aidan to the authorities in Port Nalrang."

"Thank you," Aidan says.

He and John get up and head out of the Dean's office. The Dean doesn't leave, but when Aidan glances back, he sees the Dean just staring off into space. He recalls then how close the Dean and Goliyant were. He must be taking her death quite hard.

"Are you going to bed?" John asks. It is well into the evening by now, and John gives a spectacular yawn, showing that he's tired.

"Probably," Aidan says. "Though I'm not sure I'll sleep easily tonight."

"We'll have to have dinner with everyone tomorrow before we leave."

"You think we're leaving that quickly?"

"I know so," John says. "I can see us on the road the day after tomorrow."

They are standing in the hallway, near the walkway that connects to the residential wing. The stairs leading to the fourth floor and John's dorm room are next to them. Aidan is only a few doors down the hall to his room.

"Can you see if they're going to deploy us?"

John shakes his head. "That's too far off yet," he explains. "I think it's likely though."

Aidan looks off down that hallway and then back at

his casting partner. "I'll go with you tomorrow morning to the Conscription Authority," he says.

"Get some rest," John says as he turns and heads up the stairs.

Aidan goes to his door and unlocks it, letting himself in. He shuts the door and sits down on the bed. Through the windowpane he can hear some activity in the back courtyard, no doubt spillover from the memorial service. He wonders how long before they all go their own way and Goliyant becomes a memory.

He sighs, feeling the grief inside of him. After a few minutes, he gets ready for bed and tucks himself into his highly-flammable linen sheets.

He wishes he could see the future like John can. He wishes he could see what is coming right around the corner. Because he has a feeling it's not going to be good. And if Goliyant's death taught them anything, it's that none of them is safe.

Eleven

Morvath returns to Port Nalrang about a week and a half after he killed Goliyant. He spent his time in Mosnia getting a handle on the immense power he now carries with him. And he also spent the time familiarizing himself with the spell built into the shield. He used the spell as a template to construct an identical spell. Only this one he put in the ring he always wears. The ring given to him by his father and passed down from generation to generation. The ring he would never let go of or lose. Morvath continued to carry the shield in his pocket as a backup, but the shield buried in his ring now provided his primary protection.

Back in his home, he sits in his study and pours over the contents of what he has learned in his time since taking Goliyant's power. The power sensor indicates he is a strong witch, but he would have to be near a fourth kind witch to know for certain he had captured their power. He reads through his list again and crosses off Goliyant's name. That left a few names on the list.

Thorryn Creer

Erik Satterthwait

Saknor Howells

Dalia Ekinor

~~Euphemia Goliyant~~

Nadia Oswald

Aidan Montgomery — former?

He knows there have to be at least a half dozen, if not dozen or more, of these witches out there. Likely it would be no more than that. There would be no way for them to keep their secrets otherwise. Too many voices and one would eventually speak.

Of the remaining candidates, he weighs his options. Some of them are simply out of reach. Dalia Ekinor lives in Matraize and only came up because of the unusual circumstances of her becoming a witch. He doubts he could get close enough to her without raising suspicions.

Similarly, Thorryn Creer is a renowned academic in Mosnia. If he approached him, it had better be with good reason and he better be sure he was getting the right kind of witch. That left Satterthwait who is a nomad, Howells who lives in Port Nalrang, and Oswald who is deployed.

He considers for a moment going after Oswald, but she is too insulated with the military. Howells, on the other hand, presents a unique and tantalizing opportunity. If he is right and Howells is a fourth power witch, then he would be able to gauge his own strength by approaching the man. How would he go about approaching him without setting off his alarms though? Howells is notoriously paranoid and lives in an apartment in a rundown old house in West Prekrol. Not exactly the glamor of his previous life.

An idea blossoms in his mind. He could observe the man from a distance and use the sensor to compare their powers. Then if he's right about the man he would know what to do. But if he's wrong about him, then he could leave without so much as communicating with Howells. He wouldn't raise the suspicions of the other witches if they indeed communicate with each other.

A knock on the door interrupts his reverie. His butler comes in with a witchwire note on a tray. Morvath takes the note and dismisses the butler.

He opens the green envelope. It's from another minister, Joshua Shetler. The two are friendly and he is not surprised to be receiving a note from him. What does surprise him is the contents.

> *I am organizing a trip of support to Rebluinia. We will be sailing across the Falgar and landing in Blackguard. I know with your views on the war that you might be interested in joining us. If you are, please join us at five o'clock at the Parliament Commissary on Anday, Larandy the 12th.*

The meeting is tomorrow. The message must have come while he was gone.

He sets the message down and smiles to himself. He could not have planned it more perfectly. Traveling to Rebluinia would give him a chance to get close to Miss Oswald. It would give him an excuse to be there without raising suspicions. He could still surveil Howells before leaving on the trip and possibly make contact with the witch if needed.

Morvath opens his desk drawer and pulls out the knife carefully sheathed and wrapped in a thick cloth. He had studied the spell on the blade and had come to the conclusion that it would not harm him so long as he was the one throwing it. To be extra safe, he keyed his power into the blade so that it would recognize him. It was very much his knife now.

He marvels at his work now and runs his fingers over the blade, feeling the power within. Long ago, over a thousand years ago, the first witch to imbue their magic into an object had no idea it would lead to a blade like this. It is the product of many years and many witches' work. And finally, he can be a part of that work. He can have that power for himself.

He carefully tucks the blade away and locks the drawer. He will go to Howells tomorrow. He will go before his meeting with Shetler. In the meantime, he would prepare.

Carefully, he takes the sensor out of his pocket and sets it next to his witchglass. He begins copying the lines of the spell buried in the small disc-shaped sensor. He lays the lines down in the witchglass, putting the spell into the clockwork and witchcraft device. The screen, a glass piece for which it is named, shows the spell diagram to him. He is hoping with some manipulation he can magnify the spell and make it have a larger range. Then he could use it to scan an entire crowd of people and not just individuals. He could use it to scan all of Howells's building.

Morvath leans back in his chair, satisfied at his work.

Curiosity overcomes him. He slips his ring off his finger and sets it on the desk. He activates the spell in the witchglass and watches it work. He also activates the spell in the disc sensor and compares them. They both pick up Morvath right away. That is to be expected. What surprises him is the sheer range the new spell has. He can feel the tug on his energy as it works, something that would likely tire him later, but he is satisfied with what he sees. He can register the witches who live two floors below him. He didn't realize they were low-power seer witches.

Out of curiosity, he slips his ring back on. Immediately, he disappears from both the witchglass and the sensor disc. The spell in the ring is working.

Morvath deactivates the spell. He switches off his witchglass and tucks it away along with the sensor. He has a plan, and he's content with that.

He gets up and heads to the dining room for dinner.

Twelve

Nadia can barely breathe, but she's pushing through. Her face and head are covered so thoroughly with cloth that she can't smell the desert around them. Every inch of skin, including around her eyes, is covered in some fashion to protect against the Rebluinian desert. She is wearing goggles with faintly amber-tinted glass to protect her eyes from the sand. Next to her, Elise is similarly clad, Hughes also wearing military-issue desert protective clothing. None of them are comfortable.

Since they came ashore at Blackguard, it has been hard riding for two days through the desert of Rebluinia to the oasis city of Melgarde. It is there, along the streets of the metropolis, that Ecriun forces wage their war against Rebluinian soldiers and civilians. Today, the third day of their trip through the sand, Nadia sits on her horse and stairs at the amber-tinted skyline of the city on the horizon.

Smoke rises from the buildings to the south, the place where Ecrian forces first made their incursion. Even from here, she can sense the power being poured out by all the witches fighting. Whether they were fighting to save lives or end them remained to be seen.

They continue their march towards the eastern outskirts of the city. They would make the nearest neighborhood by this afternoon. As the sun shifted in the sky, the light slowly went from behind them to in front of them. By the time they reached the city, it would be full in their faces.

Nadia glances over at Elise who glances back. They don't say anything to each other. The tension in the air deepens the closer they get to the city.

Suddenly, the line of soldiers ahead of them stops, bringing the whole convoy to a halt. Nadia looks in confusion at Elise, but none of them can see what is happening and why they stopped. But they don't have to wait long.

A wave of sand the height of a building rolls across the desert towards them. In a few minutes, it would bury them in sand deep enough to kill the entire convoy.

There is only one thing that could mean. Ecrium has a sand elemental in their ranks.

Witch after witch raises a shield around them, small measly shields that could not possibly hope to stand up to the wave coming towards them. The ground begins to destabilize beneath their horses' hooves, causing the animals to become agitated. Nadia immediately hops off her horse, Elise following suit. Around them, many other soldiers do the same.

She exchanges a glance with Elise. She doesn't need to see Elise's face to know the fear there. Nadia can feel it. She reaches out and takes Elise's hand. Her girlfriend's hand feels steady and strong in hers. And Nadia feels grounded again.

Around her, the sand becomes stone.

"I can shield us," Elise calls out, her voice straining against both the sound of the oncoming wave and the cloth across her mouth.

"I'll help you!" Nadia shouts back. And that's when she feels the ground under all the convoy solidify in response. She chose to move the earth rather than be moved by it.

Elise squeezes her hand. Then she raises her left hand up and begins to speak in witchspeak. In the intonation of witches, her voice is clear to Nadia, ringing in her ears as Elise speaks words in Old Umbrian.

Her voice rises above the din. *"Besape fetang eksyng."*

Like a blooming desert flower, a glowing shield sprouts from Elise's upheld hand. As she had felt so many times before, Nadia feels incredibly grateful for Elise's natural talent. She feels Elise pull on her power and draw it into the shield as it spreads out around the whole of the convoy. The edges come down, surrounding the line in a thick guard against the coming wave.

In their bubble of power, in the protective shield, the wave breaks over them blotting out the light of the sun. For a moment, Nadia stands with bated breath, waiting to see if the shield will hold. It buckles slightly under the weight of the sand. Elise draws more power from Nadia, throwing it into the shield. The bubble of power brightens as more of Nadia's power sinks into it, strengthening the shield.

The shield holds.

Under the shield, it is nearly silent. Nadia can hear the murmurs of the soldiers as they realize they are protected. Several witches drop their shields and move in the direction of Elise and Nadia. One by one the witches link up, hand in hand until the last person closest to Nadia takes her other hand.

From somewhere in the chain of witches, Sala shouts, "Repulsor! Do a repulsor!"

Elise looks over at him and nods. Again, she speaks in Old Umbrian, *"Tahkesh uhmso."*

The shield changes color to an electric blue. Outside the shield, the sand begins to move, to blow off the shield like it is being carried by a howling wind.

Then Elise pulls on the power within the whole network of witches. Nadia acts as a conduit for the power, her being the only one with enough strength to withstand the magic. But even with all her power and all her strength, she feels her soul burning. She doesn't know how long she can withstand this heavy of a stream.

The sand blows away into dunes surrounding the convoy. At the front end of the convoy, on the other side of the shield, stands several of Ecrium's forces. The group is small but formidable. The one person in the middle is clearly an elemental. Nadia cannot see his face because of the metal shield clearly keeping the sand out. But she sees the elemental's eyes and feels the power coming off him. Those eyes look angry.

The Ecrian forces, dressed in Ecrian brown with

metal armor over their clothes, step together in synchronized motion. It's then that Nadia realizes they are all witches. Every single one.

Nadia watches in horrified fashion as the witches synchronize their power and link with the elemental. She can feel what is coming. And she's not sure that they have enough power between all of them to combat it. They're going to take down the shield.

"Trap them in the shield!" Nadia shouts. "Quickly!"

Elise acts. With the precision of her mathematical mind, she flips the shield over and onto the Ecrian forces. The bubble surrounds them, penning them in.

A mass of power explodes within the bubble. A light so blinding she can't look at it even with the goggles fills the bubble. Elise struggles to hold the shield in place. She yanks on the power of the collective witches. Nadia falls to her knees as the power flashes through her and into the shield.

The light stops inside the shield. The repulsor must have worked. Every witch lay on the ground knocked unconscious. Only the elemental remains standing.

Elise wraps the lines of the shield around the elemental, wrapping them tighter and tighter till the elemental can't move. Yet he still struggles against the power Elise is throwing at him. He is still pulling in sand to him.

The nature of the shield changes. Elise is muttering a constant stream of Old Umbrian that Nadia can't make out. She can't even make out the words, much less the meaning. But Elise is concentrating with everything she has and pulling on their power with everything they've got.

A small sandwave comes flying at the convoy.

Abruptly it dies out.

The elemental falls to the ground surrounded by a magical cage.

Every Egrarian witch drops to their knees depleted.

Immediately, several human soldiers begin to bind the hands and feel of every witch that is unconscious. They leave the elemental for Elise who walks forward. Nadia peels herself off the ground and follows her. Colonel Ergamenes joins them. The elemental is still conscious and glaring up at them in fury. He can't move because of Elise's cage.

"Well done, Lieutenant," the Colonel says to Elise. "We'll hold him in Pratergarde."

"He'll need to stay caged," Elise says.

"Can any witch power it?"

"Yes," Elise says, "but I would use two or three at a time to keep him from breaking out."

"We have cells in Pratergarde that can dampen his power," the Colonel says.

This garners a look of horror from the elemental. His jaw works, but Elise's cage is so tight on his body that he can't even open his mouth to speak. Nadia briefly wonders what the elemental would say to them. But she dismisses it as probably something horrible.

The elemental's eyes fall on Nadia, and he glares at her. For just a moment, she hears his inner thoughts. *Blasted anchor witch*, he says. And that's all he says to her.

Of course, an elemental would pick up on her power, outside the stream of witchpower as they are. But it's still startling to be called out so specifically as that.

Colonel Ergamenes arranges a team of humans to gather the elemental. A small team of soldiers, both witches and humans, would accompany him back to Pratergarde along with the witches. Each witch is fitted with spellbonds on their wrists, cuffs imbued by a writer witch to dampen any magic by the wearer. They are powerful, but Nadia wonders if they would work on her given that her power is beyond writer power. It would take something special to bind her power. And she can think of nothing good coming from it.

"We move on now," Colonel Ergamenes orders.

Hughes helps Nadia and Elise back up on their horses before mounting his own. Nadia checks her face covering and dusts off her hands. She dons a pair of gloves and takes the reins. She looks up. Colonel Ergamenes is staring at her. He doesn't say anything, but he doesn't have to. She knows he must be thinking about ways to get her to use her power to fight. A sinking feeling in her gut tells her he is never going to let this go.

She wishes Colonel Cunningham or her father or any sympathetic party were here to curb Colonel Ergamenes's desires. She wishes she didn't feel so alone.

Elise pulls up next to her and meets her gaze. No, she's not alone. But she certainly feels isolated. And being a thousand miles from home in a foreign land did not help.

The convoy moves on, heading towards who-knows-what in Melgarde. Nadia grips the reins and spurs her horse onward, wishing again she had a different life.

Thirteen

The tension only grew as they entered the streets of Melgarde. Nadia can feel the others on edge. She is calm at this moment, calm and steady thanks to her anchor power. But she knows intellectually she should be nervous. She should be scared.

In the distance, they can hear explosions. Reverberating booms that shake the core and make the convoy nervous. Only Colonel Ergamenes seems nonchalant about the attacks ongoing to their south. Then again, he seems nonchalant about most things, but Nadia thinks it might be a front for the man's turmoil within. She doesn't care enough to read the man to find out.

The convoy heads through the city streets. There is rubble along the street's edge and clear damage to many buildings. Some of them are so badly damaged she wonders why they're still standing. A sign written in both the common script and the swirly Rebluinian alphabet hangs from a building proclaiming it once held a school. She wonders where the children have gone now. Most have likely been evacuated to the north end of the city and then onward to Pratergarde or somewhere else. This war affects more than just the people in the military. This war affects everyone.

The convoy comes to a halt in a neighborhood near the center of Melgarde. The sun has already dropped low enough that it is nearly twilight between the buildings of the city. All around her, the soldiers begin to dismount. Nadia remains on her horse even as Elise gets down from hers. From her vantage point, she sees the front of the convoy, the Colonel and his officers in what would be a lovely park on a normal day. Her gaze goes past them to the streets beyond.

It's through that slit of a view, between the gray buildings of Melgarde, that she sees their approach. And she's not the only one to spot them.

"Shield!" a voice calls out.

But it's too late. A single line of fire erupts from the roof of a nearby building. They walked right into a trap.

Without thinking, Nadia throws her hand up and shoots out a shield the half size of the convoy. It blossoms from her hand in a violent bright light arcing out away from her and over the top of the convoy. The fire hits the shield, but she doesn't quite cover the convoy in time. Some fire spills under the edges.

Witches and humans alike scramble to put out the flames. For a moment, she wishes Aidan were there to put the fires out. But they do their best with the witches they have.

Whoever fired the shot stopped immediately. That's when Nadia sees why. A contingent of soldiers wearing Ecrian brown and Ecrian armor streams out of the alleys between buildings and heads for the convoy. A knot forms in Nadia's stomach. How would she be able to defend herself and keep to her promise of not using weapons?

"Drop the shield," Elise says next to her.

She looks down and sees Elise holding a bow and arrow of glowing light. She must have created them from her power. And she is aiming the arrow in the direction of the original shooter.

Nadia closes her fist.

The shield vanishes.

Elise shoots the arrow.

In the distance, they hear a voice cry out and a man dressed in Ecrian brown falls from the fifth floor of the building. Nadia shudders at the sight.

She dismounts her horse and stands by Elise's side. Magic and weapons clash at the front of the convoy. She can't quite make out what's happening, except that they were taken by surprise, and they can only react to the attack.

"Come on," Nadia says. "I can shield them."

"I'll fight for you," Elise says.

They move forward, pushing their way to the front of the convoy where the heat from the fire makes it difficult to breathe. Nadia does not lower the cloth over her face. She knows she needs the protection from the smoke.

A fireball comes at Elise.

Nadia steps in front of Elise and raises a hand with a small shield. The fireball snuffs out on it.

Elise steps forward and throws power back at the caster. The caster goes down with one blinding shot. Elise is powerful, there is no doubt about that.

Before long, they have made their way to Colonel Ergamenes's side. The front is struggling, some soldiers already fallen to the ground. A shot comes straight at the Colonel who is shielded but not strongly enough. Nadia flings a hand in his direction, strengthening the shield in front of the Colonel. She does not like the Colonel, but she does not wish to see anyone fall. His look of surprise at her actions tells her that he knows she doesn't like him.

Elise steps forward and shoots another arrow of power at the assailant. The Ecrian soldier falls immediately. Together, Elise and Nadia step forward and begin to push back on the Ecrian forces. Nadia raises a shield with strength she didn't know she had and begins to push forward physically into the soldiers.

A single human with a sword skirts the shield and comes straight at her.

Elise shoots him without hesitation.

From their side, a blast of wind knocks Elise over. They are clearly targets of the Ecrian forces.

Nadia drags Elise to her feet.

"What was that?"

"Wind power," Nadia mutters. The shield she raised has no power against that raw element. She doesn't remember how to guard against it.

"Wind against wind," Sala says, coming up behind them.

Those words echo through Nadia, a reminder of her training back in Egraria.

"Air against air." Sala's voice goes up to be heard over the incoming wind.

Nadia hardens the air between them and the wind. The wind blast hits like a ton of bricks against her shield. The force nearly knocks her to the ground.

That's when she feels the hit to her right side. Her flank is exposed to the onslaught pointed at the Colonel's direction. Nadia looks down to see the knife protruding from her side.

"No!" Elise yells.

Nadia just sees the power coming from Elise, the power thrown in the direction of the Ecrian soldier who threw the knife. There is a flash of light and then nothing stands where the soldier once stood.

Nadia falls to her knees. She puts her hand on the knife and feels the spell there. It's a killing spell, something that reminds her of the writer witch in Avita Spring so long ago.

"Don't take it out," Sala says, crouching next to her.

Another wind blast nearly knocks him over, but he remains mostly upright.

"We need to use a repulsor, like before," Sala says, as

he examines the wound in Nadia's side.

"A targeted one?" Elise asks as she throws power around like she has unlimited resources.

"Target their armor!" Sala says.

Nadia moans as the spell sinks deeper into the wound. The wound itself is bleeding profusely, but the spell will kill her before she bleeds out if something isn't done about it right away.

"Medic!" Sala calls.

Elise grabs a witch near her, a caster by the mark on his shoulder. "Guard me!"

The soldier doesn't question anything and merely faces the oncoming Ecrian forces. He is proficient with a shield, if not overly powerful. He keeps bouncing power back at the sender.

"Lay down," Sala says. Nadia complies. She can hardly find the strength to stay upright.

From the ground, she can see Elise. She watches in pride-filled awe as Elise works. She is the prodigy between the two of them, for sure.

Elise forms a ball of light in her hands, pulling in the elements from around them. Water from the air, lines of sand from the ground below, and fire from the flames being thrown back and forth. The concentration in her eyes shows a fierceness Nadia has never seen in her lover. The pain in her side is too great for her to help, but all she wants to do is reach out and give Elise her power to use. Elise doesn't need it. She lets the power go.

Immediately, every soldier wearing the Ecrian armor flies backward some two or three blocks in the direction they came from. The few she didn't manage to hit begin to run in that direction as well.

"They're retreating!"

"Huzzah!" a cry goes up from many of the soldiers around them.

The medic arrives at Nadia's side. She remains conscious long enough to feel Elise hold her hand.

"I've got you," Elise says. She looks ragged and exhausted, but still she pours power into Nadia. She pours power into her lover.

The medic begins dismantling the spell in the knife. The bleeding slows at his direction and the spell begins to recede. Nadia feels her spirit fighting hard to remain, fighting to anchor itself.

"Stay with me," Elise says.

"I won't leave you," Nadia whispers.

"I'm going to remove the knife now," the medic

says.

Nadia braces herself.

As it moves through her flesh, a fresh wave of pain washes over her. She cries out; she can't help it.

Before the blade leaves her side, she passes out.

Fourteen

The sun is high in the sky as Morvath makes his way down the street. It is midday and enough people are heading back and forth that his presence is less noticeable. He left his steam carriage with his driver several blocks from the rundown tenant building Howells calls home. He did not need to attract that kind of attention to himself.

At the street corner he stops and stands leaning on the gaslamp post shedding measly light. The thing needs to be serviced. It is clearly not drawing enough power from the city gas. But in a neighborhood like West Prekrol, maintenance is not a priority.

Just as he is about to walk forward to a protected place in an alley across from the tenant building, Morvath spots Howells heading up the street towards him. He freezes and immediately checks the ring is intact on his hand. With the ring still in place, he steps out of the gaslight and into the shadows. Howells has not noticed him.

Howells is disheveled to say the least. His clothes are several years out of date in fashion and are rag-tag at best. The elbows have holes, and the shoes look worn to the sole. More than that, his demeanor is that of a man who has nothing to live for. He is hunched over, moving with fidgety gestures and an uneven gait. Morvath knows the man is living in poverty and is plagued by paranoia, but he had never expected it to be this bad.

The shifty witch looks over his shoulder several times as he heads into the building. The door is so dilapidated that it has fallen off its hinges entirely and is merely leaning to the side. As Howells disappears through the doorway, Morvath pulls his witchglass from his satchel and directs it at Howells's building. The glowing figure of Howells moves upward in the building, heading to the man's purported apartment in the attics.

The reading is unmistakable. The man is a fourth power witch.

He lowers the witch glass and pulls up his own readings. It's a formality. One look at Howells's

presence on the screen and it was obvious. Goliyant was a writer witch at most. A very powerful one true, but not a fourth power witch. And the comparison on the screen only confirms the truth. Howells is what he seeks.

Morvath puts the witchglass away. He has enough information, now just what to do with it. Does he go now to Howells and finish the job? Or does he wait to draw the man out? There are positives to both scenarios. On the one hand, he could easily leave Howells dead, and the man would not be discovered for days if not weeks given his hermetic nature. On the other hand, he could make it look like another robbery. Either way works and either way would get the job done.

Morvath is patient, but this is testing his will. He feels the weight of the knife at his back, tucked in his belt. The temptation is there. He stops to consider.

There must be a back door to the building. A way to get in and get out without being noticed. He doesn't know how to cloak himself yet. Some witches can do that. They can hide themselves in plain sight. He's not that practiced yet. He can conceal his nature well enough to sneak up on the man and take his power. He can do what he needs to do here.

And maybe he doesn't need to get that close to the

man until he is dying. Maybe he could incapacitate him from afar.

Morvath eyeballs the street, eyeballs the buildings across the street. The crowds are thickening for the lunch hour, and he is running out of time if he wants to do this now. Pretty soon, the busyness of the street would be no protection.

Slowly and steadily, he makes his way across the lane and to the alleyway between Howells's building and the one next door. He squeezes between a large garbage bin and the neighboring building's dirty wall. It's good he is wearing all black. None of the dirt would show and he could make it home without raising eyebrows.

The back of the building butts up against an alley that runs behind all the buildings on this street. The other side of the alley is another line of buildings, most of them constructed of brick as the older buildings in West Prekrol are. The alley continues crookedly in either direction, a few flickering gaslamps casting more shadows than light in the twilight between the buildings. He peers in either direction. The alley bends to the left, turning so he cannot see past a few buildings down. To the right it is the same, one sharp bend of the alley and the way is blocked from view.

Morvath squeezes his way around the corner of the building, making his way to the metal door at the back of Howells's building. He tries the handle, and it doesn't budge. It must be locked from the inside. That's no problem. One of the easiest tricks of writer witches is to talk things into doing things for you. He softly mutters under his breath, using witchspeak for only the third or fourth time ever.

"Unlock."

The latch clicks loudly in the quiet alley. He tries the handle again. The door gives off a shrill squeal as it opens. He looks anxiously over each shoulder, paranoid someone would come running around the corner and catch him. But there is no soul in sight and one glance up at all the shuttered windows tells him no one is paying any attention. He ducks into the building, carefully pulling the door shut.

Inside, he reaches into his pocket and pulls out the tiny disc version of the sensor. The sensor lights up in the dim building interior. He points it at the ceiling and sees the bright point light up where Howells is. He puts the disc away and makes his way through the building to the stairs. Each step feels ricketier than the last as he heads up to the third floor.

As he reaches the third floor, Morvath pulls the knife out of its sheath. He has an idea about how to approach this, but he will need to be close to Howells to make sure this works. He makes his way stealthily down the hallway through the attics till he comes to a door marked with an "H." He has no doubt this is Howells apartment.

Carefully, with a great amount of caution and delicacy, he holds the knife in both hands, the blade flat against his palm. He reaches into the metal, feeling the simmering heat of the killing spell there. Slowly and precisely, he unwinds the spell from the metal of the knife. He does not detach it completely, needing it to remain in the dagger for future use. But he does pull it out in a dim glow of red light and holds it steady.

Fortunately, Morvath can feel the spell recognize him and go quiet. It will not hurt him. Before doing anything else, he tells the spell what he wants it to do, tells it not to outright kill on contact but to kill slowly. Kill slowly enough that he will have time to get to Howells and take his power. The spell responds, turning a dark burgundy with the changes.

He lifts the spell from the knife, concentrating on pointing it at Howells's apartment.

Casually, he flings the spell at any living thing within

the apartment walls.

A thud behind the door tells him he must have been successful. He pulls the spell back into the knife and tucks the knife away. He points one finger at the lock and whispers, *"Unlock."* He hears no less than six locks click into place behind the door. He opens the door with his power, not wanting to leave an impression on the handle. He softly closes it behind him.

Howells is slumped on the floor in the middle of the cluttered room. The man writhes in pain, making no sound as he lies seizing on the floor. The man is as disheveled as he was on the street. Morvath curls his lip in response to the smell in the room. It seems Howells has not had a chance to bathe for a while.

Still. He kneels down next to Howells's dying form. Morvath lays a bare hand on Howell's forehead in a gesture almost designed to bring comfort.

The killing spell seething within Howells's body recognizes Morvath immediately. Morvath does the only thing he needs to do now. He commands the spell to enact its final measure.

Howells's heart stops. The man's eyes go vacant.

Saknor Howells, that disgraced academic and witch, is dead.

Fifteen

Morvath feels Howells's power come loose from inside him. It dives into Morvath in a tidal wave of power unlike anything he expected.

The war within Morvath begins.

The burning sensation of power sets his skin crawling and his muscles twitching. Soon he is on the ground next to the dead body, feeling the powers battle it out. There could only be one winner, and that winner would undoubtedly be Howells's power. He feels the power overcoming Goliyant's writer power, pushing it out of his body and taking over the space left behind.

Inherently, all witches have that human component. All witches have humanity at the core, and the magic is just the outer layer. It is the thing that is seen. Morvath is feeling that reality in a way that few witches ever do.

He is feeling his old humanity get pulled and warped and misshapen to accommodate the massive power Howells clearly possessed. And the fight his writer power is putting up is only making his soul twist more to accommodate the battling powers.

Then the writer power comes loose.

Every muscle in Morvath's body relaxes in response. His whole body lets go of the pain and anguish and relief runs through him. He almost cannot think straight for the pure sensation of peace settling over him. But he has to think straight. He has to pick himself up and get himself out of here.

He has to leave.

Morvath pulls himself up off the floor. The first thing he checks is the ring on his finger. The spell is intact but struggling. He makes a few tweaks to it to get it to recognize his new power levels. Then the spell settles down and seems to have no trouble concealing his power. He straightens his clothes and picks up his hat. He meticulously checks his pockets to make sure nothing fell out while he was on the floor. Nothing has, so he relaxes slightly. There can be nothing that ties him to this place.

He wipes Howells's brow to wipe away any imprint

he might have left there. Morvath is about to turn to the door and leave when the chalkboard catches his eye. A circle with seven Xs marked on it catches his attention. And next to it, written on the side are the words, "*7 anchors.*"

Anchors.

He finally has word for the kind of witch they are. Anchor witches.

He thinks for a moment and then waves a hand at the chalkboard. The contents wipe clean. He does not want anyone to find out that Howells is an anchor witch. That he is a powerful witch of the fourth kind. They can think he is a writer witch. And the Conservation Law would ensure that Goliyant's writer power would be conserved into the local witch community. So, they would only know that a writer witch had died. They would only think that Howells was a writer.

Morvath smiles to himself. He considers for a few moments and then concentrates again. This time several pages of scribbly writing untuck themselves from stacks all around the room. One by one, the pages all float across the room to Morvath. One thin notebook also loosens itself from a stack and comes to Morvath as well. He takes the stack of papers and the notebook and tucks them away in his satchel. He would burn them later, but only after he had time to study them. The pages were all the references to the word "anchor" he could summon in Howells's notes.

No doubt the man kept records of those he worked with and those he tracked as an anchor. Morvath has no doubt he would find some clues as to who the other anchors are. What Morvath will do with that information, he doesn't know yet. But he knows he needs the information. He needs everything he can find on anchors now that he has a name for them.

Once again, he checks that he hasn't lost anything or left anything behind. Once again, he makes sure he hasn't left an impression of himself anywhere. Then he heads to the door. After listening and using his witch senses, he opens the door to the empty hallway. He shuts the door softly and points at the lock. *"Lock,"* he whispers in witchspeak. Six locks all click into place.

He heads down the stairs and to the back door. There, he repeats the same effort, carefully opening and closing the door and locking it behind him. He sidles down the alleyway to the street. He walks with purpose several blocks to his steam carriage. His driver sees him coming and opens the door for him. The driver says nothing.

During the entire ride back to his home, Morvath can feel the power settling inside of him. The power is unlike the writer power he has lost now. He feels steady, strong, as if he can handle anything that comes his way. The heavy weight of the anchor power already fills him with strength he couldn't have fathomed before. Even Goliyant's immense writer power was nothing to this.

Back at his apartment he immediately takes his newly absconded belongings to his office and locks everything away in his desk. The lock has no key anymore. No one but him could unlock it after the spell he cast upon it. It was one of the easiest pieces of magic he had done so far, and it could not have been more useful.

Morvath goes to his room and orders his valet to draw him a bath. He needs to wash clean of this whole episode. He needs to feel himself again. And that is just the thing. He does feel like himself. He feels more himself than he did with Goliyant's power. He feels like the power is acting without him doing anything.

He considers for a moment that it might become a problem with the spell in the ring. The shield could only work so well, he felt. But maybe that should be his first task. He should rewrite the spell to accommodate the anchor power more fully. To keep any power leakage from happening. He would be traveling abroad and would need the protection of anonymity. He would do that before meeting with Shetler's contingent at five o'clock. It is not yet teatime, so he has time to prepare.

With the bath done and fresh clothes on, he returns to his study. The first thing he does is study the shield in the ring and make sure it is still working. Then he pulls the spell partially out of the ring and begins to make adjustments. The power drawn by the spell is not very much and certainly wouldn't be noticeable to any passing witch. But he wants to be sure. He wants to make the spell so low power that it doesn't draw any attention at all.

Morvath spends the next hour unraveling and re-raveling the spell in such a way that it self-powers. It would draw a tiny bit of power from him, but the loops of magic that go into the spell itself would continuously power the spell. He merely drops enough power into it to get it going and then it wouldn't stop as if it were a clockwork device that needn't be wound. He slips the ring back on his finger.

The next order of business is Howells's notes. He would need to burn them before his meeting. He didn't trust anyone, even those of his own staff. So, he would never leave them lying around, locked away or not. He begins reading the man's scribbly notes and scanning the writing into his witchglass for future reading. The device turned the untidy scribbles into neat text, making later study all the easier.

The time reads half past four when he finally looks up from Howells's notes. The last page he throws into the fire behind him, the previous pages already turning to ash. Even the notebook is nothing but charcoal in the fire grate. He watches as the last sheet curls at the edges with flames eating away at the ink.

What he learned in the last couple of hours is that he is not alone. Morvath has not been the only one researching anchor witches. Howells had made a great study of anchor witches and likely was the only person in the world to know all their names. No doubt he kept that information closely guarded, not even revealing it to his closest confidant, Wilhem Martinsson. No doubt he would die before giving up that information.

Morvath looks at his list of anchor witches, the real list this time, and studies it carefully. Several would be untouchable by any standard. One of them is of the royal family of Verhill, for example, and would be untouchable under normal circumstances. No doubt the Princess is heavily protected even more so because of her rare power. He would never get within a workable distance of the Verhillian Princess.

One small thing he learned for sure, something he knew already but was glad to have confirmed, is that Aidan Montgomery was an anchor witch before the power transfer happened in Umbra. Nadia Oswald is indeed an anchor witch, and a powerful one from Howells's accounts. She single-handedly turned back the Ecrian forces in the Falgar. Granted, she had some help from Montgomery and Chulyin, but it only took her anchor power to do the job. Howells remarked in his notes after meeting her that she seems to have naturally magnified Montgomery's anchor power and made it her own. And Howells noted that Oswald's power greatly outclasses his, more so than he expected.

The burning feeling of jealousy runs through him. How could this little girl, daughter of an outspoken anti-witch minister, be carrying one of the strongest witch powers on the planet? Howells admitted that he couldn't identify if she was *the* strongest, not having met every anchor, but he did question whether anyone could outclass her.

The thought makes Morvath wonder. Could a stronger anchor power displace a weaker one? It certainly could happen with other powers, with writers or casters. Why not with anchors?

He could find out.

Morvath packs up his witchglass into his satchel and locks the drawer once again. Even more so now, his meeting with Shetler is imperative to his plans to get close to Oswald. He would need to go to Rebluinia to take her power. Then he would finally have what he really sought. He would finally be the world's most powerful witch. All he had to do was kill Oswald. And that was nothing compared to Goliyant and Howells. It would be simple. Easy really.

With a slight smile on his face, Morvath leaves his study and heads down to his steam carriage. The whole ride to Parliament he feels all's right with the world now that he knows what he knows. Now that he has a plan.

Now that he knows who to kill.

Sixteen

Aidan looks over at John on his horse and the pair smile at each other. The sight of the nomadic caravan has John in a light and airy mood, a mood that is making Aidan forget his troubles. From here, the tawny-colored tents topped with brightly colored flags to signify the families of each, present a view into another life that John has chosen to leave behind. He still loves it though, something that Aidan understands and sometimes envies.

Not that Aidan doesn't have a loving family. That's not what he envies. It's the traditions of the nomadic people he envies. It's the community nature of their encampments. He wishes he had a community like that to grow up in. His family always did right by him, but he was always isolated in his family. The family witch. The one who belongs but is somehow separate. He wonders what it would have been like growing up surrounded by witches teaching him how to be the best possible witch.

They ride into the encampment, greeted genially by passersby who recognize John. They head through several dozen tents until they come to one with a red and gold flag marked with a black seven-point star. This is the Blestone flag, the family flag that has been passed down through generations.

"Well, if it isn't the wayward child," a voice calls out to them as they approach.

John slips down from his horse, a grin on his face. "Hello Uncle," he says, giving the burly man a big hug. John's uncle stands at more than a head taller than John, but they look like each other, the same gray eyes characteristic of the nomadic people looking up at Aidan.

"And you must be the famous elemental we've heard so much about," the uncle says.

Aidan dismounts his horse and smiles as he shakes John's uncle's hand. "I'm Aidan," he says.

"Reginald," he answers. To John he says, "Your mother is over at the Woodly's, but she'll be back any minute."

Almost on cue, a hefty woman shorter than John but wider than he is approaches them. Her broad smile is so welcoming that for a moment Aidan forgets he isn't family. Her bouncy curls are tied back in a black and gold scarf to match the colors of their flag.

"It's so good you came to us," she says as she pulls John into a tight hug. John welcomes the attention and hugs her back.

"This is Aidan," John says, gesturing to him.

"Ah yes, the one we've heard so much about!" she says. Rather than shake his hand, she pulls Aidan into a hug the likes of which he hasn't had since his own mother hugged him a couple of weeks ago. Even though they just met, she feels like family.

"Nice to meet you," is all he can think to say.

"Call me Asha or Momma, whatever works for you," she says as she lets go of Aidan. "And you can relax," she adds. "You're not going to set the place on fire."

John raises his eyebrows at his mother's comments.

"What do you mean?"

"I mean we *know*," Asha says, tapping her temple with a finger. "We've seen it."

Aidan smiles wanly, feeling moderately relieved to be able to relax. The tension leaves his shoulders, and he nods. "Thank you."

"Of course, darling," she says. "Come inside. Do

you eat?"

"*Mom*, of course he eats," John says.

"Just asking," she says. "I have some stew ready for you both. Come in and we'll get you fed."

She pulls back the heavy canvas tent flap and guides them inside with Uncle Reginald following behind. Aidan doesn't know what he expected, but it wasn't this. Thick heavy carpets cover the ground, muffling their footsteps as they enter the place. Cushions and pillows are strewn about the floor. Witchlight lanterns illuminate the space, giving a gentle golden glow to the plush surroundings. Everything is patterned with red and gold and the seven-point stars except the carpet. The carpet is a Mosnian rug for sure, judging from the looping, geometric design of it. Around the center tent pole, John's family sits eating stew. When they look up and see John coming in, one by one they get up to greet the wayward son.

Aidan is introduced to no less than five cousins and John's Aunt Beryl. It seems his father is across the encampment at the moment but should be back soon. Aidan can't keep track of all the cousins' names, but he shakes their hands genially and takes the stew when it's offered, sitting down on the floor cushions with the crowd.

Someone takes a Blestone colored scarf and drapes it around Aidan's shoulders. "It's fireproof," the cousin says with a smile.

His reputation must truly precede him here.

Aidan eats the hot stew, discovering that he is in fact hungry. They hadn't eaten since morning, and it is late afternoon now. The stew is filled with root vegetables and poultry of some kind, likely the wild pheasants that roam the plateau. John is eating the stew with gusto, no doubt something he ate as a child.

Asha sits down next to Aidan and looks him over. "How is your transition treating you?" she asks.

Aidan smiles in amusement. He gets this question so much. "I'm managing," he says. "I can't say it's easy, but I'm getting better."

"That's all we need, isn't it? Progress?"

He nods at her response.

"I'm sorry to hear about your teacher," Asha says. "I know you were close to her."

Aidan lets out a sigh. "She was a great guide," he says. "I could really use her guidance about now."

"Perhaps you can find another guide to help you," Asha says. She takes Aidan's empty bowl from him and sets it in the pile to be washed. "Has anyone in particular helped you since you became an elemental?"

He considers for a moment. The girls immediately come to mind and the letter he has kept with him remains close in his memory. "There are a couple," he says. "The girls I worked with before have helped."

"Why did you leave them?" Asha asks.

"I was afraid."

"Of burning them?"

"Yes," he says. By now, he is aware almost everyone in the tent is paying attention to him. Self-consciously, he wraps the scarf around himself. One of the cousins tosses him a red blanket with a smile and Aidan wraps up in it. Not for the cold, but for the feeling of comfort.

"Are you still afraid?" she asks.

Aidan glances at John who is watching him steadily. "Yes," he says. "I dream of fire sometimes."

Asha smiles at him. "You will always dream of fire," she says with the ring of prophetic truth to her voice. "But in time, you will learn to dream of other things."

"What do you mean?"

One of the cousins takes this moment to chime in. "The future is seen in fire," she says. "So, one day you'll be able to see better than any of us can."

He looks around at their earnest faces, realizing he is

surrounded by those who can see. Even if none of them is particularly strong, they all exude that kind of confidence that stems from having the sight. And he guesses all of them can see the future as opposed to the present or the past. Seeing the future brings confidence in what is to come. That there will be a future.

"Is that true?" Aidan asks John.

His casting partner nods at him solemnly. "I expect you to be a better seer than me one day."

Maybe there is something he can learn from John. Maybe Goliyant was right to pair them up. She knew so much it made Aidan wonder if she could discern the future as well.

"I know you have your doubts," Asha says, "and you're struggling with your place. But set that aside for now, for the time you are here. We see you healthy and safe here and then on your way to Port Nalrang refreshed and ready."

Ready for what? he wants to ask. The possibilities frighten him.

Instead, he asks, "Do you see me with the girls anytime soon?"

Asha goes vague in the eyes for a few moments. She looks like she is trying to peer deep into the distance.

Then she focuses on Aidan again and says, "Not right away. But I do see you together in a desert setting. I don't know where. I don't recognize it."

"They're in Rebluinia," Aidan says.

Asha shrugs. "It could be there, but I don't know Rebluinia," she admits. "And it could be awhile before you meet up again."

Aidan looks around the room at the gathered Blestones. They are John's family, but they welcomed him as if he is one of them.

"Tonight, we'll show you how we live," Asha says. John smiles at Aidan, nodding enthusiastically around another bite of stew. Asha pats Aidan's shoulders and gets up to deal with the dishes. John scoots over next to Aidan.

"Are you ok?" he asks Aidan.

Aidan shrugs, not really knowing one way or another. "I'm not sure," he says. "I'm just not sure."

John doesn't say anything, just watches as his cousins all get up and head out of the tent. After a few minutes he says, "C'mon. You should see what my childhood was like."

Aidan follows John out to the twilight of the evening. Overhead, Anax hangs in the sky, Yddril twinkling in blue next to it. For a moment, he is back in Umbra standing on the launch field as the ship takes off in the sky. For a moment, he is back to a time when he feels at peace.

Then John jogs him out of his thoughts and they go to join the cousins. There would be other times he feels at peace.

Seventeen

When Nadia wakes up, she is staring at the ceiling of a canvas tent. The cot she lies on is not comfortable, but it is better than being on the ground. She can feel a hand in hers and can sense it's Elise before she looks down and sees her girlfriend slumped over asleep.

Nadia checks in with her body. Her side is stiff but feels healed well enough. It was a stupid injury. She should have been shielding better. She could have died. She shakes her head, staring at the tent ceiling.

Beside her, Elise begins to stir. Nadia squeezes her hand. Elise looks up, jolted awake.

"You're awake," she whispers.

Nadia smiles wanly at her. "How long was I out?"

"About a day," Elise says. "We're encamped on the north end of Melgarde. The entire city south of here has been overrun by Ecrium. We're going to reinforce the Rebluinian forces heading south."

"When?"

"In the morning," Elise says. "It's getting bad down there." Her face fills with concern. "Are you doing better?"

"I think so," Nadia answers. She tries to sit up, but Elise pushes her back down.

"Rest," Elise says. "We have a long way to go tomorrow morning." Elise gets up then, stretching for a moment. "I'll go get you some food."

Nadia nods. Elise heads out of the tent and leaves Nadia on her own. Nadia turns her attention to the sounds she hears outside the tent. Some soldiers must be nearby, in other tents perhaps. Someone is crying softly out there, so quietly she almost can't hear it. Even the most seasoned soldiers have their breaking point.

Elise returns with a camping bowl and a spoon. Nadia sits up and does her best not to aggravate her wound. Though it is healed, it is healed in the sense that it feels weeks old as opposed to fresh. She would still need to rehabilitate the muscle underneath.

She takes the spoon and bowl from Elise and blows on the steaming hot stew. In a few minutes, she is able to carefully eat bites without burning her mouth. That's the last thing she needs on top of her injuries.

When she's eaten most of her stew, she asks, "Where are we going?"

"I'm not sure. The battle lines are currently about a mile south of us," Elise answers. "I think somewhere along there.

"Have we seen any other elementals?"

Elise shakes her head as she says, "No. Not that I know of. Though I imagine an earth or metal elemental would do well in this environment."

It still disturbs her that they had to face down a sand elemental. She wonders how long before Egraria's elementals get into the fight. She thinks of Aidan then and wonders briefly where he is and how he is doing. They don't have a connection to the witchwire out here except for official business. So, Nadia feels cut off from her life back home. It only makes her feel more isolated.

In the distance, an explosion goes off.

Elise opens the tent flap and looks out. She turns back over her shoulder and says, "It looks like Ecrium is closing in." Elise studies Nadia for a moment. "I'm going to go help. Will you be ok?"

Nadia strains to get up, saying, "I'm coming with

you."

"No," Elise says. "You need the rest for tomorrow. I can get Sala to help me shield. He's powerful enough on his own."

Nadia swings her legs over the side of the cot and looks for her boots.

"*No*," Elise says, going back into the tent to push her girlfriend gently back onto the cot. "You need to rest. Do it and you can help tomorrow."

Elise gently touches Nadia's wounded side. Nadia flinches at the contact, feeling tender to the touch. She concedes that she isn't in her best shape.

"Just stay here," Elise says. "Your boots and things are under the cot if you need to move. But don't go anywhere unless they make you move."

Nadia nods, her blue eyes meeting Elise's brown ones. "Please be careful."

Elise smiles, leans down, and kisses Nadia deeply. "I'll be ok."

Nadia watches as Elise ducks out of the tent. Another explosion goes off in the distance. She lays there staring at the ceiling of the tent, fear-filled and anxious. She needs to rest, but she wouldn't with Elise out there in danger.

Nadia tosses restlessly on the cot for what feels like hours, waiting on Elise to come back. Around her, she can still hear the sounds of the other soldiers nearby. The one soldier who was crying is silent now. He must have stopped or left.

She doesn't know how much time passes, just that the sky she can see between tent flaps is getting dark. Nadia peels herself off the cot and pokes her head out, looking up at the sky. She is a stranger to these stars.

A soldier goes running by, heading in the direction of the explosions. Her head whips around at the oncoming soldiers following the first.

"Hey, what's going on?" she asks one passing.

The young witch looks over his shoulder as he passes her and says, "Ecrium is falling back."

Intrigued that their enemy is backing off at all, she pulls her boots on and follows the soldiers at a more sedate pace. She does not push it, so as not to reinjure herself. As she approaches the end of the camp, her view opens up and she can see down the street the front line of soldiers. A huge shield crosses the street from building to building going up some thirty feet into the air. Elise's shield. Nadia feels a sense of pride in her girlfriend's abilities. The feeling doesn't last long.

As she watches, the shield begins to fail. Gaps begin to appear along the edges and holes open up in the middle. Fire begins to creep through from the other side.

Nadia doesn't hesitate. She begins jogging towards the fray, holding her side as she does so. She is quickly out of breath but keeps pushing forward through it. A cramp begins to form in her side. As she gets closer, she makes out Elise and Sala and several other witches all linked together. She can feel the power even from a distance.

She trips on a piece of rubble and goes down on her left shoulder. A passing soldier stops and helps her up.

"You're that witch, right?" he says.

She looks up to meet his dark eyes and curly hair and nods. "Yeah," she says. "I need to get up there."

"I got you," he says. He is a tall and burly man and lifts her up like she weighs nothing. The mark on his shoulder says he is a seer witch.

The soldier takes off running. He barely breaks a sweat and isn't even panting when he makes it up to the group of witches. "Take me to Elise," Nadia says, pointing her out at the center of the group.

Sala sees them coming and lets go of Elise. The shield, already beginning to fail, begins to come down in earnest. From her place in the soldier's arms, Nadia reaches out and lays a hand on Elise's shoulder. She immediately pours her power into the shield.

It's too late. Some Ecrian soldiers have made it through the gaps in the shield.

Sala turns to face them, raising a personal shield hugging his body. He draws a long knife from his belt. Sala weaves a spell around the knifeblade causing it to glow golden. The first Ecrian soldier to approach him dodges Sala's blow. The spell flairs against the Ecrian's shield. They spar for several minutes as other Ecrian soldiers approach. Nadia watches in awe as Sala shows his prowess, not just with the spell but with the blade.

The soldier sets Nadia down. She stays on her feet, her hand clutching Elise's shoulder. Only once did her girlfriend look back at her, so deep in concentration she is in the shield spell. An Ecrian soldier comes straight at Elise. Nadia does the only thing she can think of. She wraps an arm around Elise and raises her personal shield spell around them both. The strain on her energy immediately makes her weak in the knees. She holds firm and remains standing.

That's when it happens. Nadia feels it before she sees it. She feels the testing of her spirit, a tugging on her anchor power that she had never experienced before. Her eyes go to the Ecrian witches beyond the shield. One figure stands apart in the center of them. They make eye contact.

The other witch is an anchor.

A shiver goes down her spine. The reality around them begins to warp, the very air shimmering as if there is a great fire. The ground begins to ripple like waves on the Falgar. The shield loses its luster, the holes suddenly returning with a vengeance.

"What's happening?" Elise says, out of breath.

"They have an anchor on their side," Nadia answers.

The shield fails.

Elise and Nadia cling to each other, holding each other up. She can't collapse just yet. She needs to get through this.

The air and the matter around the other anchor witch looks sharper, more clear somehow, as if there is extra light around them illuminating them. The witches near the anchor, guarding the anchor she thinks, all look so solid and grounded and real. She knows she can solidify reality as she did with the sand in the desert. Can she push back successfully on such a practiced anchor witch?

Her soldier, the burly man who carried her, comes up next to her. Even looking at him, she can see the reality warping around him as well. Before long, they'll all be warped enough not to be who they are. It is disconcerting to see the anchor power, normally a stabilizing influence, used in such a way as to kill reality itself. She shudders to think of the extent of what could be done with it.

"What is he?" the soldier asks Nadia.

"He's like me," she says. "He's doing this and I'm not strong enough."

"I'll stop him," the soldier says.

Nadia watches in horrified fascination as the soldier heads forward, heads through the fray of Ecrian soldiers fighting Egrarian forces. He is barely touched by the fighting, seemingly dodging all the blows in a way only a truly powerful seer could. His progress is only halted when he gets to the guards around the other anchor. There, the Ecrians fight like wildcats to kill her soldier.

Fire arcs over them and lands on the shield around her and Elise. Compared to her experience with Grappley and Aidan, the fire is nothing to worry about. She uses her anchor power to solidify the air around them and the fire, starved of oxygen, snuffs out.

As the smoke clears, she can see what's become of the soldier. He's bleeding now, fighting for his life as he tears down the Ecrian soldiers. Then a blade comes down on his shoulder and Nadia watches as he throws a knife in the direction of the anchor.

Both blades hit home.

Her soldier falls like a puppet with its strings cut.

The anchor drops to the ground.

The warping of reality around them immediately ceases. Ecrian forces begin to turn tail and run, chased by the Egrarian soldiers blasting fire and air and anything they've got at them. Nadia drops the shield and falls to the ground with Elise on top of her.

"I thought I told you to rest," Elise grumbles.

"Good thing I didn't listen."

Nadia pulls herself into a sitting position and looks around. The fallen soldier saddens her. Without him they would have all been lost. She gets up off the street, her eyes still on the soldier. She wonders what his name was.

Elise gasps next to her.

Nadia's eyes go to Elise and then follow her gaze. There, some twenty feet from them, Sala lies on the ground, a pool of blood too large to be anything but fatal. Their advocate and instructor is dead.

Around them the fallen are many. There is nothing that can be done for so many soldiers who fell. So many are dead. She shuts her eyes for a moment, trying hard not to count their bodies.

Colonel Ergamenes picks this moment to approach them, fury on his face. "You could have prevented this," he says, an accusation in his voice. "You say your power is not a weapon." He gestures at the fallen anchor witch and says, "*He* used it as a weapon. You lied Oswald. This is all on you."

And the Colonel turns and walks away, leaving Nadia and Elise in stunned silence. The eyes of so many soldiers fall on them, so many of them filled with accusation.

Was he right? Could she have prevented so many of these deaths?

Elise squeezes her hand. "Let's walk back," she whispers.

And they make their way through the dead bodies and the rubble and the charred ground towards the camp. All the while the eyes follow them. And Nadia can't help but feel guilty. Can't help but feel responsibility.

What if Ergamanes is right? What if she needs to fight?

With a sinking feeling in the pit of her stomach, she ducks back into the tent and sits down on the cot. No answers, no consolation comes to her. She doesn't know what to think.

Worse, she doesn't know who is right.

Eighteen

Aidan looks on the skyline of Port Nalrang with mixed emotions. Last time he was there, it was when he was with the girls, and they were all practicing their new powers. Last time he was there, he burned Elise badly enough that it made him want to retreat to the Waste. Now, with John by his side, he doesn't know what lies ahead.

They proceed forward with caution, heading into the city through the neighborhood of Upper East Herren. Past the sleepy residential district consisting of adobe houses reminiscent of those in Courtthostur, they enter Sheocag Bazaar. Here, the brick buildings line wide streets jam-packed with seller's tents. Even with the bombings and the unrest in Port Nalrang, this neighborhood never quits. On this Epday, the street bustles with buyer and seller alike.

Aidan and John carefully steer their horses through the crowds, crowds that separate for them as they pass through. Nobody wants to be trampled by a horse. They come to the south end of the Bazaar and leave the bustling crowds behind. It is late evening and the gas lamps of Port Nalrang are beginning to come on.

To keep matters simple, Aidan had reached out to Edgar Oswald and requested they stay with him. Otherwise, they would need to stay in the Conscription Authority barracks and Aidan is not keen on that kind of close quarters. Mr. Oswald had accepted the request on the condition Aidan doesn't burn down the building unless it is absolutely called for. The man's dry sense of humor only got drier the more contact they had with him.

Together, they arrive at Nadia's building. Salter meets them at the front door to the Oswald apartment and welcomes them in. They make their way through the apartment to the living room where Edgar Oswald is waiting. Aidan is immediately drawn to the window where he can see the wide vista of Port Nalrang buildings, all lit up with electricity for the night. Between the buildings, the view of the Falgar is dark. He can't see south to where the girls are.

"How was your trip?" Mr. Oswald asks as he puts his witchglass down.

"Lengthy," Aidan says, taking a seat across from Mr. Oswald. John sits next to him. "I stopped in Avita Spring to see my family. And in Courtthostur, but I'm afraid that wasn't a happy visit."

"I'm sorry about your teacher," Mr. Oswald says. Aidan had written to him, explaining the circumstances of his delay. "I can't believe such a strong witch was taken by surprise, but I guess anyone can be caught unaware."

"They still haven't found the killer," John says. Salter hands him a cup of tea and John takes a deep drink of it.

"I doubt they will," Mr. Oswald says.

"Why do you say that?" Aidan asks, alarmed.

"Because the killer probably wasn't native to Courtthostur. They probably went there specifically to kill Goliyant and left long before her body was found. Wherever they are, they're smart enough to cover their tracks."

Aidan has to admit he's had similar thoughts. He wonders who would be crazy enough to attack a powerful writer witch like Goliyant and can't imagine it was anyone local. All anyone would say is that they would keep looking.

Salter pops in then to let them know dinner is ready. The three of them head to the dining room and sit down together. Dinner is an informal affair, none of them changing and the food is familiar to them. Just vegetables and meat, something simple.

When they finish their dinner, Aidan asks, "Can I use your witchglass?"

"Of course," Mr. Oswald says. "It's back in the study."

Aidan nods. The three of them get up and head out of the dining room. Mr. Oswald bids them goodnight and goes in the direction of his bedroom. John follows Aidan to the study.

"What do you need the witchglass for?" he asks.

"I just want to check my messages to see if the girls have sent anything," Aidan says.

"Would they even have access to the witchwire where they are?"

"I don't know," Aidan answers, "But I hope so."

He pulls up the messaging center on the witchglass in Mr. Oswald's study. His messages come up and there is nothing from the girls. Chloe and Alex had both sent messages, as did his mother and one of his cousins, but nothing from the girls. It's likely that John is right, and they don't have access to their messages or even just a witchwire device there. Still. He'd like to reach out to them anyway.

He glances up to see John wandering the study, reading the titles of Mr. Oswald's book. Aidan sits down at the desk and begins writing out a message on the clockwork keyboard. The clattering attracts John's attention.

"Are you messaging them?"

"Yes," Aidan answers. "It's the least I can do."

He types out the message:

> *I am at your father's home. John is with me. I will keep you updated on whether the CA will send us south as well. I hope you are safe and doing well. And I hope to see you soon.*

The message is short but sufficient. He honestly doesn't know what else to say right now. So, Aidan sends the message and shuts down the witchglass.

"We should go to bed," Aidan says.

John nods in agreement and they head out of the study. Salter appears out of nowhere to show John to his room and Aidan takes his old guest room. Once behind the closed door, goes to his travel bag. From deep inside, he pulls out the carefully wrapped glass pendants he made for the girls. He had given one to his mother, and she immediately got a chain to wear it on. He wonders when he will be able to give the other two to Elise and Nadia.

Aidan puts his bag aside, deciding to fully unpack in the morning. He washes off in the water closet and gets ready for bed. He tucks himself between the linen sheets, feeling oddly at ease with his fire abilities. Before long, he has dozed off.

The morning comes and Aidan wakes to the sunlight streaming into the bedroom. He forgot to shut the curtains last night. Groaning at the early hour, he gets up and goes through his morning routine. Fully dressed, he heads to the dining room to find Mr. Oswald seated at the head of the table reading over his witchwire paper.

"How did you sleep?" he asks Aidan. John is nowhere to be seen.

"Pretty well actually," Aidan says. It's true he didn't even dream of fire last night.

"Good," Mr. Oswald says. "I understand you and John are going to the Conscription Authority first thing?"

As if he heard his name, John comes into the dining room just then, smiling tiredly at them both.

"Yes, we are," Aidan says. "I need to check in and

John needs to get assigned."

"Well, if they give you any trouble, you know to refer them to me," Mr. Oswald says.

In surprise, Aidan says, "Thank you." He doesn't know what else to say to that kindness. Mr. Oswald really doesn't need to stick his neck out for them; they aren't his children. But having a politician and renowned lawyer on their side would certainly be an asset.

Salter comes in just then and hands them a green witchwire envelope. While personal messages come through on the witchglass, if you have one, official information still comes via the little green envelopes from the main witchwire office. Mr. Oswald, a look of surprise on his face, takes the envelope. He opens it and his normally impassive expression vanishes for one seriously alarmed. He sits up straighter in his seat and seemingly reads the message again and again.

Aidan exchanges a look with John. He asks, "Is something wrong?"

Jogged out of his thoughts, Mr. Oswald looks startled, as if he had forgotten both Aidan and John are there. "Yes," he says cautiously. "Nadia was injured."

"What?"

Mr. Oswald hands Aidan the message, and he reads

it over. No wonder Mr. Oswald read it several times. It is only two lines long.

> *It is the Conscription Authority's duty to inform you that Nadia Oswald has been injured in battle. She is recuperating at this time.*

Like Mr. Oswald, Aidan reads it several times before handing it to John.

"They don't say much, do they?"

"No," Mr. Oswald says. "I'll be riding with you to the Conscription Authority. I want more information."

John sets the message down. "I suppose it's good they say she's recuperating," he says.

"Yes, but what was the nature of her injuries?" Mr. Oswald is irritated. He sets his napkin on the table in frustration. "When will you two be ready to go?"

"In a few minutes," Aidan says immediately. He can tell the man is impatient to leave.

"Then let's go," Mr. Oswald says. He abruptly gets up from the table and heads out of the dining room.

Astonished at his behavior, Aidan and John sit for a moment before snapping out of their bewilderment and getting up.

"I guess they wouldn't have written if she wasn't going to be alright," John says softly as they head down the hallway.

"I guess."

At the door, Kaye, Nadia's lifelong companion, looks at each of them with foreboding in his eyes. He had been by Nadia's side through thick and thin and he should have been with her in Rebluinia. He should have been allowed to accompany her.

"We should go," Mr. Oswald says.

Aidan and John don their coats and follow Mr. Oswald out the door. They head down the lift and to the steam carriage that Kaye starts up. They head out of the carriage house and towards the Conscription Authority.

An odd sinking feeling fills the pit of Aidan's stomach. He looks out the side of the carriage and watches the people as they pass them on the street.

He blinks and the cityscape disappears for a wide expanse of desert sand. The sun is setting in the sky and the moons are rising. He doesn't know where he is, but he turns his head to the left and sees Nadia smiling at him. Then he blinks, and the desert is gone.

He's left wondering if it was vision or just wishful thinking. He's not sure which. And he's not sure which is worse.

Nineteen

The sun rises on another day and Morvath is ready for this one to come. Over a week after he took Howells's power, he stands on board the ship the ECAS *Raelle*, watching as the black cliffs of Rebluinia come into view. The ship approaches the harbor of Blackguard, chugging along at a moderate clip. The water is not still today on the Falgar. The waves are capped by white in some areas, the boat rocking unsteadily as they move forward. Still, Morvath is unphased. His new anchor power steadies him in the face of what would have shaken him before.

His colleagues chalk his unruffled nature to his previous travels. And it's true, his previous travels do have something to do with him being used to traveling. He has sailed on the Falgar before. He has never felt seasick, unlike some of his colleagues.

"We'll be anchoring soon, sir," a Lieutenant says to him as they pull between the hulking cliffs of Blackguard Bay.

Morvath looks over at the tan Lieutenant with the tawny hair and nods. "Thank you," he says. "Should I go inside?"

"Only if you wish to, sir," the Lieutenant says. He salutes and heads back to his duties.

Morvath continues to watch the approach of the coastline, now filled with the buildings of Blackguard. The black stone used to build buildings, cut from the quarries near the city, is complemented by the glittering of steel and glass. The high tower at the center of town juts far above the rest of the skyline. That is the Governor's Palace of Blackguard. Morvath looks forward to meeting him, the Governor having a reputation for a steely personality. He is not a favorite with the diplomats but does his job so well in this port city that he has not had a serious political challenger for six years. Morvath, plenty familiar with the political machinations of Egraria, is looking forward to wading into those of Rebluinia.

Behind him, the anchors drop off the sides of the ship. The steam engines grind to a halt and the ship begins to slow. Soon, the weight of the anchors draws the ship to a standstill, only the up-down motion of the waves rocking the boat.

"Still out here, I see," a voice says behind Morvath. He turns to see Shetler looking green in the gills. He hasn't adjusted to sea life adequately.

"Yes," Morvath says with a smile. "I'm reminded of my travels to Humsea in the eastern Falgar." Nostalgia fills his voice, something he does not try to hide.

"Were the waters less choppy than these?"

"It was so calm out there, you could easily fall asleep on the ship deck," Morvath says.

"That sounds nice," Shetler says. He grips the railing of the ship and looks out at Blackguard. "I'm looking forward to being on solid ground again."

"Oh, I can't agree with that sentiment," Morvath says with a smile. "I have wanted to sail to Verhill and Humsea and even through the Notrium straits again. It's been too long."

"The price we pay for being politicians, I suppose," Shetler says. He holds a handkerchief up to his mouth and looks like he might wretch at any moment.

"You should sit down, or have one of the medics look at you," Morvath says.

"I already have," Shetler grumbles. "When do you

think we'll be on shore?"

"Soon I should think," Morvath says, scanning the horizon. "Ah, here comes the Governor's delegation now. You shouldn't have to wait long."

"Good," Shetler says. "I don't know how much more I can take of this."

Amusement fills Morvath's features as he says, "Just think of the journey home."

Shetler grimaces. "I can't," he says. "It'll make me throw up."

Morvath chuckles. "Go sit down and rest for now. It'll be an hour or so before they can get you on land."

The man concedes it's the best idea and heads back inside.

Morvath continues to watch the progress of the delegation coming their way. They are on a small steamboat,

coming alongside the *Raelle*. As Morvath watches, a ladder is tossed down to the smaller ship and several members of the delegation climb up, leaving a few sailors aboard below to hold the boat steady.

The delegation heads inside and Morvath thinks it might be time to join them. He follows them at a distance and heads into the ship. Of the four delegation members who came aboard, two are witches, and strong caster witches he thinks. He can't quite make out their power levels with the spell masking his own, but he's fairly confident in the assessment.

One of the witches turns back and smiles at him genially. "Are you one of the ministers, sir?" he asks.

"Yes," Morvath answers, introducing himself to the witch.

"Oh, I've heard of you," the man says. "I'm Leif Morelli, caster witch liaison to the Governor."

"Pleasure," Morvath says. "You've heard of me?" he asks, falling into step with the witch.

"Yes, well, in these times it's unusual to find a human so supportive of witch causes, especially one in your position," Morelli says.

"You mean with all the tension between both sides?"

"And Ecrium's new decree about witches," Morelli says. "Have you heard?"

"No."

"They're requiring all citizens to register as human or witch or elemental and be subjugated to government control," he says.

"What does that mean?"

"It means we have a lot of work to do," the other

witch delegate says, interjecting into their conversation. "They want full control over their citizenry and want to do the same to Rebluinians."

Morvath studies the other witch, another caster as far as he can tell. He is a stockily built individual, muscular and no doubt someone one wouldn't want to get into a fight with. The fierce-looking witch stares straight at Morvath, but Morvath doesn't flinch. The witch eventually nods in approval, and they head into the room where the rest of the Egrarian ministers are waiting.

Morvath immediately goes up to Shetler and asks, "Still green?"

The man is clutching a glass of water and indeed looks ready to throw up at any moment. "I'm managing," he lies.

"Gentlemen and lady," a human delegate begins, acknowledging the one female colleague who made the trip, "We will arrange to have you all brought on shore and taken to the Governor's Palace as soon as possible. I understand there is some urgency to the request." His eyes go to Shetler who is clearly in distress. "We will have you removed to the mainland within the hour."

The relief that goes across Shetler's face is almost comical. Morvath genuinely feels sorry for the man.

The second human delegate steps forward to explain the procedures. Morvath listens to the man, but his mind is on other things. The approaching audience with the Governor for one. The fact that they are about to set foot on Rebluinian soil for another. He has not been to Rebluinia in nearly a decade, and it was certainly in better circumstances than this.

Part of him is worried about what's to come. But every time he worries about something, his anchor power flares inside him, and he immediately calms down. He's not sure if this new instinct is a good thing or not. He wonders if it is taking away from some survival instinct he needs.

The delegates wrap up and Shetler gets up delicately from his seat. Morvath smiles to himself at the man's discomfort. They are disembarking and heading to shore now.

"I envy your steadiness," Shetler mutters to Morvath.

Morvath just smiles in response.

They head out to the deck where the ladder hangs over the side. His baggage would be brought on shore later, though he does not have much of it to be concerned about. His most important possessions are in his pockets and on his finger.

Once in the small boat, the delegates join them, and they push off from the *Raelle*. Morvath takes a last look at the ship that bore him across the vast expanse of the Falgar Sea. It is unlikely he would be returning on the same ship.

Then Morvath turns his face forward, towards the approaching expanse of cityscape and black cliffs flanking it. The boat chugs along, the steam engine at the back sputtering a bit as they traverse the whitecaps. Shetler looks even greener, if that's possible, and is clinging to the side of the boat like his life depends on it. He doesn't have to wait long though. They pull alongside a pier and the boat ties up to a post. A gangway comes down to connect the boat to the shore. Shetler is the first off. Morvath follows him.

As Morvath sets foot from the gangway to the pier, he feels the instability of the sea slip away. He feels the anchor power settle down and relax within him, no longer working to hold him steady and strong. The world itself no longer wavered, so he no longer needed to fight to stand firm. The muscles all throughout his body relaxed, the tension slipping away.

He stands tall as he walks the length of the pier to the cobblestone street that meets it. There he turns back, waiting for the delegates and the other ministers to follow. As they join him, they turn up to the shadow of the city, looking to the tower that is their destination.

Morelli leads the way up the street to several steam carriages waiting. They all squeeze into the contraptions. The drivers begin to steer them down the street.

For a moment, Morvath has a wave of nostalgia, seeing the brick buildings and the merchant's tents all lining their path. But the streets that were lively and vibrant when he last came here are dampened by the tension in the air. The shadow of the war dims the spirit of this usually active city. For that he is angry. He is angry that it has come to this and that the Ecrians dare shake the foundations of the world.

Like a soothing wave of warm water, the anchor power asserts itself and dampens his anger. Morvath turns his gaze to the tower again and lets go of his feelings. He lets go of the turmoil within.

There would be plenty of time for revenge.

Twenty

Nadia marches onward with Elise by her side. They are crossing the southern end of Melgarde, the city in shambles around them. Nadia marches reluctantly, her soul tired of fighting and tired of being made to fight.

The past several days have been harrowing. Colonel Ergamenes has been relentlessly pushing her to do more, be more. She longs for a time when she was sitting in an observatory on a creaky stool, trying to understand the universe.

The worst part is knowing that she could do things that the other anchor could do. That she could do what he did, but she is so totally untrained that she can't even figure out how to attempt it. And now with Sala dead, with her teachers long left behind, she is on her own with only Elise by her side. She is left to figure it out by herself.

Story of her life.

Nadia discovered that war is just a long walk, a long slog punctuated by moments of terror and angst. Her power sizzles within her, unable to rest now that she is constantly in danger. With the anchor abilities still out of her reach, she cannot seem to calm it down. She feels stable and certain, but she cannot use the power to control the reality around her. Maybe she never would.

The convoy comes to a halt. Nadia and Elise stand near the front, several soldiers flanking them on either side and behind. The street before the convoy is empty, and Nadia can't make out why they stopped. She watches the street warily. The pressure of being the most powerful witch in the convoy weighs down on her.

An eerie silence settles over the city block. Nadia can hear every breath Elise takes despite the cloth covering her mouth. She can hear the thrumming of her own rapid heartbeat in her ears. Something is coming. She doesn't need to use her seer abilities to know that. She can feel it like electricity from a rainstorm.

The earth begins to vibrate below their feet. The sand so pervasive in desert cities begins to shake loose from the ground and go into the air. Through her amber-tinted goggles, Nadia sees the wave of sand coming. She has a sense of deja vu as she watches the wave come from down the block. She is suddenly back in the desert, watching the sand elemental raise a wave like it's nothing to do so.

Elise's fingers go to hers. They clasp hands and raise their free hands to the sky. A shield forms. The sand begins to pummel the hardened air some fifty feet above them. Nadia extends her abilities out further and further, pushing the air and sand back away from them.

Arrows rain down on the shield, testing the strength of Nadia's power. Anger wells inside her. Anger at herself and at the apparent elemental the Ecrians have. How is it they have so many unique and rare powers under their control? How is it they have so many powers on their side? She sets her questions aside and concentrates on everything she knows about her own power.

In the past, all she has worked with is calming dissonance, steadying chaos into calm. Back on the Falgar Sea so long ago it feels like a dream, she used that power to send the Ecrians home. She used it to break up battles and calm the fray. Perhaps she could attempt something similar. The best she can do is try.

"Can you hold the shield?" Nadia asks Elise. "I want to try something."

Elise nods and Nadia feels her girlfriend take over the powering of the shield. Elise's jaw clenches visibly as she stands up under the weight of the spell. Nadia has confidence in her abilities though and lets go of Elise's hand.

Nadia walks forward to the front of the Egrarian forces, almost right up to the shield. The shield ripples in response to her presence, feeling the flexing of her anchor power as she nears.

From her memory, she points to the ground and draws out the spell circle with fire. A burnline traces where she points, making a shaky version of the spell Elise had drawn in chalk on the boat. This time, she left off the two circles for Elise and Aidan. Nadia kept her own circle. She steps into it and takes a breath.

From within, the anchor power pours out of her into the diagram. She is struck by the familiarity of the feeling, reminded as she is by the time on the boat on the Falgar. The charred lines on the cobblestone begin to light up, the sand that is everywhere in Melgarde blowing back from the force of the magic.

As the power pours out of her, shaking her to the

core, she feels the spell beginning to work. The magic of it causes the ground to vibrate in a way the boat hadn't before. Is it because she is less powerful than the three of them together? Is it because she is more forceful because of her anger? She would never know the answer. Nadia just kept going.

Just when the magic has built up so much she doesn't think she can hold it any longer, she finally directs the spell. Nadia raises a hand and points a finger in the direction of the Ecrian soldiers. She finally speaks.

"*Return home.*"

The spell breaks free and goes flying towards the Ecrians—

—only to rebound back onto her.

It takes every ounce of energy in her body and soul to keep from falling over under the crushing weight of that spell. But she manages to stay standing.

This time, with more force, she punches the air in front of her, directing the spell aggressively towards the Ecrians.

"*STOP!*" she shouts in witchspeak.

Her voice carries on the spell, ricocheting

And from down the block, carried on the wind, she hears a voice whisper, "*No.*"

Like a wave on the Falgar, the spell hits her and knocks her to the ground. Her head hits the cobblestone, and she blacks out for a moment. When she wakes up again, she feels disoriented and dazed. Around her the Egrarian forces are drawing back. Whether from her spell or from the fact that the Ecrians are advancing, she's not sure.

"No! Stop!' she shouts.

"We have to fall back," Elise says. "I can't hold the shield."

Nadia looks and sees the shield beginning to fail. She backs away from the hardened air. Just on the other side, Ecrian forces push forward, waiting for the shield to fail. They have her in their sights.

She falls back to Elise's side. They begin backing up together.

"Get back," a soldier next to her says. "Fall back."

Elise grabs Nadia's arm. They turn tail and begin running up the block as the shield fails.

An arrow shoots past them. Fire burns the air around them. Nadia ducks her head as they turn up a side street and away from the main fray. Several soldiers run with them. They turn another corner, and the sounds of the battle diminish. They run in the direction of the convoy, looking to rejoin the rest of Egrarian forces.

Something hits Nadia from behind square in the back, but she keeps running. Elise falters beside her, slips and falls. Nadia immediately stops and pulls at her girlfriend's hand to get her up and moving. Then she sees Elise's leg. There's no way she's going to walk on it with it twisted at that angle.

A piece of rubble lands next to them narrowly missing Nadia.

She looks up at the oncoming Ecrians and a single individual stands apart from the rest. She raises a hand. Nadia barely gets the shield up in time to block the bricks that fly at them from all angles. They have a stone elemental on their side. And she looks angry.

Can Nadia hope to match an elemental power for power? She doesn't have a choice.

"You have to fall back," the soldier says.

"No," Nadia answers. "I'm not leaving Elise."

She looks down at her girlfriend. Elise's face is twisted with pain and terror. She looks back up at the oncoming Ecrian forces. And she makes up her mind.

Nadia steps forward, between Elise and the elemental.

"You can't!" Elise gasps out.

Nadia doesn't have a choice.

She reaches deep within her, pulling the anchor power to the surface. She couldn't think of anything to do with it. She just stands her ground and throws as much power into the shield as she can manage. A brick hits the soldier in the head, and he falls to the ground.

Nadia stands alone.

A second individual joins the stone elemental. Together, they raise hands in Nadia's direction. Sand begins to rise in response to their call. The second individual is the sand elemental who was attacking the convoy earlier.

Nadia clenches her jaw, determination and anger fueling her. Lines of power begin to push in on the shield. She can see them and their incursion, the places where they seek to get to her. She doesn't know if they're trying to kill or capture her. She just knows their intentions are bad.

For just a split second, she glances over her shoulder and realizes the Ecrian soldiers had surrounded her. They are moving in, their witches throwing power at the shield to bring it down. She's running out of time.

The fiery red lines out power eat away at the shield. Nadia pushes back on the power with everything she's got. It's still not enough.

The shield collapses.

The lines of power encircle her, burning through her clothes and singeing her skin. She falls to her knees, all the energy going out of her. She can't move, she can't flex her power outside of her body. The spell they cast is to hold her steady and bind her powers.

"Hold her," one of the witches says.

"She's an anchor," the sand elemental says. "You'll need to adjust."

Just how many people know about anchors now? The secret seems to be out everywhere. Worse, they seem fully capable of identifying her as an anchor.

A line of power goes over her mouth and gags her. She can't move her arms or her legs. She falls to the ground.

"Good," the stone elemental says. She leans over Nadia, her long braided hair falling to the side as she studies Nadia's prone form. "This one is powerful. She'll make a good asset."

"What about this one?"

Nadia can just barely see Elise out of the corner of her eye. Elise is shielding herself, but she is on the ground clearly in pain. She looks up at the surrounding witches with fear in her eyes. No doubt her strength would give out before long.

"They're coming," a witch says.

"Take the anchor," the stone elemental says, a cold look on her face.

"What about the scribe?" Likely their word for writer witch is scribe. Once again, how can they be so easily specific about what kind of witches they are? Is there a spell for that?

"Leave the scribe. She's as good as dead anyway," the stone elemental says.

Fury seethes in Nadia. "Don't touch her!" she tries to say.

Cold malevolence fills the eyes of the stone elemental. "Don't worry. We have other plans for you."

Nadia struggles against the bonds and feels the power flexing to contain her. She digs deep inside, seeking to pull the root of the anchor power out to help her. But the power is muted, dimmed by the spell. And there's nothing she can do.

A burly witch picks up Nadia and carries her over his shoulder. She spots the approaching Egrarian soldiers, but it's too late. All she can do is watch the receding body of Elise on the ground. She sees the flickering shield over Elise's body snuff out as they turn a corner and head away from the fray. She has no idea if her girlfriend is alive or dead.

Twenty-One

In an encampment in Pratergarde, Morvath and the other ministers gather in a large tent with Colonel Cunningham and several others from the military. Outside, a sandstorm is blowing through the desert city, and they are all dressed for it. Morvath's cloth face covering is draped around his neck at the moment so he can drink his tea. The others have done the same. He exchanges a look with Kerensa Chalke, the only woman in their company, and they clink cups out of sheer chaotic insanity. The cheerful clinking of cups feels so out of place in such a serious environment, but they can't help but break the tension.

The news from Melgarde is not good. The city is largely overrun by Ecrian forces, the Egrarian and Rebluinian combined forces being driven back at every turn. They were all forced to retreat to the northern end of the city, the fighting taking place in every street south of there. And as Colonel Cunningham is explaining, the forces on the Ecrian side are composed of more witches than they thought possible.

"It's not just that they are witches. It's that they are mostly casters and writers," the Colonel explains. "And the few seers they have seem inordinately powerful ones, able to escape our oncoming forces at every turn."

"What do you mean?" Shetler asks.

The Colonel leans on the table in front of them, studying the city map of Melgarde. "From what we can tell, the Ecrians compose their units mostly of caster or writer witches with a powerful seer assigned to them. They also employ their elementals to extreme effect," he adds. "They have more elementals on their forces than I've ever seen. I wonder about how they got them."

"You mean, maybe they're not doing this purposefully?"

The Colonel sighs. "We just don't have enough information," he says. "But I would be surprised if any of these elementals was a born elemental."

A stunned silence fills the room. Morvath exchanges looks with Shetler and Chalke and the other ministers.

"You mean they're killing elementals for their powers?" The shock is apparent in Chalke's voice.

"It's happening in Egraria right now. We have a string of murders all seemingly for power." The speaker, Minister Harrison Withlow, is grim-faced and worried. "It's not like it hasn't happened before."

"But to see it on this scale, where they're actively killing elementals for their powers . . ." Chalke trails off. She doesn't need to say it. It violates the unspoken rule to respect others' powers. It violates the basic taboo against power theft. There's a reason murders for power carry heavier sentences than plain murder. To violate the Central Dogma feels so wrong.

"They're not just using slaves, they're killing people," Withlow says.

"We haven't proven that they're using slaves," the Colonel says. "But all reports point to yes. That they're using enslaved humans in their labor camps." He straightens up. The Colonel says, "The Vacancy Principle is powerful and tempting. It's not surprising the Ecrian government has taken this stance of power theft. They aren't going to go easily, I'm afraid."

Morvath glances down at the map of Melgarde and the markings showing the military's encampments.

"When will our elementals get here?"

"We have several who are preparing to leave Port Nalrang now. But as you know it'll take a week to cross the Falgar," he answers. "In the meantime, we have to hold them off as best we can with the forces we have."

The main tent flap opens and a major steps through, quickly closing the flap behind him. He lowers his face covering and raises his goggles before saluting the Colonel. Then he hands a message over to Colonel Cunningham.

The Colonel opens it, and tension immediately fills his brow.

"They've taken some of our people," he says.

"What? Who?" The questions come from Shetler.

"A few of our strong witches." There is a pause. "Nadia Oswald has been taken captive," the Colonel says.

Morvath works to hide his alarm. He is surrounded. He cannot reveal his true feelings here. And this is a concerning development. Such a valuable asset in the hands of the enemy is a terrifying thought. "Captive, not killed?"

"Correct," he says. "We're not sure if it's for ransom or something else. We have heard nothing from the Ecrians." A dark look comes over the Colonel's face.

"When did this happen?"

"About three hours ago," the Colonel says.

Anger fills Morvath at the delay in notification. "I know her father," he explains as a way to dismiss his interest in her. "I know she's got strong writer powers," he says, concealing his knowledge of her anchor abilities. "I shudder to think what they can do with them."

"Yes," the Colonel says. "She has extraordinary power." The way he says it and looks at Morvath makes him wonder if the Colonel knows Nadia is an anchor.

"I gathered as much when I met her back in Port Nalrang." Morvath shakes his head. "Maybe I can be of some use here. To negotiate?"

The Colonel's eyebrows go up. He looks around at the other military and ministers present.

Shetler nods at Morvath in agreement. "I think that's a good idea," the minister says. "It's got to carry some weight that we're part of the Egrarian government."

"Can you get me to Melgarde?" Morvath asks. Internally he is screaming at this turn of events and possibility of getting close to the anchor witch.

"Yes, that's no trouble," Colonel Cunningham says. "You'll have to have an escort."

"Will the Ecrians even recognize a negotiator?"

Chalke asks.

"We can try," Colonel Cunningham says. The look he gives Morvath betrays his doubt. But their hands are tied. The best they can hope for is a prisoner exchange or to pay a ransom for Oswald.

The Colonel turns to the major and directs him to prepare a convoy to take Morvath to Melgarde. He also scribbles a message and says to send it over the witchwire to the Ecrian authorities. They have a way to contact through direct messaging and they would need to use it for this situation.

"Minister, we can send you as soon as tomorrow," the Colonel says to Morvath.

"Can we not go today?" It is, indeed, before teatime. They have some time to head down there.

"You would have to camp along the road to Melgarde," the Colonel says. "I'm not sure that would be wise given the prevalence of elementals in their ranks and the way they've been attacking the road to Melgarde."

"Are they skirting the city?" Chalke asks.

"Yes," he says to her. "They bypassed the city a while ago to blockade the road. The Rebluinian forces managed to hold them back, but they hold the western side of the city."

"I just want to get started," Morvath says. "I don't like sitting and doing nothing."

The Colonel looks at him appraisingly. After a moment of staring, the Colonel then says, "You'll have to go now with Major Hannesko. You might be able to ride through the night to get there, but I don't imagine you'll be there before midnight at the earliest."

Morvath nods. "I can handle that," he says.

"Then go with Hannesko and get your belongings together, whatever you're taking with you. Keep it minimal. We can only send you with a minimal escort," the Colonel says.

"Would you like one of us to come with you?" Shetler asks.

Morvath considers for a moment. He considers what he intends to do to Nadia when he gets to her and thinks it best to keep witnesses to a minimum. "I think I'll be fine with the military escort," he says.

Shetler nods and extends a hand. Morvath shakes it and the hands of the other ministers.

"Be careful," Chalke says. "We don't know what they really want and you're human."

"I will be," Morvath answers. "I'll be careful." To Major Hannesko he says, "Let's get going."

He raises his face covering and lowers his goggles and follows the Major out of the tent. They head through the blowing sandstorm to Morvath's tent. Inside, he packs up what few belongings he thinks he'll need into a small bag. Just a change of clothes and a few other accouterments. Then he checks the spell on the ring is intact and the disc is securely within his inner pocket. He's ready to go.

He ducks back out of his tent and follows Major Hannesko. Finally, he would get the chance he is looking for.

Twenty-Two

Only two days after arriving in the city of Port Nalrang, Aidan found himself leaving again. He apologized to Mr. Oswald for using him like a free hotel, but there was nothing he could do about the Conscription Authority sending him abroad. So, he and John left the great metropolis and headed south across the Falgar.

The lack of information on Nadia's condition motivated Aidan to head south. Mr. Oswald couldn't get any more information about her condition. Only that she recovered from the injury. So, when the Conscription Authority decided to send him abroad, he didn't argue. He just required that John be by his side. John obtained a commission as a sergeant, but the rank doesn't matter to John. It matters that they go together.

And together is how they arrived in Blackguard. By

the time they got there, rumors had begun to spread about the state of the war. None of it could be verified, but some of it was concerning to say the least.

About a day after they arrived in Blackguard, they traveled down to Pratergarde. The journey took them the better part of a day to complete, going through the desert as quickly as was safe for them to do.

Aidan finds himself meeting with Colonel Cunningham early in the morning on an Epday. The days have started moving quickly since they left Port Nalrang. The voyage across the Falgar felt like it took barely any time at all.

John stands with him in the tent, clearly the lowest ranking soldier present. But John holds his own, adhering to protocol and being respectful of the Colonel whom he had never met before.

"We received a disturbing report yesterday," Colonel Cunningham says. He dismisses most of the other soldiers but allows Aidan and John to stay. "Can I assume John knows the truth about your transition?"

"Yes, he knew well before it happened," Aidan says, surprised that Colonel Cunningham even asked.

The Colonel nods in response and lets out a tight breath. "This may come as a shock to you, but yesterday

Nadia Oswald was taken by Ecrian forces," the Colonel says.

Aidan feels like the ground has gone out from under him. His breath freezes in his lungs. He can't move because of the shock.

"Sir, what exactly happened?" John asks what Aidan can't seem to find the words to ask.

"There was a surprise attack with two elementals," the Colonel says. In response to John's surprised reaction, he waves a hand and says, "The Ecrians have more elementals and high-ranking witches in their ranks than I've ever seen anywhere."

"How could you let this happen?" Aidan asks, breathless. "Where is Elise?"

Colonel Cunningham straightens up. "I suppose that's fair to ask, but you should watch your tone," he says warningly. "Elise Chulyin is recuperating at the medical camp in northern Melgarde."

"What are they going to do with Nadia?"

The Colonel studies them for a moment before saying, "We've gotten reports that they're using the Vacancy Principle to transform as many of their soldiers as possible into witches. They don't have much respect for humans."

"That's why they had the human protests back home," John says, a look of dawning on his face.

"Yes," Colonel Cunningham says. "It's no secret Ecrium is particularly prejudice against humans."

"What's being done to get Nadia back?" Aidan asks suddenly.

"Minister ap Gwynedd is going to negotiate for her release. He's already in Melgarde," the Colonel says. He lets out another tight breath, a look of concern on his face. "We're concerned they are going to use her for another power transition."

"You mean they're gonna kill her," Aidan nearly shouts.

The Colonel looks taken aback at the raised voice, but then he seems to let it go. "We're also planning an extraction," he says.

"You're looking to retrieve them, sir?" John asks.

"Yes," Colonel Cunningham says. "They've only taken witches, leaving humans behind."

"I want to help," Aidan says.

"And so you shall," the Colonel says. "I called you here to assign you to the team of witches going in. John, you can go as well," he adds.

"I won't go anywhere without John by my side."

"I am aware," the Colonel says tightly. He seems to be holding himself back. "Your partnership will not be disrupted. Go to Melgarde and find Elise. She will tell you everything she knows about the witches and elementals who captured Nadia. The intelligence officers there will do the same. Your orders are to *discreetly* extract Nadia from the Ecrian camp to the south of Melgarde."

"Do you really believe diplomacy will fail?" John asks.

"I would rather err on the side of caution." The seriousness of Colonel Cunningham's tone is enough to suggest he doesn't think it will succeed.

The Colonel spreads a map on the table between them. He puts some weights down on the edges and smooths the middle. The center of the map is the metropolis of Melgarde. The densely packed lines show the neighborhoods labeled throughout. He pulls out a pencil and marks an "X" to the south of the neighborhood Zofria Heights. The road to Ecrium cuts through the area, no doubt the reason the encampment is down there.

"The Ecrian army has taken this part of the city completely," he says, indicating an area about midway through the city called Balustrode. The city is overrun.

There is no denying it. "You will have to make your way around the city exterior," he indicates a path around Braker's Ridge and through the southern end of Melgard. They would have to somehow cross the path to Ecrium and make their way into the encampment.

"It's not going to be easy," Aidan remarks.

"Nothing is," John says.

"You'll have a team with you, some of our best casters. Don't get caught," the Colonel says seriously.

Aidan nods. "We should get started."

"Go to Melgarde now," the Colonel says. "You should get there by evening. You can infiltrate the camp overnight."

"Yes, sir," Aidan says.

"Dismissed," the Colonel says. "Send in the Major."

John leads Aidan out of the tent. They indicate to the waiting major to head back into the tent. They criss-cross their way to their tent and head inside.

"Do you think we can do it?" Aidan asks John. He values his partner's opinion. And his sight.

"I think there's a fighting chance," John says. "But I can't see anything, if that's what you're asking."

"I think I had a vision recently," he says. "But I'm not sure whether it's a vision or just imagination."

John smiles. "That's the usual problem with seer powers." He pauses, then asks, "What was the vision?"

"It was of me in the desert standing next to Nadia. She was smiling," he says.

John tilts his head to the left and seems to think for a moment. "Well, let's take it as a good sign then," he says finally. "Let's take it as a sign we'll find them."

They finish packing up what they need. Neither of them has many belongings with them, just some clothes really. And they close up their tent to be used by the next soldiers.

They make their way through the camp to the place where horses are kept. A sergeant salutes Aidan and helps them get equipped for the long trek to Melgarde. They take their time checking that everything is correct and ready to go. Then they get a package of food from the mess tent and get ready to ride. The whole trip would take them the rest of the day, but they have the time, and they are motivated to get it done.

As they are about to mount their horses, a young lieutenant in Rebluinian uniform comes up to them.

"You're the fire elemental?" he asks Aidan.

"Yes," Aidan answers. He gives his name and introduces John.

"I'm to ride with you to Melgarde and make sure you don't get lost," he says. "I'm Anwas Cecil."

Aidan nods and says, "Pleasure. We should get going."

"I'll get my horse," Lieutenant Cecil says. He leaves then and comes back some ten minutes later with his brown mare, ready to travel. "Follow me," he says. "I know the way through the worst of it. We may have to cut across the desert to avoid the Ecrian army."

Aidan exchanges a look with John. Neither of them likes that idea, as Aidan can tell. "If you think it's best," Aidan says.

"You'll see what I mean when we get halfway down," the Lieutenant says. He steers his horse towards the southeast end of the encampment and leads them to the road to Melgarde.

Aidan secures his cloth face covering and goggles and keeps his opinions to himself. He doesn't know the Lieutenant. He doesn't trust him. There's nothing to be done though but follow him along the way south.

He just looks at John who looks back with worry in his eyes.

Aidan just hopes whatever is causing the foreboding feeling can be seen before it happens. He just hopes John can see before it makes it to the now.

Twenty-Three

When Nadia awakes, she has no idea how long she has been unconscious. She only remembers being knocked over the head sometime on their journey from the streets of Melgarde to the Ecrian encampment. At least she assumes she's in the Ecrian encampment. She is tied up on the sandy floor of a ubiquitous tent, still bound with power beyond her capabilities to break through. One look around and she knows she's in deep trouble.

Nadia cranes her neck to look around the tent. The sun is bright outside, bright enough it must be afternoon. The tent flutters gently in the wind. There is no one in the tent with her, but she can see boots just outside. She might be alone, but she is definitely being guarded.

For a moment, she struggles against the lines of power trapping her. But it isn't even flexing enough for her to move that much. The gag is still in place, and she can feel another line of power around her forehead. They have her trapped thoroughly.

Now what?

Perhaps she can break the lines from within. Perhaps she can use her personal shield to break them. Maybe if she used the repulsor it'll be strong enough to break the lines from the inside. It would be difficult to produce the shield close enough to her skin to not be immediately snuffed out by the power trap. But it was worth a try.

Nadia reaches deep down inside her for the crux of her anchor power. She pulls it to the surface. Immediately, the power trap flares around her, reacting to the presence of her power. She pulls back slightly and thinks the power into her skin. The power trap calms down.

The boots of the guard outside move. She freezes. She stops everything she's doing and just waits. But the guard doesn't seem to do anything except shift his position. So, she focuses again on the shield.

For a moment, she can't remember how to do the repulsor. For a moment, she struggles to think of anything useful. Then she takes a breath. There's no point in trying to rush it. She has time to get this right.

She raises the shield again, putting it barely over the top of her skin, sitting so close to her that it's beneath her clothing. She works to just hold the shield in place and put enough power into it to keep it from failing right away. Then she changes the schema of the shield. She makes it a repulsor, causing the color of the shield to change from a faint blue to a foreboding red.

The power trap reacts right away. It flares up in response to the incursion of the shield. But Nadia is relentless. She pushes her shield outward until she can feel the weight of the power trap in her mind. The trap is trying to sink into her to get her to stop. She pours more power into the shield, more than she thought she could handle, and works to hold it in place.

The guard outside shifts again.

Forget it. It's now or never.

She violently pushes the shield out from her body, struggling with the bonds the whole time. Nadia wriggles her body, thrashing against the strong lines of power. The power is unbelievable, but it did take several witches to hold her. Even so, she's surprised at the strength of the bonds.

The light from the lines of power gets brighter. She

pushes harder and harder, willing the shield to work, willing the shield to break the power. But it's fighting her. It's fighting her hard. Maybe if there was a witch actively monitoring it, her power would not be working right now. Maybe they would be able to prevent her from taking it down. But there is no one here.

The power begins to flicker around her, tested by the strength of her shield. And it begins to fail.

The boots outside shuffle and she panics, throwing even more power into the shield.

The lines of power vanish.

Nadia pulls herself up off the sandy floor.

What's next?

"I will see her," a stern voice says from outside the tent. "I want proof of life."

"She's in here," another voice answers. The second speaker sounds annoyed. "We've kept her intact. Her power is too valuable to throw away haphazardly."

"'Intact?'"

"We have not removed her anchor power yet," the second speaker says.

"It's atrocious what you do to your witches," the first speaker says, indignation in his voice.

"Only the worthy should hold such power," the

second speaker replies coldly. A shiver goes up Nadia's spine. She backs up to the back of the tent.

The flap opens and in walks two men.

"Morvath!" she says in surprise.

"She's loose!" the second man says.

Her guard comes bolting in and attacks her immediately. He is a strong caster witch for sure, throwing power at her like he had enough to burn. Plus, he's a burly man. He outclasses her physically though her shield is holding. She is pinned to the ground immediately.

She switches her shield back to a repulsor.

The burly man flies off her into a tent pole and slumps to the ground.

Then she sees that Morvath has attacked his companion. Morvath cut his throat with a long dagger that seemingly came out of nowhere. The sight of so much blood shocks her.

Morvath wipes off the dagger and stows it away in a hidden pocket. "We need to get out of here," he says. "Now."

The commanding voice jars Nadia into action. She gets up from the ground.

"Thank you," she says.

"I was coming to negotiate for your return, but it looks like you didn't need much help," he says in amusement. He checks outside the tent flap. "We might have to fight our way out of here."

"Where are we?"

"The Ecrium encampment south of Melgarde. We're on the edge of it though, so we might be able to escape into the desert," he says. He opens the tent flap. "Let's go."

Nadia steps through the flap.

A burst of power hits her from the right. Morvath grabs her arm and drags her past several tents before more Ecrians notice what is happening. They start taking hits from every side.

They run, run as fast as they both can through the camp towards the desert. But just when she thinks they're going to make it to the edge of the sand dunes, a large hit knocks them both off their feet.

Nadia flips over on her back, her shield over her. She reaches a hand out and extends the shield over Morvath, knowing he can't defend himself.

They're surrounded. Their caster witches and writer witches close in around them. Nadia hits one of them with a blast of power so strong it knocks the hulking soldier backwards. She sits up, Ecrian soldiers all around them. She stands up, ready to face whatever is to come.

A hand comes down on her shoulder.

She feels a blade plunge into her back.

She falls to the ground, her shield failing.

A moment later, she loses consciousness.

Twenty-Four

Lieutenant Cecil comes to a halt past the halfway point between Prartergarde and Melgarde. Aidan exchanges a look with John as they draw even with the Lieutenant. They have come to a slight rise in the landscape that looks down on the dunes below, the dark imprint of the road curving into those dunes and disappearing into the horizon. Fuzzy on the horizon and amber-tinted by his goggles, he can see the outline of Melgarde's skyline. They would probably get there within an hour.

"What is it?" John asks the Lieutenant.

The Lieutenant is looking through a spyglass down at the valley below. He takes it down from his eye and hands it to John next to him. "Follow the road to where it disappears behind the dunes. You can see the tracks in the sand on either side."

John complies and nods his head. He hands the spyglass over to Aidan who mimics his motion and finds what Lieutenant Cecil described. There are distinct impressions of footprints in the hills where the road disappears from view. He passes the spyglass back to the Lieutenant.

"What do we do?" John asks.

"We go around," he answers. "We'll have to cut through the dunes." He turns his horse around and heads back down the ridge. Some halfway, he stops and turns off the road onto a beaten-down track. Maybe it was once a proper road, but it had fallen into disrepair. Their horses take the trek into the desert landscape and around the nearest dune out of sight of the road.

John falls back slightly, maintaining a distance from Lieutenant Cecil and keeping pace with Aidan. He feels grateful his casting partner is next to him because he truly doesn't know the Lieutenant and he just has a sense of foreboding.

They trudge along the beaten down track heading west then south for maybe an hour. They can no longer see the main road behind them, but they can occasionally see the Melgarde skyline ahead of them. But that only happens when they come to a rise in the landscape and can see the valley ahead of them. On the downside of the dunes, they can only see the sand ahead and behind.

As they come to one such rise in the land, Aidan is not paying attention to where they are going, distracted by the rock outcroppings on either side of them and the dunes running right up to the stone. The landscape, while empty of human life, is still beautiful.

John comes to an abrupt halt, staring ahead. Aidan stops next to him, his gaze going to where Lieutenant Cecil has disappeared around a bend in the road.

"Can you shield us?" John whispers.

"Not like a witch can," Aidan whispers back. "What is it?"

"We're not alone."

Cautiously, they make their way forward, urging their horses to go slowly.

John ducks.

A blast of power from behind goes flying over his head.

Aidan raises a fire shield, the only thing he can think of to protect them. It unnerves the horses immediately and both he and John fight to keep control of the beasts. Leaving the shield in place behind them, the wall of heat and flame recedes as they push their horses forward.

Aidan is leery of what waits for them just around the bend in the road.

They walk right into the net.

A lattice of power spans the road ahead of them as they turn the corner. A second lattice falls behind them almost immediately. They are trapped.

Aidan reaches out and takes John's hand like he had so many times in the past. He connects with John's limited seer power and grants John access to his further ranging power.

Can a seer witch and a fire elemental cast spells? Can they bridge that divide and somehow break free from the spell surrounding them? They could try.

John would have to cast. Aidan can no longer sense spell magic. It's beyond his abilities now. But John could, as he had so many times before, with Aidan's assistance.

His casting partner points in the direction of the lattice and says in witchspeak, "*Unravel.*"

The lattice begins to unweave itself.

From beyond the net, both ahead and behind, witches in Ecrian uniforms come out from behind the outcroppings. Lieutenant Cecil is among them. And he is not in bonds. He is with them. Lieutenant Cecil is a traitor.

They have to set that truth aside for now and somehow get away from these Ecrian forces. Somehow get away from half a dozen or so witches. There is no telling what they would do to a seer witch and a fire elemental if they got their hands on them.

The lattice behind begins to creep forward, touching the horses as they come closer.

Aidan points at the lattice ahead and directs his fire into it. Between John's assumed casting power and the lines of fire coming from Aidan, the lattice collapses.

They take off at a gallop towards the Ecrian witches.

"Stop them!" Lieutenant Cecil shouts.

Another figure joins the fight, stepping out into the road ahead of them. Aidan immediately recognizes another fire elemental.

He can't even think as he parries flame and fireball and lines of fire coming at him from the fire elemental. This elemental is far more practiced than he is. Aidan feels outclassed by this individual.

He borrows John's seer abilities and peeks a second into the future to block the next blow before it comes.

They ride forward past the fire elemental who is

astonished at the quick reaction.

"Follow them!" a voice calls out.

Aidan looks back once to see Lieutenant Cecil following on his horse. That traitor led them right into the trap. He knew they would follow him into the desert and right into the space where Ecrian forces waited.

"We have to get back to the main road!" John shouts next to him.

Aidan doesn't question his partner. They come around a bend in the track and see the main road ahead of them. "Can we make it?" Aidan asks.

"If we hurry!"

They push their horses on, making them gallop as fast as they can on the dirt track. They lose sight of the main road a few times with the twists and turns of the track. Then they make one more turn and there it is ahead of them. Their pursuers are still following them, still trying to catch them. Lieutenant Cecil is well ahead of the rest.

Aidan lifts a hand to blast fire at him when a shot of power goes past him, taking Lieutenant Cecil off his horse.

Aidan turns back to see Rebluinian soldiers running up the dirt track to meet them. The Ecrian forces begin

to fall back, heading back into the protection of the dunes.

John comes to a stop as their horses make it to the main road. Both beasts are panting from the exertion. He draws even with John and looks around them.

A Sergeant comes forward and raises a hand to his face, removing his goggles and face cloth. Aidan does the same. The Sergeant looks up at Aidan on his horse and says, "Identify yourself."

"I'm Aidan Montgomery, fire elemental to the Egrarian Army."

John lowers his face coverings as well and answers, "John Blestone. Seer witch."

"You're lucky," the Sergeant says. "We've been seeing this kind of ambush a lot recently." He extends a hand to Aidan and says, "Meilir Harries, of Rebluinia." He is human, judging from the lack of power present in the handshake.

"We need to get to Melgarde," Aidan explains. "As quickly as possible."

Sergeant Harries nods and waves his soldiers forward. It is a mixed group of witches and humans, all armed with the Rebluinian bows slung along their backs. He looks around at the masked faces, watching as they watch him.

"We'll escort you," Sergeant Harries says.

The soldiers mount horses on standby next to the main road. Aidan and John ride in the center of the group, with Rebluinian soldiers at their front and their back. They head in the direction of the Melgarde skyline.

Aidan has no idea whether they are safe or not.

Twenty-Five

One powerful blast knocks out all the Ecrian soldiers. It's truly a shame Nadia could not control her power that well. One well-timed blast from her and she could wipe out this whole camp with her power. But Morvath knows that's not the way.

He stands over her body, his long dagger plunged into her back. He kneels down and pulls the dagger out of her, turning her body over. He checks her pulse. She's still alive, but the pulse is faint. It's only a matter of time.

Another blast of power hits his personal shield. He looks up and sees the Ecrian soldiers coming. He can't sit here waiting for Nadia to die. And if she dies too soon, he's going to lose her power. He makes a split decision.

Morvath picks up Nadia and turns and runs into the desert. Nadia is bleeding out in his arms though. She has completely passed out. As they come to the top of a dune, fire and power scorching the sand around him, he sets Nadia down, turns back and blasts the oncoming Ecrians with enough power to drive them back. Then he turns to Nadia. She is barely alive. He considers the consequences of what he's about to do. The military is searching for them. He is the last one with her. Would they trust the Ecrians if they told the Egrarian military that he stabbed her? He isn't sure.

He swears out loud as the blasts continue to come.

Morvath kneels down next to Nadia, his shield bowing out around both of them in a dome of power. He has no choice. He hasn't studied it, but he will have to heal her. At least enough that she can die later and not right this second. He knows from experience the transition of power will incapacitate him temporarily. He can't do this now.

He turns Nadia over onto her stomach and places a hand on her bloody back. He calls up his anchor power and thinks through what he wants to happen. He wants her bleeding to slow but not stop completely. Slow enough that she'll still bleed out later.

"Bleeding slow. Healing incomplete."

The reverberation of witchspeak echoes through him. He feels the power come out of him. Morvath feels the strain of having to hold both the shield and the healing in place. He has to maintain both power levels carefully not to underpower one of them.

A large explosion of power crackles on the shield.

Nadia is stable.

Morvath picks her up and heads into the desert. The high afternoon sun bears down on them, but as they cross over the ridge, their followers cease to chase them. Still, he keeps running until he is over the dune and onto the next one. He sees an outcropping of rock to his left and heads that way. By the time he reaches the outcropping, he is panting from the effort of carrying Nadia the whole way.

He sets Nadia's prone body down along the outcropping and leans against the stone surface. The girl is still unconscious from the blood loss, and likely would be for quite a while. Morvath slumps down into a sitting position next to Nadia. He's not sure what to do now. He was forced to save the person he wants to kill, and he doesn't know what to do.

He pulls out the power sensor from his inner pocket

and takes a reading. The reading for Nadia is off the charts. Howells was right. Her anchor power is distinctly more powerful than Howells's power. He wonders about why and if the power is only as strong as it is because it belongs to her. It almost doesn't matter though. He still wants her power for himself. He still wants that strength.

Morvath pulls the dagger back out.

He contemplates his situation once again. It would be exceedingly difficult to get away with killing her here. On the one hand, he is out in the middle of nowhere and could attribute her death to the Ecrians. On the other hand, he would be questioned for not coming back with her alive. He debates his options and makes his decision.

Morvath stows the dagger again.

He sits back against the outcropping, feeling defeated and annoyed. The sand shifts around them with the desert breeze. He looks out at the expanse of desert and pulls out a compass. He knows he is somewhere east of the encampment, between the camp and the road to Ecrium. He could easily make his way back to Melgarde proper and make his way to the north end of the city. The tricky part is what to do about Nadia.

After considering for a few minutes and thinking about what could be done, he picks Nadia up again and begins making his way north. He comes to a rise in the landscape and can see both the encampment behind and the city ahead. He trudges along in the direction of the city.

After about an hour of straining to keep going and carrying Nadia, he is exhausted but has made it to the outskirts of Melgarde. He crossed the road to Ecrium and headed into the southern end of Zofria Heights. Then he stopped in a back alley filled with debris from previous Ecrian attacks and hunkered down between a large trash bin and a pile of garbage.

Morvath checks Nadia's wound. It seems to have clotted enough to keep from bleeding out, but Nadia is still in rough shape. She's pale from the blood loss and still unconscious. He's concerned she won't make it back to camp at this rate. But he has to keep moving. If they're caught, they would both be killed. Nadia for her power, and Morvath because they think he's a lowly human. He picks Nadia up again and starts making his way down the alley.

At the end of the alley, where it meets the main street, he stops and looks around. There, across the street, is the green sign of a witchwire office, a local communication center useful because most of Melgarde is not wired like Port Nalrang is slowly becoming. He is slowly realizing that there is no way he can make it to the camp on his own. Maybe the witchwire is still usable.

As quickly as he can, he darts across the road. He opens the deserted store front door and goes inside, setting down Nadia on the floor by the door. He locks the door and closes the curtains across the door's window.

The room is dim. He goes to the nearest wall and flicks on the light. Mercifully, the lights come on. That means the witchwire will still be working as well; it requires electricity and magic. He pulls out the witchwire device from below the shelf of the store. He has no idea who to send the message to.

From another shelf, he pulls down a heavy book of witchwire numbers. He flips through to the page showing all of Melgarde's witchwire offices. Morvath runs a finger down the page until he finds the one he's looking for. The Egrarian military is currently encamped in the neighborhood of Argent Gardens. He finds the directory number for the witchwire office located on the north side, betting that the office is not only still standing, but still functional. It's a long shot, but he has to get out of here. He can't keep running on his own.

He clicks on the clockwork part of the witchwire device and feels the buzz of the magic part come on automatically. The genius Eiriana Elley who invented it made sure that the device could be used by any person, human, witch, elemental, or even spirit. It would require no magic other than what was inside the device. Elley's design had been improved upon, but largely remained the same as its first invention.

On the typewriter-like keyboard, Morvath strikes the keys in the correct order: MG1736N6. The numbers stood for "Melgard, Argent Gardens North, Wire Office 6." He picks up the receiver and puts it to his ear silently hoping the receiver on the other end would pick up.

"Argent Gardens North," the voice on the other end says.

"My name is Morvath ap Gwynedd and I am a minister of Egraria trapped in southern Melgarde," he says by way of introduction.

An intake of breath tells Morvath he has the listener's attention. "What can I do to help?"

"I need a message sent to the Egrarian military outpost in Argent Gardens."

There is a pause and the sound of paper shuffling as the listener gets ready to record the message. "Go ahead."

"I am trapped at the Zofria Heights South fifteen witchwire office," he says, double checking the office location on the side of the location directory. "Designation M-G-one-two-five-three-S-one-five. I need immediate rescue. I have an injured soldier, Nadia Oswald, with me."

After a pause and the sounds of scribbling, the listener says, "Anything else?"

"Tell them I will remain at this location as long as I can, but I'll head north if needed."

"Got it. I'll send it over right away," the speaker says.

"Thank you," Morvath remembers to say. The line goes dead.

He leaves the witchwire device on in case of a callback. But he shuts the lights off in the building. Morvath goes back to Nadia who is still unconscious. He checks her wound again, the wound he himself inflicted. It has clotted over enough that she is definitely not going to bleed out, but he thinks he should heal it slightly more.

Nadia stirs just then, before he can enact a bit of magic, and looks up at him.

"Morvath?" she says groggily. "What happened?"

"Don't move," Morvath says. "You're injured and we're trapped."

"Where are we?"

"A witchwire office in south Melgarde," he explains. He's not sure how good her sense of Rebluinian geography is. "The Ecrians got through the shield, and one stabbed you. I managed to get us away before they could kill us."

"What's going to happen?" she asks.

"I contacted the witchwire office on the north end of Melgarde, near the camp," he explains. "Presumably they'll get the message to the right authorities and send them to get us."

She nods her head slowly. "How long?" There is worry in her eyes.

"Not sure," Morvath says. "But I think you're stable enough for now. I just don't want to risk carrying you any further."

Nadia nods again, her eyes blinking slowly. After a moment of clearly struggling to stay awake, she passes out again. Morvath is left looking at her prone form and wondering why he didn't kill her when he had the chance.

He stands up and checks out the window, studying

the empty street. If she dies with him, they won't question it now. But he can't very well use the dagger again. It leaves a slight impression, and the wound would be too fresh. He taps his pocket where the dagger lurks. No, this was a golden opportunity that he squandered because the Ecrians were too many.

He lowers the curtain again, shutting out the view of the street. He's not worried. There would be other opportunities.

Twenty-Six

As they approached Melgarde, the city seemed to leap right out from the distance to surround them. Aidan rides forward with the Rebluinian soldiers towards what he presumes is the Egrarian encampment in northern Melgarde. They enter the neighborhood of Argent Gardens and make their way to the central park the neighborhood is built around. There, they can see the tents of the Egrarian army set up, covering the entire park and several blocks surrounding it.

Sergeant Harries escorts them all the way to the command tent set up in the centermost part of the park. Aidan dismounts and thanks Sergeant Harries for both his help and his guidance coming to Melgarde.

"You're welcome," Sergeant Harries says. "I need to report the incident to my superiors. Watch your backs out there."

"We will," John answers, also dismounting from his horse. They watch the Rebluinian soldiers move on, heading towards the west end of camp.

Two guards make them wait outside the command tent while a third goes in to announce their arrival. The third guard pops back out a second later to wave them in. Aidan and John step through the tent flap into the relative dimness inside. Once his eyes adjust, he is surprised to be facing Colonel Ergamenes.

"Lieutenant Montgomery," the Colonel says by way of greeting. "And Sergeant Blestone. Your timing couldn't be better."

"What do you mean?" Aidan asks, forgetting all the necessary formalities of speaking to a superior officer.

"We just received a witchwire from Minister ap Gwynedd. He managed to extract Nadia from the Ecrian camp," the Colonel explains.

"That's a relief," Aidan says.

"It's not over yet," the Colonel explains. "The Minister is trapped in a witchwire office in Zofria Heights, near the heart of Ecrian territory."

"Have you sent a team to rescue them?"

"They've already left," Colonel Ergamenes says,

much to Aidan's surprise. He knows the Colonel dislikes Nadia.

Aidan glances over at John. "What can we do?" he says.

"I believe your orders were to debrief Lieutenant Chulyin," the Colonel says. "She is recovering in the medical tent."

Aidan has never felt so dismissed in his life. The Colonel clearly wants to just get rid of them for now. So, he and John both salute the Colonel and duck back out of the tent.

"Well, that was a letdown," John says.

"I'm not too surprised," Aidan answers. "He seems to always go against Colonel Cunningham if he can."

They walk away from the command tent and head in the direction of the one with the medical shield on it. The red "X" with a circle around it is the universal symbol for medical care and can be seen on most hospital buildings back in Egraria. They head into the tent.

They approach a woman with both caster witch and Egrarian Medical Corps patches on her shoulder. The bold red "X" of the medical logo in this case has the healing hands symbol emblazoned over it. They ask the healer where they can find Elise. Rather than point them in the right direction, the healer walks them down the long ward to her bed.

Elise looks up as they get closer. She doesn't smile, but merely looks more alert, as if she had been waiting for them.

"You made it," Elise says.

"Yes," Aidan says. "Not without trouble, I'm afraid."

"What do you mean?"

"We were ambushed along the road from Pratergarde," John explains.

She looks surprised. "I had heard that has been happening," she says. "I'm glad you made it safely."

"We were told to talk to you and get your account of what happened," Aidan says.

Elise looks confused. "I already gave my statement to Colonel Ergamenes himself," she says.

Aidan and John exchange a look and Aidan rolls his eyes. "I think the Colonel was trying to get rid of us."

Elise lays back. "I don't like him," she says emphatically. It's unlike her to be so blunt about it. "I don't trust him, but I do believe he will get Nadia back."

"We were just told that Minister ap Gwynedd found her," Aidan says.

"Oh! We met him!" she exclaims. "We met him at dinner on our last night in Port Nalrang. He works with Nadia's father."

"Somehow that makes sense then," Aidan says. "Seems like he would be motivated to find his colleague's daughter."

"Are they back yet?" Elise asks.

"No, they're trapped in a witchwire office in Zofria Heights," John says. "But the Colonel said they sent out a party to retrieve them."

"You don't seem worried," she remarks to John.

"I'm not," he says. "I can see her getting here by nightfall."

"Ah, to be a seer with decent range," Elise says. "Meanwhile, I get my leg broken by a power blast," she says, gesturing at her right leg. It has clearly been healed but is still bandaged up. "I'm stuck in this cot for another couple days."

"Why didn't they take you too?"

"I don't know," Elise says. Her eyes go to John, and she says, "Does he know?"

"He knew first," Aidan says, immediately understanding what she meant.

Elise lowers her voice. "I think it's her anchor

power they wanted," she says. "They knew right away what she was. It seems like it's common knowledge in Ecrium."

Aidan sits down on the bed next to Elise's. He looks up at John and shakes his head. "How much longer is the secret going to be kept?" He rubs his forehead. "And how are we supposed to protect anchors if the secret gets out widespread?"

"It's not common knowledge in Umbra," she remarks. "But I wonder now how common it is to know. I wonder if more people know than we suspect."

"The Unnamed Church has protected them for centuries," Aidan says. "It's literally on their crest."

Elise nods. "'With grace we protect thee'," she quotes the motto on the crest.

They had all become members of the church by default when their power switch happened. They were all too valuable as targets for other witches and humans that the church offered protection months ago. But they were too public of figures to be able to accept. They all had to rely upon the military to keep their secret and to keep their promise.

But even now, as Aidan recounts every person who knows about the anchor power from him or Nadia, the list is getting exceedingly long. Perhaps it is only a matter of time before it becomes common knowledge everywhere that anchors exist. How safe would they be then? How safe would Nadia?

Further, Aidan wonders who the other anchors are. Wilhelm Martinsson remains in Umbra working with Kensa Chulyin-Siku on the ship going to orbit in a few months. He remains isolated and protected in Umbra. But then there's Howells who doesn't have any protection at all. He is alone and exposed. Perhaps people suspect he is an anchor already.

But that still leaves the question of who the other four are, if there are indeed only seven of them total. Would it be in their best interest to remain hidden?

Elise is watching him closely, as if she can read his thoughts. She is such a prodigy of a witch that he doesn't doubt she probably could if she tried.

"I think you're right," she says suddenly.

"What? What is Aidan right about?" John asks.

"He's wondering if the other anchors, the other four we know about, should remain hidden," she says. "But I think Howells knew who they were. So, I think it would be best if he destroyed his records, so no one else can find out."

"I think it'll be a while before we can tell him that," Elise says. "I don't know if you've noticed, but none of us has communication with anyone back home."

"I noticed," Aidan grumbled. "We don't even have basic witchwire news."

Elise leans back into her pillow again. "If we knew anyone from the church here, they could get the message to him."

"We don't though," John says. "At least I don't."

"Same."

"We would need to find an avatar of the church, someone who acts as liaison to the outside," Aidan says. He is by far the most familiar with the church, having been born an anchor witch and under their protection since birth. He was approached by them at an early age and sworn to secrecy about their existence, even from his family. It was difficult to hide from his family, but he understands the necessity now.

"But who?" Elise asks.

"I don't know," Aidan says. "We need the help though."

A nurse walks by and they all hush immediately. When he has gone further down the ward, Elise says, "Maybe I can get a wire out with my diplomatic connections. I'll have Hughes contact our Port Nalrang contacts."

"That might work," Aidan says. "Where is Hughes?"

"He only left a few minutes before you got here," she says. "He'll be back shortly."

"Should we let you rest?" John asks.

"Probably," Elise says. "Though I'm keen to get out of this bed."

"All in good time," Aidan says, getting up from the bed. He clasps Elise's hand, thinking of the time in the Waste when her and Nadia's letters were his only connection to humanity. He is grateful for her friendship even more so now.

"Be careful out there," Elise says.

"We will be."

Aidan follows John down the length of the ward and out of the hospital tent. They are immediately thrust back into the turmoil of the war zone. Again, Aidan wonders when he will next feel at peace.

Twenty-Seven

Morvath fidgets as he waits. He keeps checking the street for any sign of the Egrarian rescue party. They should be here soon. It's been hours since he sent the message. Hopefully, they got it and are coming. In the meantime, he is trying not to worry too much.

He looks down at Nadia who is unconscious again and thinks he needs to find something to bandage her wound. He goes back behind the counter and starts rummaging through drawers and cabinets to try and find a medical kit. Most places like this would have a basic kit on hand in case of an emergency. He finds one in the lowest drawer of the counter and takes it over to Nadia.

She looks up at him groggily. "What's going on?" she says, her voice straining from the effort.

"I'm going to try to bandage your wound to keep

you going till our rescue gets here," Morvath explains. He gently helps her turn onto her side. "This is going to hurt," he warns her as he brings out some antiseptic cleaner to wipe the area down with.

She winces as he wipes the area but handles it like a trooper. She is as strong as he expected her to be.

Next, Morvath brings out bandages and applies them to the area with medical tape that keeps the gauze in place. He is not sure how good of a job he did, but it would have to suffice till help arrived.

"Do you need anything?" he asks.

"Some water?"

"I'll see if I can find some."

Morvath searches through the back of the witchwire office, going through what looked like an employee respite room. He finds snacks there and a glass water tank for employees to drink from. He opens cabinets until he finds a glass and fills. He brings it back out to the main room.

A dark figure stands in the open doorway.

Nadia is passed out on the floor.

Morvath's eyes go from the figure to Nadia and back again. His senses tell him the person is at least a caster witch. They are so heavily cloaked he can't tell their gender or anything else about them. He only knows their presence is menacing.

"What do you want?' Morvath asks, immediately hostile.

"What are you doing here?" the voice answers.

Morvath doesn't answer. He just stares at the figure.

The figure takes a step forward, still in shadow by the door, but closer now.

"You're Egrarian." The remark is not a kind one. And they raise a shrouded hand at Morvath.

He reacts immediately. He drops the glass and draws the dagger while casting a shield. In one swift motion, the blade comes free of his jacket, and he dodges the blast of electricity thrown his way. He wasn't expecting a plasma witch. He throws the dagger.

It hits home.

The figure clearly wasn't expecting him to have power, much less to have a spelled dagger. They slump to the ground near the door.

Morvath immediately checks that the figure is dead. He pulls back the hood to find a young male soldier, his eyes open and vacant. Morvath sheaths the knife.

He goes to Nadia and checks her vitals. She's still

alive, just passed out. Good. She didn't witness his necessary use of magic. He gets up and checks the street again, looking down the way for any sign of the Egrarian forces. Then he shuts the door and locks it. They would probably be coming in the back anyway.

A bang at the back of the office jolts Morvath. He pulls out his dagger and heads to the back room. The bang goes off again. He freezes, realizing the banging is on the other side of the door. He gets closer to the door, waiting.

Someone knocks on the other side.

He opens the sliding peephole cover in the door and peers out. He sees several Egrarian soldiers on the other side. At least he hopes they're Egrarian soldiers and not Ecrians masquerading as Egrarians. Only one way to know for sure.

"What's today's code word?" he asks through the door.

"Courtthostur," a voice calls back, naming the town in the central plateau. He nods and shuts the peephole. He unlocks the door and lets the half a dozen soldiers in.

"Is one of you a healer?" he asks.

"I am," a caster witch says. She is probably in her thirties, her hair pulled back in a dark bun. Her sharp, dark eyes look at Morvath with concern.

"Over here," he says, leading the healer to where Nadia is still unconscious on the floor. "I bandaged it as best I could."

The healer kneels and examines her. "You did a good job. The bleeding has stopped," she says. "I can heal her, but she will still be weak and need rehabilitation."

"Do it," a tall Corporal says. He is the ranking soldier in the group. Morvath is surprised they didn't send a more experienced team to rescue him and Nadia. Perhaps the authorities didn't think they were worth retrieving.

The healer works the chant known to all caster witches that acts as a basic wound healing. No doubt this healer had used it many times before. He watches diligently to capture their prowess with the spell. He is not a healer, but knowing how to heal would be useful knowledge. In only a few short minutes, the healer has closed the wound completely. She takes the medical kit and cleans the area thoroughly before putting it away.

Nadia revives, her eyes fluttering and looking around at them. "What's going on?" she asks.

"They're here to rescue us," Morvath says. "Can you

stand?"

"I can try," she says, wincing as she tries to sit up. Morvath reaches down and helps her to her feet. She leans on him, barely standing.

"I can carry you," Morvath suggests. He is strong enough to do it.

"Perhaps that might be best," she says. "We have a long way to go."

"We should get going," the Corporal says. His whole demeanor is rushed and nervous. Morvath can't blame him. They are in a war zone deep in enemy territory. They need to get back up north as soon as possible.

Morvath lifts up Nadia, and she slings an arm around his neck, holding on tight. "Thank you," she whispers. "For finding me."

Morvath doesn't answer. He doesn't say he would have gone after her anyway, he would have sought her out no matter what for her power. He doesn't say any of that. He just follows the soldiers out the back of the witchwire office into the back alley and onto the street.

For about an hour, they move through the streets without incident. They stick to the alleys and the narrow lanes between the tall buildings of Melgarde. The sun is beginning to set and twilight has fallen in the city itself. The shadows provide some cover to their passage. Their gray uniforms keep them from being noticed.

They make it out of Zofria Heights like that, managing to get halfway through Balustrode before they see Ecrian soldiers ahead of them. The group of soldiers is clustered in an alleyway, hidden from sight but by no means safe. With Morvath and Nadia at the center of the group, they make their way back up the alley to the cross passage between the back of the buildings. There, they stop and assess.

"Analysis," the Corporal says.

"We have to go around," one of the privates says.

"Where?" another argues. "We would have to go all the way over to Barking to make it around."

"Can we get across without them seeing us?" a third asks.

"Maybe," the Corporal says. He looks over his shoulder, up the passage between buildings to where another alley cuts through. "Private Jannsen, go up the passage and scout out their location for the next few blocks." Private Jannsen, the first to speak, heads down the passage. The Corporal studies Morvath for a moment. "I don't suppose you've ever been cloaked by a witch before, have you?"

"You mean have I ever had a spell put over me?" Morvath asks. The Corporal nods. "Yes, I have," Morvath admits. "In Matraize, by a writer witch." Which is true, but not entirely honest. It wasn't Matraize, but it was a writer witch. Goliyant was very much a native Egrarian.

"Can you manipulate spells?" the Corporal asks.

"I don't have enough magic in me," Morvath lies.

The Corporal looks at Nadia in Morvath's arms and says, "Are you up to cloaking two people?"

She looks tired and rundown, but she says, "I can. It will be easier if you cast the spell and I just maintain it."

The Corporal waves forward another private, this one with a caster witch patch on his arm, the hand and star symbol prominent. The caster witch places a hand on both Nadia and Morvath. He does his best to stand absolutely still.

A tingling feeling indicates the spell taking hold. He feels the spell in the ring react to the cloaking spell. But it doesn't do much more than simmer for a moment before settling down. He's surprised the spell reacted at all.

With everyone cloaked and ready to go, the Corporal gives them instructions. "We are going to circle the

Ecrian troops and avoid detection by sticking to the alleys as much as possible," he says. "Bennett, Harlow, you two will take point. Jannsen, Smythe, bring up the rear." He looks at Morvath. "Stick with me and Weslaw," he says, indicating the healer. "We'll flank you on either side." He looks around the group. "Everyone ready?"

The group murmurs their assent.

"Let's go."

They head down the alley and towards the street. Morvath has no idea how they're going to make it back to camp.

Twenty-Eight

They make it out of the alley without much incident. And they make it down the block, passing some Ecrian soldiers as they go. Morvath is tense as he moves with the soldiers, as they move as a unit north through town. He is surrounded by them, but that is by no means a guarantee of his safety. He would have to trust their abilities to protect him. He couldn't risk using his own abilities and exposing himself as a witch.

They are about to turn a corner when Bennett and Harlow freeze and back up. Not the optimal location to stop. They are exposed along a street in the shadow of a building. The streetlight is out, but there is still enough light from the nearby lights that they could be seen. The night is approaching but not fast enough.

"What is it?" the Corporal whispers.

"About thirty soldiers," Bennett says. "Too many for the cloak to hide us." Indeed, the cloak is only meant to confound casual glances. It simply made the individual cloaked, a part of the background environment and thus ignorable. There's no telling if it would work on direct scrutiny, and it certainly wouldn't work on so many soldiers at once.

"Jannsen and Smythe, lead us back to the side alley we passed. We need to regroup."

They follow the Corporal's instructions and begin to head that way. Once down the alley a good distance, far enough to be in near total darkness, Morvath sets Nadia down for a moment to rest.

"What do we do now?" he asks quietly.

"We need to go around," the Corporal says. "There's no other way." After a moment's pause to think, he says, "Jannsen, can you and Smythe go down the alley further and see where you end up? See if you can circle behind them?"

The two Privates head down the alleyway and disappear into the darkness. The remaining four soldiers and Morvath and Nadia wait in tense silence as the minutes tick past.

"What will we do if there's no way around?"

Morvath asks.

"One thing at a time," the Corporal answers. Morvath nods, accepting the assessment. There is no reason to plan for another contingency if that contingency is not needed.

A group of Ecrian soldiers passes on the street. Morvath and the rest all huddle down behind a trash bin and hope the darkness conceals them. Fortunately, the soldiers pass without incident. Their passing makes it obvious they can't stay there for too much longer.

"Why did you go after Lieutenant Oswald?" Weslaw asks in a soft whisper.

Morvath simply says, "I know her father."

"Oh," Weslaw says. "I had wondered why you would risk your life for her."

And Morvath realized that he did, in fact, risk his life for Nadia. Or at least risked his life to kill her. He wonders about that now. Would he get another chance to take her power? Would there be another golden opportunity like the one he just gave up? He would have to wait and see.

"I'm impressed with your bravery," Weslaw whispers.

"I'm not brave," he says in reply. "I'm just an idiot

who doesn't know when to quit. Nadia is the brave one."

"Why do you say that?"

"Because by the time I got to her she had already escaped her bonds. She would no doubt have made it out of there in one piece without me," he says. Morvath shakes his head, trying to show surprise and disbelief. "If she didn't have to protect me, no doubt she never would have gotten injured."

"How did you face down so many witches?"

Morvath reaches into his jacket and pulls out the knife. "Don't touch it," he warns. "It has a killing spell on it. I got it from a writer witch in Matraize a long time ago. It seemed like a good idea to carry it here." And while most of that is true, it isn't the whole truth. It is all he is willing to tell them though.

"Be careful with that," the healer says. "You never know if the spell will turn on you too."

Morvath nods sagely. He can't tell them the spell has been rewritten to protect him specifically. He can't tell them he has the power to rewrite spells at all. He just agrees that he has to be careful and stows the dagger away in his jacket again.

"Where are Jannsen and Smythe? It's been long enough, they should be back by now," Bennett says.

The Corporal exchanges a dark look with him. "We'll have to follow them down the alley and hope we don't meet any trouble," he says. "Bennett take point."

Bennett is a caster witch and likely a skilled one, given the marksman patch under his caster badge. The rest of them form up behind him and begin moving as a unit down the alleyway into the darkness. Every small sound feels magnified in the dark alley. It feels as though every movement could give them away at any time.

Just as the tension is killing him, Bennett comes to a complete halt. A shadow moves in the dark ahead of them, a shape almost indiscernible from the surrounding dimness. He holds onto Nadia tightly, knowing he might have to take off running.

"It's us," a voice whispers. And just as Bennett is about to cast a spell—what Morvath couldn't tell—the shadow steps forward and Jannsen comes into view. Smythe is right behind him, looking over his shoulder as he approaches.

"What took you so long?" the Corporal snaps.

"The Ecrians got too close for comfort," Smythe explains. "But we found a way around. We have to go down about five blocks, but we can make it."

They begin moving in that direction, heading for the

next building to hide behind. From around the corner, down a cross alleyway, they hear the Ecrians marching. Quickly, each of them darts across that alleyway to keep from being seen. Then they head further down into the dark passage and away from danger. All they can do is hide. There's too few of them to defeat such a formidable enemy like the Ecrians.

Once again, Morvath reflects that it's a shame Nadia is so unpracticed as an anchor witch. One blast from her and she could take out the whole platoon. But she's injured, and that isn't an option. It's certainly not an option for Morvath to do something about it.

Morvath follows their lead and keeps his mouth shut. He knows better than to speak the truth right now. It would only get him into terrible trouble.

About five blocks down, they pause at a junction with another alley. Jannsen and Smythe head down the alley to the main street. Once they have taken a good long look at their surroundings, they wave the group forward. Morvath lofts Nadia for a moment, adjusting her. She slings her arm over his neck to help.

The group scuttles out of the alley and down the street. They head down the street, straight north. They turn one more corner and find them: a group of

Rebluinian soldiers battling with a small group of Ecrians in the middle of a city park. They are trapped with no way out but through the fray.

"Weslaw, no matter what happens, escort the Minister and the Lieutenant back to camp. I'm putting them in your direct charge," the Corporal says.

"What are you going to do?" Morvath asks.

"We're going to keep you from getting caught." The look on the Corporal's face suggested he would do just about anything to prevent that from happening. "Let's go," the Corporal says.

They start at a light jog that turns into a run.

"This way!" Weslaw calls out, leading them to the right and north away from the bulk of the fighting.

As Morvath watches, the rest of the soldiers attack the Ecrians from behind. The few Ecrians that are blindsided by the attack are made up for by the clearly strong writer witches that return the attack. He only watches long enough to see the Corporal fall, dead before he hits the ground. Then he is following Weslaw, running as fast as he could to keep up with her. They have no time to lose.

They make it through the park, dodging Rebluinians who see their uniforms and don't pay them any attention.

On the other side, Morvath spares one glance back to see that the others have fallen as well. All five soldiers dead in a matter of a minute or two. They are no match for Ecrium's forces.

"This way!" Weslaw calls as they head down a sidestreet and up what is marked as the entrance to Argent Gardens. They get maybe a few blocks up before the healer stops and hunches over, heaving in deep breaths.

Morvath stops too, turning to face the direction they came from should any soldiers come for them that way.

"We're only a few blocks off from the camp," Weslaw says.

"So close," Morvath mutters.

"I know."

So close the Corporal and the others could have made it. So close their deaths were needless.

"What was the Corporal's name?"

"Heartson," Weslaw says. "Reginald Heartson."

Morvath files away the name in his memory. He would write to the Corporal's family later. He knew he would.

"We should keep moving," Weslaw says, jogging him out of his thoughts.

Morvath agrees and they begin jogging up the street, this time at a more sedate pace. They only have so far to go and only so much energy to spare. And they have time. They have an abundance of time. Unlike Heartson and the rest. Unlike the Rebluinians who even now are beginning to fail in their attempts to hold back the Ecrian tide.

He turns his back on the Rebluinian fight. There's nothing to be done about it now.

Twenty-Nine

Aidan is left wandering around the camp with John, waiting for an assignment. He is a touch surprised he hasn't been sent to the front lines already, what with Ecrium's excessive use of elementals. But that isn't his call to make. So they find a tent they can share and take the time to change from dusty, desert clothes into a cleaner uniform. There is not much to be done about the pervasive sand, but at least he can feel slightly cleaner for the moment.

Aidan and John both leave their bags in the tent, though they mostly contain clothes and nothing valuable. The only valuables Aidan has anymore are the pendants he created for the girls that he has yet to give them. And those he keeps in his pocket.

They walk through the camp in search of something

to do, or just in search of some food as neither of them has eaten yet. The sun has gone down by the time they make their way into the camp mess tent. The food is nothing to write home about, but they eat the stew and flatbread with gusto to avoid starving to death in the desert. Once again, the hot food doesn't bother Aidan.

As they finish their meal, a commotion outside the tent catches their attention.

"What's going on?" Aidan asks a passing soldier.

"Minister ap Gwynedd made it back," the soldier says. "They say he brought back that captive witch Oswald."

Aidan and John look at each other and immediately clean up their trays and head out of the tent. They move through the crowd towards the front. They can't get close enough to make out the view of the Minister before he heads into the medical tent. So, they just have to wait for the crowd to thin before heading towards the tent flap. Once there, a nurse stops them and asks what their business is.

"Is it true he brought back Nadia Oswald?"

The nurse glances over her shoulder and says, "Yes, but I can't let you see her just yet."

"You don't understand," Aidan says. "She's a

partner of mine. I've worked with her before."

The nurse studies him and seems to make a decision. "Fine, but don't get in the way. She was badly injured."

Aidan and John push past the nurse into the tent. One glance to the right and there she is with the Minister in the ward opposite Elise's. They head into the ward and hang back, waiting to hear the news. The Minister looks up, sees them standing there, and steps aside to talk to them.

"You wouldn't be the elemental, would you?" he asks somewhat rudely to Aidan.

"Yes," is all he can think to say.

"You're the person she got the power from?" he asks.

Aidan nods, staring at the unconscious Nadia in the military cot. "What happened to her?"

"She was stabbed," the Minister says. "In the fight to get out of the camp." He shakes his head. "She was shielding both of us and I couldn't help."

Sympathy fills Aidan at the sight of the Minister's guilt. "Do you know Nadia?"

"Slightly," the Minister says. "I know her father from the Ministry, and I met her in Port Nalrang before

she left."

"I wondered why you were so adamant about negotiating for her return," Aidan says. "What did they want with her? Why capture her rather than kill her?" he asks.

The Minister looks over his shoulder at Nadia and the healers surrounding her. She is still unconscious, but still the Minister moves them away from the group. "Let's talk over here," he says, leading them to the vestibule area between wards, far enough to be out of earshot of Nadia should she wake. Once out of earshot, the Minister continues, "The thing is, we know somewhat what they do with their captive witches." The Minister lets out a tight breath.

"What is it?"

"They kill them for their power," the Minister says. "They're either using the Vacancy Principle or the Replacement Principle in their favor. They take a human and make them a witch or take a lower caste witch and make them a stronger one. Either way, they're killing their prisoners."

Aidan's stomach drops. "So, if you hadn't gone after her, she would have been killed," he says.

A wry smile fills the Minister's features. "I'm not

sure," he says. "She had gotten out of her bonds by the time I got to her. It was only a matter of time before she escaped."

Aidan and John exchange a look, John's eyebrows going up in surprise.

"Sounds like her," Aidan remarks.

"She is very powerful, even for the kind of witch she is," the Minister says, with a waggle of his eyebrows.

Aidan's eyes widen. "You mean . . . ?"

"Yes," the Minister says. "The Ecrians don't hold back that information. It's common knowledge in their country."

"So, it's only a matter of time before it's common knowledge in Egraria," John says.

"Yes," the Minister says. "And I take it that's why she became what she is. Because she got it from you." He looks at both of them for confirmation.

Aidan doesn't answer but suspects his non-answer is enough of an answer for the Minister.

"Well, either way, she's back and safe now," the Minister says.

"Thank you, Minister ap Gwynedd," Aidan says.

"Call me Morvath, if you please," the man says.

"What exactly is your position? I'm not up on

politics."

Minister Morvath smiles wryly. "I'm the Human Minister of People," he says. The irony of someone so situated in human affairs becoming aware of the existence of anchor witches is not lost on Aidan.

"So, it really is only a matter of time," John remarks.

"I'm afraid so," Minister Morvath says. "But I won't be the one to reveal them. Ecrium has already done that for us."

Aidan shakes his head in annoyance. Had he still been an anchor he would be thoroughly concerned. As it is, he is completely unamused by the probability that Nadia's life just got more in danger. As if any of them needed that.

"I'm going to check on Elise and let her know Nadia is back," Aidan says suddenly.

"May I accompany you?" Minister Morvath says.

For a moment Aidan almost says no, but then he nods and accepts the fact that the Minister is in on the secret now. There was no way around it. So he leads them into the second hospital ward and down the line of cots to where Elise sits up waiting for them.

"What's going on?" she asks immediately.

"You know Minister Morvath?" Aidan asks. He

takes a seat next to Elise again, John taking the one opposite while Morvath continues to stand.

"Yes, we met in Port Nalrang," she says. "What's going on?"

"Minister Morvath managed to rescue Nadia. She's in the other ward being healed," he explains.

Alarm crosses Elise's face. "What happened? When can I see her?"

"She was stabbed," the Minister explains. "She was protecting both of us and she got stabbed. But she's being healed. She'll be alright," he adds as she looks even more alarmed.

"She'll be alright?"

"Yes," John says. "She's in the next ward and is still unconscious, but we can make sure they put her next to you."

"I would prefer that," Elise says immediately.

"I'll go talk to the nurse," John says, getting back up. He heads down the hospital ward towards the nurse.

"Minister Morvath knows," Aidan says abruptly.

"You mean . . . ?"

"Yes, about Nadia's real power," Aidan explains.

Minister Morvath takes John's seat next to Elise. She looks him over before saying, "You know the kind of

danger she's in then."

"I do," Minister Morvath says.

"Then you know why it shouldn't be made public knowledge?"

"I think that ship has sailed," the Minister says regretfully. "Ecrium knows about them, and it is common knowledge there. They use this kind of witch to their advantage on a regular basis. I think it's only a matter of time before the whole world knows in earnest."

"But can it be delayed? And can the identity of such individuals be protected?" Elise asks.

"I believe it can be," Minister Morvath says. "In my position, I see the status change from human to witch on a regular basis. It is my job to know the numbers of humans versus witch and elemental et cetera." He acknowledges Aidan sitting across from him. "But the kind of chaos this could cause is concerning. The kind of upheaval this could bring, with witches exposed for knowing the secret and protecting their own . . ." he drifts off and shakes his head. "I'm honestly not sure how it will be taken."

Elise looks over at Aidan, nodding soberly about the coming crisis. "You think they'll be sought out and killed for their power," she says.

"I do," Minister Morvath answers.

"Is there anything we can do?" she asks Minister Morvath.

He shrugs in response. "Continue to hide both your former—" he indicates Aidan— "and Nadia's current nature. Hide who and what you are."

Elise shakes her head. "I didn't trust it when Colonel Ergamenes said he would keep it a secret. But it turns out our enemy is the one we should be worried about."

"One should always worry about the enemy," Minister Morvath says. The words ring true, but Aidan silently wonders who their real enemy is.

John comes back down the hospital ward then. "I got them to agree to put you next to each other," he says to Elise. "When they're done checking her over, that is."

The relief on Elise's face says more about how the girls feel about each other than any words she could express.

"We should give you space and let you rest," Aidan says.

"I've rested enough," she grumbles. "It's time to do something."

"I'll see what I can do about that," Minister Morvath

says. "I need to brief the Colonel anyway."

Seemingly satisfied, Elise nods and sits back on her bed. "Come visit later?" she asks Aidan.

"Of course," he says. "I'll need to check on both of you."

He and the Minister both get up from their respective beds. Aidan clasps Elise's hand for a moment before bidding her goodbye for now. Then he, John, and the Minister head out of the hospital ward and back to reality.

Thirty

When Nadia wakes up, it's full dark outside the tent. She can tell because the electric lights in the tent are dimmed down for nighttime. She blinks a few times to get her eyes to clear. She is laying on her right side, facing the bed next to hers. And in that bed is Elise.

It takes her a moment to remember everything that happened in the past few days. From the attack that led to her capture, to Elise falling with a broken leg, to Morvath appearing seemingly out of nowhere to rescue her. Then she remembers the knife going into her back and winces at the memory. She flexes her left shoulder, feeling the muscle's tenderness in her back. She is healed, no doubt, but she is not back to her full self yet.

Elise rolls over and faces Nadia. She blinks and see's Nadia is awake. Immediately, her girlfriend sits up and puts a hand on Nadia's left shoulder.

"How are you feeling?" she whispers. "Should I call the doctor?"

Nadia shakes her head. "No, I'm ok. I'm sore but I feel like I'm healed."

Elise puts her hand to Nadia's cheek. "I'm so glad you're back and you're better," she says. "I was so worried, my love."

Nadia reaches up to put her hand over Elise's hand. "I love you too," she says softly. "I was so scared you had died."

"I didn't think for a second you were dead," Elise says. "I think we would know if the other had gone."

"Is that sentiment or magic?" Nadia asks.

"Both I think." Elise smiles at her and leans down to kiss her. Then she says, "You never know the extent of magic between two people who love each other. Love is the ultimate magic, after all."

"Sentiment, then," Nadia says with a smile. "But I think you're right."

"Aidan and John were by earlier," Elise says.

"Aidan made it down here?"

"Yes, the pair of them have been here for a day or so," Elise says. "They came down directly from Port

Nalrang."

"Will they come by again later?"

"I'm sure they will."

A few moments pass in silence. A nurse comes into the ward. She spots Elise sitting up and heads directly to them. Elise sits back to make space.

"How are you feeling?" the nurse asks Nadia.

"Alright, just sore and stiff I think," she answers. She studies the nurse's calm demeanor, spies the caster crest on her shoulder. She must be a healer herself.

"Your healing is complete," the nurse says. "It might take a couple days to feel totally back to normal. You should keep moving, let the muscle feel like itself again."

"I will."

"In the meantime, get some rest," the nurse adds. She tucks Nadia in, the feel of the thick linen sheet and wool blanket a welcome warmth against the chill in the night air. She hasn't been tucked in since she had a governess as a child.

"Thank you," Nadia says.

The nurse adds, "Ring if you need anything." She indicates the small clockwork bell at the head of the bed. It would set off a device in the nurses' rooms to notify them that a patient needs assistance. Then the nurse heads back down the ward and leaves them alone again.

"We should both sleep," Elise says.

"I'm not really tired yet," Nadia answers. She considers her feelings and says, "Can you stay up with me and talk for a bit?"

"What do you want to talk about?"

"Anything but this war," she says. She is tired of the weeks they've been in this environment.

"Where do you want to live after all this is over?" Elise says.

Nadia thinks about it for a bit. Then she says, "I honestly don't know. Someplace that is ours though. Someplace that belongs to both of us."

Elise takes her hand. "City or country?" she asks.

"Country? Maybe a small city," Nadia says, thinking of Avita Spring. She wouldn't necessarily want to live in her hometown though.

"Someplace familiar or someplace new?"

"That I'm not sure of," she says. Then she pauses and adds, "What about Coreton?"

"What would we do there?"

"Drink tea and teach at Fernsby probably," Nadia says with a smile. "We'll finally get to see Atley and Dean

Aagard again." Part of her is nostalgic for the days she lived at Fernsby. But she wouldn't necessarily go back there.

"We would both need to go to university to become teachers though," Elise reminds her. Neither of them had been given a chance to start their university schooling properly yet. The closest either of them got was the time they spent at the observatory only a month or so ago. It felt so much longer ago too.

"Would you study mathematics?" Nadia asks her. She already knows the answer.

"Of course," Elise says. "Mathematics and writer witchcraft. I would probably blend the two. What about you?"

"I would probably study advanced caster craft, get into the theoretical stuff a bit," Nadia says. "I'm not as good at math as you are. I would like to teach the next generation of anchors though."

"That sounds like a noble calling," Elise answers.

"I need to learn first," Nadia grumbles. "I'm clearly out of my depth where anchors are concerned."

"You mean with how strong the Ecrian anchor was?"

"Yes. If that soldier hadn't killed him, we would

have lost."

"How many anchors do you think there are out there?" Elise asks.

"I don't know. Maybe a dozen, I would think," she says. "Maybe more because of the war going on. I think anchors show up when needed."

"That's what Howells said," Elise says.

"I think he might be the only person to know who all the anchors are," Nadia remarks. "At least the ones that were willing to reveal themselves." She thinks for a moment, her mind drifting to the far reaches of their world. "I do wonder who they all are."

Elise smiles. "They could be anyone. A princess or a pauper." A look of whimsy comes across her face. "I wonder if Matraize has one," she says suddenly. "They have so many writers, an anchor could hide in plain sight."

"Or would be an obvious anchor in such a setting."

"What do you mean?"

"Well," Nadia says, thinking of Howells again, "my anchor power recognized itself in Howells. As if we were both cut of the same cloth. I think an anchor would be too obviously different from a writer. Or at least too obviously powerful."

"I'm too biased to notice the difference between us," Elise says.

"You also have a strong writer power, which makes the difference more subtle."

"You think it's that strong?"

"I know it is, my love," Nadia answers. "I've seen you use it."

Elise lays back down on her side, pulls the sheet and blanket up over her shoulder. Nadia watches her get comfortable.

"When do you think we'll get out of the hospital?"

"In a day or so, I would think," Elise says. "They are ready for us to get back into the fray."

Nadia grimaces. "I'm ready for the war to be over."

"I'm afraid we have a long slog ahead of us before it ends," Elise answers. Her expression is that of someone facing the inevitable, not liking it, but being strong in the face of it anyway. Her strength gives Nadia strength.

"We'll be ok as long as we can fight together," Nadia says. "I still hate violence."

"What happened when Morvath got to you?" Elise asks suddenly. Nadia thinks she must have seen something, a brief snippet of a vision perhaps.

"I think I killed someone," Nadia whispers.

"An Ecrian soldier?"

"Yes. He attacked me and I used a repulsor shield to repel him," she explains. "He flew through the air and hit a tent pole. I don't know if he's alive or dead."

Elise reaches out and they hold hands across the gap between their beds. "I'm sorry," Elise says. "I wish it didn't have to be this way."

"That's why I want a quiet life after all this is over," Nadia says. "A life without fighting in it."

Elise nods in agreement. Nadia sighs. "I guess we should rest."

"Tomorrow is another day, and the boys will be back," Elise says.

"I'm looking forward to it."

And then Nadia pulls the blanket up closer to her neck, snuggling down into her not-completely-uncomfortable bed. Across from her, Elise remains awake, her eyes watching Nadia. Slowly, Nadia drifts off to sleep.

Thirty-One

About mid-morning the following day, Aidan and John came to visit Nadia and Elise. They brought news about the latest campaign against the Ecrian forces. The trouble with those campaigns is simply how outmatched they were against Ecrium. They couldn't possibly defeat an army composed completely of witches and elementals.

"How do they have so many of them anyway?" Elise asks. The girls are sitting around eating a late breakfast as they chat about the day's events. The other patients in the ward pay them no attention.

"As I understand it, being human in Ecrium is tantamount to being a slave," John says. "Supposedly, humans have to earn their way to witch status and some of them never make it."

"That's so ridiculous. Being human does not make

you less of a person," Nadia grumbles. "Nor does it make you superior to witches." She had spent her entire life listening to anti-witch propaganda in her home, and she hates all of it. She hates the anti-witch propaganda and the pro-witch movement. True equality is the only way forward.

"Where does that leave elementals? How do they have so many of them?" Elise wonders aloud. Nadia knows her girlfriend is more of a mathematics specialist than a historian. John seems to be well-read on the topics of politics and history though and is educating them.

"They catch elementals from the southern deserts and other places where they can be found," John says. "It's well-known that Ecrium hunts down elementals."

"But *why?*" Elise shakes her head. "It's such a violation of basic free will. How do they even feel about spirits?"

John's face turns grim. "That's the most disturbing part," he says. "They capture spirits and use them for their power."

The thought disturbs Nadia. Capturing and killing people for their power felt so taboo. What kind of sick people are they?

"Can we believe all the propaganda?" Aidan asks

softly.

"Much of it," John answers. "A lot of my reading comes from primary sources of Egrarians who visited Ecrium a decade or so ago. They wouldn't have been biased by a war yet."

"But they would be biased by their nationality," Elise says.

Nadia takes a bite of a buttered roll and contemplates that. There must be a grain of truth to the stories they've heard about Ecrium.

"Yes, but these are primary sources," John continues. "They might be biased in their opinions of what they see, but they are recording what they see."

Their nurse walks over then and interrupts their conversation.

"Lieutenants Oswald and Chulyin, you'll be discharged after breakfast," she says.

Nadia is surprised. She is still sore and generally uncomfortable. She thought they would hold her for another day or so.

"Already?" Elise asks.

"You're needed in the command tent as soon as you're discharged," the nurse says. To the boys she adds, "I'm told to relay to you that you're expected there now."

As much of a surprise as her discharge is, Nadia certainly wasn't expecting them to call up the boys since they had not been using them till now.

"Why?" she asks the nurse.

"I haven't been told, but I suspect it's to issue new orders." The nurse smiles sympathetically at them before walking back down the ward.

"I guess we should get going," Aidan says to John.

"I wish they would make up their minds what they're going to do with us," Elise says. "I don't feel like they *know* what to do with all of our respective powers."

"I suspect that their not knowing is about to come to an end," John says. He and Aidan get up from the ends of their beds.

"We'll see you later," Aidan says. They had given the girls the location of their tent so they could be found later on.

Nadia watches as the boys leave them to the rest of their breakfast. She proceeds to finish her rolls and her porridge and the rest. They would need the sustenance today to face whatever is coming. She drinks her tea, finding the familiar beverage comforting.

She flexes her shoulders and arches her back to feel the healing of the wound. There's no denying that it needs more time to get back to normal, but it is healed. She swings her legs over the video of the bed and reaches under it for the bag containing her belongings. It was brought here from her tent after she was brought in by Morvath.

Morvath is one person she needs to see. She needs to thank him for coming after her and bringing her back. Without him, she would have bled to death out there and her power would no doubt be in the hands of some Ecrian soldier. As Nadia gets dressed in her uniform, she contemplates what she will say to Morvath when she gets the chance to speak to him. She can't think of anything to say other than thank you.

Once she and Elise are fully dressed, they gather their things and head down the ward. The nurse stops them to check them out of the hospital, but otherwise they are free to get moving.

It has been about an hour since the boys left them. Since they would likely be back at their tent by now, Nadia and Elise agree to head that way and drop their things in the boys' tent. But when they get to the tent marked with the number Aidan and John told them, the place is deserted and they're nowhere to be found. Nadia and Elise exchange a look, neither of them sure where the boys are. Still, they drop their bags in the tent and head for the command tent.

When they get to the command tent, they're announced and waved inside. Inside, they find Colonel Ergamenes and Nadia is immediately tense. But the Colonel isn't the only one there she recognizes. Morvath is waiting off to the side, and he gives her a little half wave when she makes eye contact with him.

"Lieutenant Oswald, we have an assignment for you," the Colonel says. "I'm sending you to the front lines to see if you can help Rebluinia hold the line."

Nadia's jaw drops.

"I don't want to hear one word of complaint," the Colonel reprimands her preemptively. "Lieutenant Montgomery is up there waiting for you to join him."

"Understood," Nadia grumbles. She's honestly not sure she's fully healed enough to be fighting, but it appears she has no choice.

"We have reports of a force of soldiers coming up from Zofria Heights," the Colonel continues, including the whole room with his words. "We understand that several elementals are present in their ranks as well as high level witches like Lieutenant Oswald here."

More anchors?

The eyes in the room all find Nadia. She feels like a spotlight is shining on her anchor witch patch, the only one like it in the ranks of the Egrarian military. Part of her wants to cover it up and hide who she is. Part of her is afraid she'll never be able to again.

"Your assignment is to anchor the troops," the Colonel says, using the forbidden word. Nadia is livid. How dare he go back on their agreement of never revealing what she is to anyone? She finds this unacceptable.

But what can be done about it right now? Her father is back in Egraria. She doesn't have anyone to back her up. There's nothing she can do.

Some twenty minutes later, the Colonel dismisses them and Nadia steps out of the tent with Elise by her side. They've taken maybe five steps when a voice calls out, "Nadia!"

She turns back to see Morvath coming towards them. "Morvath," she says. "Thank you for everything." She walks up to him and gives him a hug. He looks surprised but hugs her back.

"Think nothing of it," Morvath says. "I know you would do the same and anyway we can't let anything happen to you." He pulls back from the hug. "Your father would kill me if he knew I let something happen to you."

Nadia chuckles, a strange and jovial sound in this grim time. "He probably would."

"You're headed to the front?" he says. He knows she is, but it seems as if he's confirming she's not running away or anything.

Nadia lets out a tight breath. "Yes, I am," she grumbles.

"Be careful," he says. "I hope we can get dinner together when you come back."

"I hope so too," Nadia says.

"Miss Chulyin, you be careful as well," Morvath adds kindly.

"I will, sir," Elise says. "We should get going."

Morvath shakes Elise's hand and gives Nadia another brief hug. The familiarity is new, but well warranted she thinks. With him having saved her life, she thinks they might be friends now.

Nadia takes Elise's hand. Together, they walk away from Morvath and the command tent. At one point Nadia looks back and sees the sad look on Morvath's face, an expression she thinks might be because of the danger she's heading into. She faces forward again and keeps walking.

They head towards the front.

Thirty-Two

Fire burns. It sucks the oxygen out of the very air they breathe. Embers crackle in the air, flames lick the ground around them.

Aidan stands alone. Fire sizzles at his fingertips, his control moderate at the moment. Next to him John is linked with a caster witch and they are holding a shield in front of Aidan. Between the two of them, their power is sufficient to hold the line against the casters. He doubts it would work against a writer witch or an anchor witch.

The line of Ecrian soldiers is coming. They form a tight flank across the road in front of him, their own shields glittering in the morning light.

He lifts his hands and calls the fire to life. The fire compresses down into a dense ball of fire that struggles against his grip to break free. He lofts it and sends it in the direction of the Ecrian soldiers. Aidan watches as the fire bombs them and spreads to encompass the entire street. Flames engulf the Ecrian soldiers, and he watches as they burn as well.

Then the fire stops.

The flames completely snuff out and as he watches, the soldiers begin to rise again, untouched by the fire. Aidan swears comprehensively.

"What is it?" John calls out.

"I think another fire elemental," Aidan responds. And he has no idea how to fight another of his kind when he himself can barely control his own power.

A cannon blast of fire so strong it rips through the shield comes flying directly at Aidan. He reacts instinctively, throwing his hands up to block the flames. And the flames respond to him as if he had cast them himself.

Fire circles Aidan. He sees John and the surrounding casters back off from him as he gathers the fire in a river around him. The fire continues to concentrate in a ring until it is again fighting against his control to go where it wants to go.

Aidan throws the fire back at Ecrium.

Immediately, it snuffs out.

It's only then that he spots the fire elemental. A tall woman with dark hair and dark eyes walks through the Ecrian soldiers directly at Aidan. She looks to be in her thirties. Fire cloaks her hands in a level of control that Aidan immediately envies.

On either side of the woman walks an Ecrian soldier, each casting a shield so strong it distorts the view of the woman. They must be writer witches to pull power that strong. Or could they be anchors? Could Ecrium really have that many anchor witches? Not for the first time, Aidan wonders just how much they don't know about anchor witches.

"Shield!" Aidan calls out.

The surrounding casters redouble their efforts. John steps close to Aidan and says, "I'll help you." Then John's eyes go vague. Aidan steps forward to guard his casting partner.

Aidan draws fire into himself, careful not to let it burn John. He creates a starburst pattern in front of him made of lines of concentrated flames. Each line contracts into the center, concentrating there.

"Now," John says.

Aidan shoots the fire forward.

The fire engulfs the Ecrian elemental and her

guards. The elemental ducks and the fire goes blasting past her to the soldiers behind. Aidan is stunned she was able to dodge it.

Then he watches appalled and flat-out impressed as she gathers the fire to herself from the surrounding street. As Aidan watches, he sees the flames coalesce around the elemental, forming a sphere of fire that only a fire elemental or fire spirit could survive in.

"She's here," John says softly behind him.

And there, with Elise by her side, Nadia stands next to him.

"Together," Nadia says. "Like we did on the Falgar."

"We don't have time to draw the diagram," Aidan says.

"I know," Nadia answers. "It won't be as effective, but we can at least slow them down."

"How about just getting them to stand still?" John asks as another blast of fire hits the shield.

"That could work!" Elise shouts over the roar of the fire. Elise takes Nadia's hand who takes Aidan's hand. John's hand goes to his other one. The four of them link their powers together and face down the oncoming Ecrian forces.

Nadia takes the lead. It is her power that would guide this. He feels her pull on his fire power and can't quite believe the strength in her now. It is even more so than that night on the Falgar. She really has come into her own with the anchor power.

A diagram of light appears in the air between them and the approaching enemy. The diagram looks similar to what they drew on the boat deck back on the Falgar. But this one was distinctly different. A circle for each of them occupies the outside ring.

A line of power shunts out from those four points on the diagram and connects with each of the four of them. The brightest line is Aidan's; the dimmest, John's. As it connects with Aidan, for a moment, he feels the old sensation of witch's power and can understand it. But the sensation does not last. Neither does the understanding. It remains beyond him now.

The tug on his power becomes more insistent. The power pulls from him, diving into the shunt and brightening his section of the diagram. The same happens when each of their powers infuse the diagram.

Nadia takes one half-step forward, the rest of them holding in their places. She leans forward, staring intensely in the direction of the diagram and the shield.

The diagram increases in brightness until it is nearly blinding. But even with the blinding light in his eyes, Aidan can see their shield beginning to fail.

"The shield," John gasps out. He is still holding it in part with Aidan's power to help.

"I got it," Elise says. She reaches her left hand forward past Nadia, and a line of power comes out of her towards the shield. One glance at her and Aidan can see the strain on her face. The power drains from her from two outlets. No doubt she is feeling it.

Elise's effort works. The shield holds up against the bombardment of fire and power from the elemental and her flanking witches. Her dark eyes look coldly at them, meeting Aidan's gaze. He wonders if she got her power from another elemental. He has no doubt she did, as most of their elementals did.

Aidan realizes the surrounding soldiers on both sides have been fighting this whole time, stepping through the shield by using their own. The Ecrian forces keep creeping closer, fighting their surrounding Egrarian and Rebluinian colleagues. He doesn't know how much longer they'll last. Ecrium's forces are overwhelming them. Too many witches in their number. Too many casters and writers fighting for them.

"Ready?" Nadia calls out over the sounds of the firebombing and the fighting around them.

"Ready!" they all say.

Nadia yanks on their powers, dragging even more energy out of each of them. The lines of the diagram immediately flare to blindingly bright. Aidan squints until his eyes adjust to the brightness. On the other side of the diagram, the shield fails and Ecrian soldiers head directly for them. Aidan squeezes Nadia's hand in warning.

The spell ignites.

He doesn't hear what Nadia said in witchspeak to trigger the spell. Whatever she said has worked. The soldiers coming directly at them stop dead in their tracks. They stand still and don't move. The elemental stops using her power completely and stands still. The anchor witches look the least affected by it, but even they stand stock still in the middle of the road.

A cheer goes up from the Rebluinian and Egrarian forces.

"Quick!" Nadia shouts. "Tie them up!" Then her knees buckle and Aidan and Elise struggle to hold her up.

The soldiers around them snap into action. As Aidan doubles over, feeling the fatigue of such a strong casting, he looks up to watch the soldiers tie the hands of every Ecrian soldier. Next to him, John sits down in the sand on the road.

"Are you ok?" Aidan asks.

"I'm exhausted," John says. "I'm completely wiped out."

Aidan suspects John's seer power was overwhelmed by the three higher powers linked with him. He lets go of John's hand and lets his partner rest. He lets go of Nadia's hand and straightens up. Nadia looks ragged. Elise isn't much better, having held two spells at once. Aidan feels like he's the least affected by the spell casting.

"Well done, Lieutenant," a voice says from behind them. Aidan turns around to find Colonel Ergamenes approaching. "We should be able to do a prisoner exchange for our captured soldiers after this."

Nadia nods and says, "I hope so."

"You all look terrible," the Colonel says. "Go get some rest. We'll call you when we need you again."

A look of dismay crosses Nadia's face. Aidan has no doubt she is annoyed by the Colonel's presumption that they would enact the spell again. He wasn't sure how feasible it is to fight one battle at a time using the spell to stop the oncoming forces. Then again, what choice do they have? They're severely outpowered by the Ecrian army. There's nothing they can do but keep fighting.

He pulls John to his feet and lets the seer lean on him as they walk their way back to camp. Likely, they would all sleep for hours after this one. He is looking forward to the uncomfortable army cot. He just wishes he was going home.

Thirty-Three

This is his only chance. Morvath knows he needs to take it while he can. He knows once they get back to Egraria, there would be no opportunity for him to be alone with Nadia. He would never get another good shot at this again.

He stands in his tent, getting himself ready. Like that night when he went to see Goliyant, he dresses in all black, a hood drawn up over his head. He wears a black cloth covering his face, protecting his identity. He tucks the dagger into the sheath at his belt, folding his cloak over it to protect it from view. He is ready.

Rather than go out the main flap of the tent, he pulls back the back flap where it backs up against a back alley of sorts. He is situated in the middle of the camp, near to the mess tent and far from the infirmary. He would be making his way to Nadia's tent, closer to the infirmary side.

He ducks out of the tent and beings weaving his way down the back alley. He would pause behind a tent, check that no one was watching, and then dart across the gap between tents as quickly as possible. The gas lamps in this area are still working, for the most part, so he doesn't have a lot of darkness for cover yet. By the time he makes it past the mess tent, darkness deepens around him. The tents in this part of the camp house soldiers of lower rank. Thus, they aren't given prime locations near the working lamps.

Morvath darts across yet another gap between tents and takes stock of where he is. Nadia's tent is two rows from him. He will have to put both her and Elise Chulyin into a deeper sleep before he tries to enter the tent. He pulls out the power sensor from his pocket and reads the surrounding witches. Nadia—and Elise even—stand out among the rest of the military. Their powers are just significantly stronger than the average witch in the military. No wonder Ecrium is beating them so badly. If Ecrium's army is made up mostly of caster and writer witches, he can't imagine how Rebluinia will ever manage to defeat them.

He puts the sensor back in his pocket and heads down the tent "alleyway" till he draws even with Nadia's tent. He would need to cross two walkways before he gets to the back of it. Cautiously, he sticks his neck out and looks around. No one can be seen. He hustles to cross the gap. On the other side, he repeats this process crossing the second walkway and finally comes up to the back of Nadia and Elise's tent.

After listening for a moment to uninterrupted deep breathing, he concludes that they're both asleep. He would need them to remain asleep for his plan to work. He checks the dagger and checks his other belongings. Everything is in place. Nothing has moved, and he hasn't dropped anything. He is ready.

Morvath reaches out and places a hand on the canvas of the tent. The rough material yields to his touch, only barely buckling in as he touches it. From within, he gathers his power to the surface. The ring still in place, the spell still shielding him, he begins to cast the sleep spell. As he does so, the power of the ring flares for a moment, then settles down. It becomes acquiescent to the power he is putting out. Then he's finished, the casting is done, and he is ready to let it go. He pushes the spell into the tent and into the minds of Nadia and Elise.

Now for the hard part: getting into their tent from the back without accidentally knocking it over.

Carefully, he unties two knots on the right back corner of the tent, untying the bottom and the middle ones. Morvath is tall, but not so tall he can't stoop down and go into the tent that way. He peeks in and sees the girls fast asleep. Morvath slips into the corner of the tent, drawing the flap closed behind him.

Nadia and Elise have shoved their bunks together and are tucked all cozy under the thick army blanket. He almost feels bad at the idea of breaking up this cozy scene. But he is here to accomplish a mission.

Quietly, Morvath unsheathes the dagger. He steps closer to the bed and pulls back the blanket over Nadia. Elise's arm is over Nadia in an unconscious embrace. He moves the arm off Nadia's chest. Elise doesn't even stir once. He has no doubt the sleeping spell will hold Elise. He's not sure it will hold Nadia. He considers for a few moments before proceeding.

Morvath places a gloved hand over Nadia's mouth. He draws back the blade and plunges it directly at Nadia's heart.

The blade stops one inch above her chest.

At the contact point with the blade, he can see the

radiating lines of a shield. She must have shielded herself in her sleep.

Undeterred, Morvath draws back the blade and brings it down again.

It meets resistance again.

He leans onto the blade, trying to use his weight to bring it down into Nadia's body. But it's not working. The dagger won't budge. It's as if her shield is made of brick or stone. He even thinks those substances would yield where this shield will not. He pulls the dagger back noting that the blade is getting a slight bend in it from the force of the shield's resistance.

Morvath stands there thinking, his hand still on Nadia's face. That's when he realizes his hand is under the shield. Perhaps he is going about this wrong. He pushes the dagger down on the shield. This time, he moves it slowly. This time, the shield almost seems to let the dagger go by. But not quite. He can't get the dagger below a certain level. Like half an inch off her chest.

He pulls it back and stands up for a moment, shaking out the hand that has been on her mouth. The strain of holding multiple spells in place and trying to physically use the dagger are taking a toll on him.

Maybe that's the answer. He's using the dagger

physically. What about magically? The killing spell sits right there in the blade, ready to be used. All he has to do is get it past Nadia's shield and it should kill her. But first he has to get the blade past the shield.

He covers her mouth again. This time, he thinks his way down into the spell in the blade. Slowly, he begins to lower the dagger into the shield. It resists at first, but then gives way a bit as he presses down lower. The blade is going to make it this time. It wouldn't stab her at this rate. But he can still use the killing spell.

Slowly and carefully, he unravels the killing spell from the dagger. Inky black and red lines of light seep out of the blade, creeping into the shield over Nadia. The shield reacts immediately. It brightens and fights back.

Nadia's eyes open.

The sleep spell has failed at last. Good thing Morvath came in disguise. He holds her down by her mouth, keeping his hand clamped over her jaw so she can't call out. Her eyes go to the dagger and widen. Nadia begins to panic.

Morvath draws back the blade and brings it down one more time. This time it breaks through most of the shield, but the killing spell still can't break through. It seeps out over her into the shield covering her body in dark light.

Nadia's hand goes to Morvath's wrist, keeping the dagger from going any lower. He is going to lose this fight. He knows it. Through his contact with Nadia, he can feel her power waking up within her. He can feel the blast she is about to throw in his direction.

He hits her. Hard.

The pommel of the dagger has blood from her head on it. But it's enough to get her to let go. She slumps back down on the cot and seemingly falls into a stupor. Morvath pulls back from the cot. Is there any more to be done tonight? Is this really his last chance to get her power?

There is no choice. He needs to go back to his own tent before anyone finds him and before Nadia wakes again. He only caught her unaware. He doubts he could defeat her in a one-on-one battle.

He sheathes the knife.

Meticulously, he checks all his belongings again, making sure nothing is lost or disturbed. With everything accounted for, he opens the back flap of the tent and ducks out into the alley. He turns around and carefully ties the tent back together.

He hurries away in the direction of his own tent.

Thirty-Four

Nadia jolts awake.

Her hand immediately goes to her chest and to her mouth. Both the dagger and the hand are gone. Was it just a dream?

No.

She feels pain in her head where the person hit her.

Another jolt goes through her.

Elise.

She tries to sit up but can't seem to move very well. Her head is swimming from the injury. She's probably concussed. Somehow, she rolls onto her side and puts a hand on Elise. She's alive, just asleep. Deeply asleep.

"Elise!" she says, shaking her. Her girlfriend doesn't move.

She pulls herself up on the cot. She sits up in the

dark tent.

"Medic!" she shouts. "I need a medic!"

She moves her legs over the side of the cot, grabs the central tent pole, and drags herself to her feet. She makes it to the tent flap, still woozy, and stumbles out into the walkway.

"Medic!" she shouts again.

The pounding of boots on pavement signals the approach of the two soldiers on sentry duty tonight. The first one makes it to her and kneels down in the dirt next to her.

"Oswald?" he asks. "What happened?" She looks up at the soldier who looks concerned at the sight of her blood.

"There was someone in our tent trying to kill me," Nadia gasps out. "Elise won't wake up."

The soldier signals his companion to go into the tent and check Elise. The second soldier disappears into their tent. Another soldier is running up to them now followed by a medic.

"Sound the alarm! Someone broke into our camp," the soldier says. To Nadia he asks, "Did you get a look at them?"

Nadia winces as the medic begins to poke at her

head wound. "Not really," she answers. "They wore a mask and gloves." She pauses as the medic applies a piece of gauze. "I didn't even get a good look at the dagger he used."

"He tried to stab you?"

"My personal shield kicked in," Nadia explains.

The second soldier comes out of the tent carrying a still-sleeping Elise. "She's just asleep as far as I can tell," the soldier says. "We should get them both to the infirmary."

"I'll stay and start the investigation when the team gets here," the first soldier says. "Go ahead and take them."

"Can you stand?" the medic asks Nadia.

"Sort of," she says.

The third soldier offers to carry her. She assents and they head towards the large hospital tent.

Around them, a flurry of activity kicks up. Nadia is carried from the tent to the infirmary and watches as soldiers bustle past. What was a quiet night has turned into a flurry of activity.

Once inside the tent, Elise's former nurse immediately sees to her. She must be working the nightshift as it is after midnight. The soldier lays Nadia on a vacant cot, the other laying Elise down next to her. A nurse-healer comes out from behind a curtain at the far end of the ward and heads to them. The first nurse continues seeing to Nadia's head wound.

About twenty minutes pass as her head is disinfected, healed, and bandaged for good measure. She is concussed, and there's not a lot magic even can do about that, but she is alive and otherwise unharmed.

"What's wrong with Elise?" she asks the nurse.

"Looks like a heavy sleeping spell," the nurse-healer says. "We can wake her, but it might be best to let it run its course. She should wake in the morning."

"What if she doesn't?"

"Then we'll try a spell to break the current one," the nurse-healer says kindly. "For now, just concentrate on resting and healing."

The curtain to the ward swings open and flutters shut behind the three soldiers that enter. The ranking officer, a Major, comes forward and says, "Can you tell us more about what happened tonight?"

"Major Dixon, is this necessary right now?" the nurse-healer asks. "She needs rest."

Major Dixon answers, "Yes. We need as much information as possible while it's still fresh in her mind."

Nadia looks between the two of them, and then just says, "Oh, for goodness's sake. I'm well enough to talk."

"What do you remember about the assailant?" Major Dixon asks, taking a seat at the end of Nadia's cot and pulling out a writing pad and a pencil from an inner pocket.

"He was tall I think?" she begins, squinting her eyes to concentrate more. "He had a dagger that had a killing spell on it."

Major Dixon nods and scribbles down the information. "What kind of dagger?" he asks.

"I'm not sure," she says, closing her eyes. "I think it had a jewel on the pommel. Maybe a red one?"

"Good," he says. "What else?"

"Whoever it was wore gloves and a mask and black clothes," she says. "That's as much as I remember."

Major Dixon finishes writing down everything she says before standing up. "We are searching the camp," he says. "But I'd be willing to bet your assailant is long gone. We're going to station two guards around you at all times." He nods at the sergeants next to him. Both sergeants go to the front of the tent and head outside to stand guard. The Major adds, "Try to get some rest."

He heads down the ward and out of the tent.

Nadia can't imagine falling asleep with everything that happened. But she lays back in the cot anyway and tries to shut her eyes. She ends up staring at the ceiling of the tent in the dim infirmary light for what feels like hours before she finally exhausts herself enough to fall back asleep.

When she awakens, it must be early dawn. The light coming in the gaps of the tent walls has the overly bright early morning feel to it. She rolls onto her side, turning to look over at Elise. Her girlfriend is still asleep. She wonders how long the spell will take to wear off.

The healer-nurse comes over to her cot then.

"How are you feeling?" she asks.

"Better, but still groggy," Nadia answers.

The nurse checks her vitals and adjusts Nadia's blankets. When she's finished, she asks, "Can I bring you anything?"

"I'm hungry," Nadia says. "Can you tell me when Elise is going to wake up?"

The nurse smiles as she says, "As far as we can tell, it was a particularly strong sleep spell put on both of you. We think the reason it didn't work as well on you is because you outclassed the caster's power. Miss Chulyin is in no danger. She is just asleep."

Nadia nods and thanks the nurse. "Has anyone come by?"

"Just Mr. Hughes," the nurse says. "If you're up for visitors, I know a couple of your acquaintances are eager to look in on you."

"I think I can handle visitors."

"I'll get some breakfast for you," she says. She walks away, adjusting her nursing uniform as she goes. She disappears through a partition at the end of the ward. After a few minutes, she comes back carrying a small tray of food. Behind her, two figures follow down the ward. The first is Hughes, and the second is Morvath. She expected the first, but not the second.

"Morvath?" she asks.

"Are you alright?" he asks, concern on his face.

Nadia struggles to sit up, but both gentlemen tell her to stay laying down. She adjusts anyway and turns on her back to look up at them more easily. The nurse sets the tray of food down next to her cot and brings over a stray pillow from another cot so she can prop herself up at least. Then the nurse sets the tray across her lap and leaves them alone.

"I am still groggy, but I'm much better than last night," she says. "I had a concussion." The healers

healed the brain injury last night, but they had warned her she might feel out of it for a couple of days. She certainly felt that would be the case.

"What am I going to tell your father if you keep getting injured," Morvath teases.

Nadia musters a smile but asks, "Have you been in touch with him?"

"Not recently," Morvath says. "I can send him a witchwire if you like."

As Nadia just realized, Morvath must have diplomatic privileges. "Could you send a message from me too?"

"Of course," Morvath says. "When you're ready, I'll send the message."

"Thank you."

"How is Elise?" Morvath asks, including Hughes in the question.

"She is deeply asleep," Hughes answers. "The spell seems to have been a strong one."

"When will she wake up?"

"They don't know," Nadia answers. "Soon I hope."

"Will you write to her parents about it?" Morvath asks Hughes.

"I already have," he says. "I keep them apprised of

her situation."

"Thank you," Nadia says sincerely. Then she looks down at the standard army food, this time a light porridge and some bread and what looks like cactus fruit from the locals.

"We should leave you to eat and rest," Morvath says.

"Take it easy," Hughes says. He and Morvath turn to go back down the hospital ward.

Nadia lifts a spoonful of hot porridge to her mouth and blows on it to cool it down. She takes a bite and feels the warmth go through her. She is ravenous. Between her shield and the concussion, she burned a lot of energy. She downs the porridge, using the bread to sop up the rest of the broth.

As she finishes her meal, the nurse comes back and takes her tray, tucking her blankets around her more. Then the nurse leaves and Nadia settles down into the cot to rest. She feels safe for the moment, but she doesn't know how long that will last.

Thirty-Five

"Do you think it's possible to do that kind of casting?" Colonel Ergamenes asks Aidan over the strategy table in the command tent. He is flanked on either side by two majors, both of whom are built as formidably as the Colonel himself.

Aidan says, "I'm no longer a witch, but what I know it would be possible. I just don't know how many witches it would take to cast on that scale." He looks at John next to him and adds, "Elise Chulyin would be the one to calculate that." It's true that of all of them, Elise's mathematical prowess would be sufficient to the task.

"We have another writer witch who can take a look while Chulyin recovers," the Colonel says. "Can you work with him to expand the diagram?"

"Yes," Aidan says immediately. He may not be a

witch any longer, but it's not like he's forgotten everything about being a witch.

"Good," the Colonel continues. "Here's the plan then. We will coordinate with Rebluinia and gather as many casters as possible. The mission will take place tomorrow before dawn."

Aidan nods in acknowledgement.

To the Major on his right, he says, "Find Captain Dyrams. He is working near the front lines. Pull him back."

"Yes, sir," the Major says. He salutes the Colonel and leaves the tent.

"When Major Carlson is back with Captain Dyrams, I want you two to develop the necessary diagram. If Chulyin wakes before we are set to go, we will have her check your calculations," he says decisively. "Understood?"

"Yes, sir," Aidan answers.

"Dismissed," the Colonel says.

Aidan and John both leave the tent. When they step outside, John turns to him and asks, "Now what?"

"I would say we go visit the girls, but we just did that."

"Let's get some food then," John says. "We have a

long day ahead of us."

"And possibly a long night."

"Probably."

They head for the mess tent and spend the next hour or so eating and getting their strength up. As they're finishing their meal, the Major shows up with presumably Captain Dyrams in tow. The Captain is tall, with salt and pepper hair and dark eyes. He is probably in his forties and shows the confidence of someone in their prime.

"Lieutenant Montgomery, this is Captain Dyrams," the Major introduces them. The Captain shakes their hand and then sits at the table. The Major excuses himself and heads out of the tent, presumably heading to the command tent.

The Captain pulls out a notebook and sets it on the table in front of them. "What can you tell me about the spell?"

"Everything," Aidan answers somewhat cockily. "I worked it twice. Once as an anchor and once as an elemental."

The Captain hands over the notebook and a pen. "Can you sketch out the essential diagram?"

Aidan nods and takes the notebook and pen. He begins drawing the series of secant circles with the pen.

After about five minutes of concentration, he hands back the notebook and pen. The Captain studies the design for a few minutes before scribbling some notes in the margins.

"We're gonna need some bigger paper," the Captain says suddenly. "Come with me."

He gets up from the table, leaving Aidan and John scrambling to keep up. The Captain leads them out of the mess tent and through the maze of tents to another admin tent. He leads them inside where they are greeted by a middle-aged woman with a tidy coif and glasses and captain's bars on her shoulder.

"Captain! What do you think you're doing?"

"I need space to work on a diagram," the Captain explains. "I know you won't mind," he adds in what can only be described as a charming manner.

The woman shakes her head. "Use the table at the back and don't move *anything* from the surrounding tables!" she says forcefully.

"You're a gem," Captain Dyrams says.

She rolls her eyes.

The Captain leads Aidan and John to the back table in the tent.

"Where are we?" Aidan asks.

"This is the Centralized Logistics Administration," the Captain says.

"*Way* above my rank," John remarks.

The Captain looks at him with a mischievous smile. "Just don't tell anyone." He begins to sketch out the diagram on a large piece of parchment, using a pencil so they can erase and change the lines as needed. Aidan picks up a pencil and helps him. When they have the full diagram out in front of them, the Captain steps back and studies it. "You believe your friend Lieutenant Chulyin would be of some help, correct?"

"No doubt," Aidan answers. "She's a mathematics prodigy."

"Then we'll see if she's up for reading through the calculations later," the Captain says. "Provided she's awakened," he adds darkly.

Aidan feels annoyed at the implication that she might not awaken. She is, after all, just asleep. She probably doesn't even remember the spell being cast on her, much less the trauma afterwards. She could be awake already.

"I have an idea about how to expand the diagram to accommodate the increased load," the Captain continues. He sketches out a series of circles on the paper, all tangent or secant to the main diagram. In the circles, he draws a "C" or an "S" for the various caster and seer witches they could call on to pull power. He scribbles some of the symbols Aidan is familiar with but has largely forgotten over the past six months, each representing a different piece of the magical working. When the Captain finishes his sketches, he stands up and asks, "What do you think?"

Aidan studies the diagram for a bit, following the lines with his eyes until the scratchy sketch goes blurry. Then he straightens up and turns to John. "I think we need Elise. Can you go see if she's awake and up for coming down here?"

"We can go to her," the Captain says.

Aidan nods. "Yes, that might be the better option."

"I'll bring her back if she's up for it," John says. He heads out of the tent and leaves the current and former writer witches to mull over the diagram.

About twenty minutes pass before the tent flap opens and closes again. This time, both Nadia and Elise follow John into the tent, smiling when they make eye contact with Aidan. He straightens up from the table and turns to them as they come in, giving each of them a hug.

"Are you alright?" he asks them both.

"Enough," Nadia admits.

With a grin, Elise says, "I'm fine. I feel well-rested."

"Can you take a look at what we've got so far?" Aidan asks. He leads Elise and Nadia over to the table. "This is Captain Dyrams. He's been working on expanding the spell."

Elise studies the diagram for about five minutes without saying a word. Then she asks for a pencil and begins making adjustments to the circles and the symbols. She erases some, adds others, and keeps adjusting until, some thirty minutes later, she straightens up and stretches her back.

"I think that'll do it," she says. "We just need enough volunteers to make it work. About twenty, I would say."

"We'll get that," the Captain says. "Colonel Ergamenes has put out a call for volunteers and we've had a good response."

"No one likes that we're losing the war," Aidan mutters.

"For real," John agrees.

"Are you satisfied?" the Captain asks Elise.

She studies the diagram for a moment before answering, "Yes. I am. I'll be out there with you to cast it."

The Captain nods as if he is expecting that. With Nadia going out, it is almost expected that Elise would as well. He begins transposing the diagram in ink to another parchment. Elise picks up a pen and helps him transfer it. They spend about another fifteen minutes working meticulously before fanning the ink dry. Then Captain Dyrams rolls up the parchment and binds it with a strip of leather.

"Will you be ready an hour before dawn tomorrow?" the Captain asks.

"Of course," Elise answers. Aidan assents as well and Nadia and John just nod. They have no choice but to be up and ready to go.

"I'll take the diagram to Colonel Ergamenes and round up the volunteers," he says. "Be ready tomorrow morning."

Aidan and Nadia and John all salute him. Then the Captain leaves.

"I guess we should get some sleep," Aidan remarks.

Elise snorts. "Not me," she says. "But let's go get food."

They head out of the tent and over to the mess tent, the afternoon having whiled away while they worked. They would have an early start and likely a long and trying morning. Aidan feels like they deserve a normal night for once. They hadn't had one in such a long time.

Thirty-Six

The march continues. The convoy circled Melgarde to avoid any contact with Ecrium forces before getting to their encampment. Even circling the outskirts of town, they are not completely protected from Ecrium and find themselves hiding periodically.

Nadia walks slowly with the rest of the twenty or so witches they got to work with them. In her mind, she goes over and over the diagram again and again, trying to remember every aspect of the spell. One subtle nuance wrong and they would fail. She knows this from their previous attempts. However, the fact she has going for her now is the knowledge of how it works. And the knowledge that so many witches would take the risk of making this walk.

Captain Dyrams walks with her now, though they are

both silent. Aidan walks with Elise and John just ahead, their boots crunching on the gravel of the city's outskirts.

"How much longer?" she asks the Captain.

"Not sure," he says. "Probably another hour I would think. Are you getting tired?'"

"A bit," she admits. "But mostly I'm just anxious to get this done."

"Understandable," he says.

Up ahead, the leading soldiers call for a halt to the convoy. Immediately, everyone including Nadia moves to the sides of the road and into the shadows of the nearest buildings. With twenty-plus people in the group, it's difficult to hide them all. But they divide up and manage to find places along the alleyways and buildings' shadows.

"What's going on?" Nadia whispers.

Aidan and Elise are next to her and both shrug. A message gets passed back from the front of the group, whispered one person at a time.

"We're going to split up and go around the next square. There's no way we can hide from the Ecrian soldiers up ahead."

Captain Dyrams says, "Stay with me. We'll go down that way and head around on the dune." He indicates the alley that cuts crosswise to their own. On either side, falling down houses line the streets. Down the alley Nadia can make out the sand of the nearest desert dunes, their sand maintained by some magical process that keeps them from overwhelming the houses.

"Ready?" he whispers, once the first groups begin to break off.

"Ready," Nadia whispers back. Together with Elise and Aidan, John and Captain Dyrams, she heads down the alley, catching a glimpse of the other three groups heading in another direction as they go.

"Over the dune?" Elise asks.

"Yes."

They jog down the alley between the houses and past their backyards directly up the side of the dune. At the top, they can see the encampment in the distance, just a sliver of the tents viewed between the dunes. They head over the crest and down the far side, the view disappearing as they go.

About an hour passes before Captain Dyrams directs them back towards the edges of town. Nadia is panting from the effort of climbing up and down the dunes. They head back towards the southern end of Zofria Heights, to the point where the encampment comes close to the city. As they climb the last dune, another group of witches startles Nadia as they approach. Before long, several groups have all conglomerated together on the dune. A quick headcount confirms that all the witches are accounted for.

"Form up," Captain Dyrams directs the group. He is the ranking officer, though he is less practiced with the spell than Nadia. The troops seem more willing to accept his direction than that of a teenager's.

As the soldiers fall in line, Nadia watches them do so. On the other side, Elise watches the group expertly and tells Nadia through gesture and nod of head where she needs to make changes. Nadia complies. She circles the group, directing them to make adjustments on where to stand. Then Captain Dyrams, Aidan, and Elise all weave in and out of the group, drawing on the sand with fire and power. The scorched earth eventually comes together to form the diagram of the spell. Captain Dyrams checks the diagram against the parchment he carried all the way from the Egrarian camp. Satisfied, he stows it away and signals to Elise, Aidan, and Nadia to take their places.

Nadia steps carefully to the center of the diagram, her power being the most integral to the working. There they stand, the twenty something witches all on the top of the dune ready to work the spell. She nods at Captain Dyrams, who nods back giving the go ahead to get started. Every witch in the diagram braces for energy pull. Every witch has a weapon out, ready in case the Ecrian witches notice them and head their way.

Nadia looks over at Elise on the edge of the diagram. Her girlfriend nods at her and she nods back. They're as ready as they're going to be.

She begins by drawing power from within. The rising tide of power within her spills over and makes her skin crawl with tingles. She looks down and sees the power pouring from her hands, the strength of the magic she wields barely controlled by her. She opens her closed hands and lets the power fall to the scorched-earth diagram around her. The lines light up almost immediately, power glowing in the ground and sending light into the air.

"Here they come!" Captain Dyrams shouts. He is at the top of the dune with the best vantage point. Immediately, Nadia sees him cast a shield spell linking with casters around the outer exterior. Again, Nadia glances over to see Elise has linked as well. She is on the outer tier. Nadia sets that aside to keep her focus on the power around her. Elise is in danger, but there is nothing Nadia can do but get this spell complete.

Refocusing on the spell at hand, Nadia links with all the witches around her through the diagram lines. She feels the link sync with each of them one at a time, each witch's power being made available to her. Slowly, so as not to send anyone into shock, she siphons off the power from the other witches in a trickle so slow she barely feels it. But the power is enough. It saturates the diagram, lighting it up brighter and brighter until it is nearly blinding around her.

Light circles her, circles her arms and her body. Blind to that which is tangible around her, she finds herself seeing the energies of the Egrarian and Rebluinian witches and the Ecrian witches coming from the other side of the dune. She can see the light of those witches in town miles from her position, the cluster of witches near the north end far from where she stands. She can make out the bright lights of the strong witches and one particularly powerful witch at the Egrarian encampment that makes her wonder. But she doesn't have time to think about that. She has a spell to cast.

Power explodes around her. This power is that of the Ecrian soldiers. They've arrived and are throwing power around like they have it to burn. Her senses blocked out by the power she wields; Nadia calls the power forward and pushes outward into the shield to help the writers and casters protect against the enemy. But it's not enough. The sand beneath their feet begins to shift.

Nadia stamps her foot.

The sand hardens in response. Under all of them, the individual grains of sand come together to form stone. The scorched-earth diagram, bright with power, burns through the stone around them.

"Hurry Nadia!" Elise shouts over the fray. Briefly, Nadia sees her throw power at an Ecrian witch, but she is no match for the anchor witch. A blast of power takes Elise out.

Nadia screams.

The power surges around her, yanking on the strength of all the witches in the diagram. She is not alone. And she can do this. She brings her hands together. The light explodes outward, washing in waves over the soldiers surrounding them, blasting everything in sight.

And that was it. That's all it took.

As if in a zombie-like state, the soldiers begin to

march away from the dune, away from the Egrarian and Rebluinian forces. Without looking back and without protest or seemingly any control over themselves, they head down the road to Ecrium.

Nadia watches long enough to be assured they are walking away from them. Then she collapses onto the hardened earth as it turns back to sand. From the ground, her cheek scraped by the sand, she sees her girlfriend's fallen form. Elise is not moving.

She blacks out.

Thirty-Seven

Seven witches fell. Not counting Nadia. Aidan doesn't know what to do. He holds Elise in his arms, waiting for a medic. The wait feels like eons.

Captain Dyrams crouches next to Nadia, throwing primitive healing magic at her like her life depends on it. It does. But the magic keeps slipping off of her, as if she is beyond his magic somehow. She lay there dying and there's nothing any of them can do with the tools they have.

A flash of vision comes to him again. Of Nadia smiling in the desert, at peace and happy. Maybe it's not a vision at all. Maybe it's where she is now. At peace.

They can't die. Neither can die. Elise's heart has stopped. But she can't die. Not now. Not when they've finally made progress. Not now. Not ever.

Fire fills Aidan. Tears fall and immediately evaporate from his burning skin. He is reminded of his time in the Waste, the time when he was alone and lonely. He is reminded of what it felt like to lose control. But this isn't that. This is something else. This is magic beyond even what he has in him now. He feels the power growing within and finds himself giving in to the strength of the magic. There is nothing holding him back now. He can feel the changes coming on.

Fire ignites on his skin, surrounding Elise's prone form. His uniform burns. Her uniform burns. He clutches her to his bare chest. He surrenders to the power within. There is nothing left to do now but let go of all his latent fears. Let go of everything holding him back. Let go of his pain and his caution and his will to stay human as much as possible. There is nothing left to do but surrender. So that's what he does. Aidan surrenders.

Fire erupts around them, surrounding them and seeping into Elise's body. It doesn't burn her. The opposite happens. It awakens her, her eyes opening and reflecting the light of the fire surrounding them both. He looks at her eyes, fiery tears falling from his own, and wonders how he could ever love anyone like he loves her in that moment. Her kind words kept him going in the Waste. Her kindness kept him from falling away from humanity. And she's alive in his arms.

He draws her closer to him, his lips touching her forehead in an intimate kiss. Elise wraps her arm around his neck and embraces him. There is nothing more that needs to be done.

Or almost.

Gently, so gently, he sets down Elise on the ground, the fire parting between them as he rises. Elise's own fire gentles as he lets her go, but carries on burning in a delicate glow. The light from her feels as gentle and kind as her spirit. Perhaps that's the way it works with elementals. Perhaps that's why his light was also so harsh. Because his own spirit is harsh.

Aidan stands and walks over to Nadia's prone form. The sand burns beneath his feet, but he doesn't feel the need to calm the fires within. He just knows what he can do and what needs to be done now.

Captain Dyrams looks up at him, desperation on the older man's face. There is pain in his eyes, the kind of pain that comes from being helpless, from feeling useless. Aidan smiles at Captain Dyrams. He kneels beside Nadia and takes her body into his arms. She is dead. She is dead. She is dead. There is no life in her body, nothing holding her to the world. Except the flicker of power still within.

Once again, Aidan lets the light take over, lets the bright power from within seep deeply into Nadia's body. Her clothes burn away just as Elise's did. Her skin glows from the contact with the extreme power sinking into her now. Her body awakens little by little, the power coaxing out Nadia's own anchor power and forging it into something so much more than just an anchor's power. But somehow, she doesn't change as Elise did. Somehow her anchor power stands up to the spirit power Aidan pours into her. Somehow, she is made whole and still an anchor. Still herself, resilient as always in the face of terrible things.

Nadia opens her eyes. No longer a clear and vibrant blue, they shine a golden yellow powered from within. She blinks tears away, lines of water falling from the corners of her eyes.

"Aidan? Did you save me?"

Aidan lets out a sob. A desperate sound of relief. "I think I did," he sobs out. "I think somehow I did."

"Elise?"

"She's ok too," he says, crying despite the flame

around him. And it isn't really fire, is it? It is so much more than fire. It is light.

"They need to get back to camp," Captain Dyrams says. "We all do."

From somewhere behind him, their reinforcements arrive along with the medics they so desperately needed a few minutes ago. Aidan carefully picks up Nadia, one arm under her bare legs and the other behind her shoulders. He pulls her close and whispers in her ear before anyone can hear, "I will love you and Elise forever. Remember that."

Then he stands up with Nadia and turns to the oncoming medics. Elise joins him, now wrapped in Captain Dyrams's coat. She lays a hand on Nadia's head and kisses her forehead. The move is so intimate Aidan wants to look away. But he is carrying Nadia and has no choice but to witness their love. A love he feels himself.

"Can you tell me what happened?" the medic asks Aidan. The healer doesn't seem phased by Aidan's form. He behaves as if he has seen spirits up close his whole life.

"She collapsed after enacting the spell," he explained. "Her heart stopped."

The medic probes Nadia's neck, checks her eyes.

"And you revived her," he says. It's not exactly a question the way he says it.

"Yes," Aidan says. "I've never done that before."

The medic nods in understanding. "Can you carry her back to the camp with me?" he asks.

"Yes," Aidan answers. "Can you look over Elise too?" He nods in Elise's direction to indicate her. "She was hit with a spell. I had to revive her, too."

By now Elise's fires have died down and are calm throughout her. She is as far as Aidan can tell a calm fire elemental, which is unusual to say the least.

The medic follows Aidan's direction and looks over Elise. Satisfied that she is not going to keel over at any moment, he instructs them to walk with him back to camp. He takes his own jacket off and covers Nadia with it to provide her with some modesty. Aidan hadn't even paid attention to that.

The medic leads them down the dune back into the city. At one point, Aidan looks over his shoulder to see Captain Dyrams watching them go. No doubt they make an odd trio: a witch, an elemental, and a spirit. But somehow Aidan thinks it's more than that. He thinks it might be what just happened that is prompting Captain Dyrams to stare after them. The unnerving sight of watching someone dead come back to life might have something to do with it.

He follows the medic into the city, his bare feet crunching on the gravel, and they begin to cross Zofria Heights. By the time they walk into the Egrarian encampment, Aidan is tired of the stares. There is nothing he can do about it though. He is too obvious a target of staring. His very skin glows softly now. Not as brightly as when he enacted his power. No, it's more of a gentle glow reminiscent of a sunset.

Once in the camp, they head directly for the infirmary. When they get inside, all three of them are admitted and immediately examined. Aidan carefully lays Nadia down on a cot and takes the one next to her for himself. Elise sits on the edge of the cot on the other side of Nadia.

"I don't even know what to make of what just happened," she says.

Aidan closes his eyes but says, "Neither do I."

"Why didn't I become an elemental too?" Nadia asks.

"I don't know," Aidan admits. "All I know is your anchor power pushed back. And I don't think spirits can give up their power the same way."

Nadia's face becomes pensive, but she gives a spectacular yawn. "I'm going to need to sleep when they're done with their exam."

"Me too," Elise says.

"I don't know if I *can* sleep," Aidan says mostly to himself. Even so, he closes his eyes and lets the sounds of the nurses working soothe him.

When the healers and nurses have checked out all three of them, Elise and Nadia are told to get some rest and take it easy. Aidan is told to do what feels right for him. So, he keeps laying on his cot and staring at the tent ceiling, contemplating his existence such that it is. Before long, the sounds of deep breathing come from both cots next to him and he is sure the girls have drifted off to sleep. He only wishes he could do the same.

Thirty-Eight

When Nadia awakens, every muscle in her body aches. She doesn't know if it's from the spellwork or from dying and being brought back to life. Either way, she doesn't want to peel herself from the cot. She turns her head to the left and to the right only to find both Elise and Aidan are gone. She has so many questions for them, mostly for Aidan, but she guesses they'll have to wait till they get back.

A person clears their throat, and she looks down at the foot of the cot and realizes that Morvath is standing there. She blinks, looking at him. Something isn't right with her vision. There's a vague outline around him, a halo of sorts that might just be an aberration. She blinks a few times, but it doesn't go away.

"Where are Elise and Aidan?" she asks.

Morvath moves to Aidan's cot and sits down. "They left yesterday," he says. "You've been asleep for two days."

Nadia's eyebrows go up. She is suddenly alert, all exhaustion falling away from her. "Two days?"

"The healers assume the spell took it out of you," he explains. "Something about you doing a lifetime's worth of work in only a few minutes."

"Was it that much?"

"You channeled more than any witch on record," he says.

Nadia looks off in the distance, her mind going back to the feeling of all that power running through her. And all the things she saw with that vision. An artifact of that vision might be what's causing the halo around Morvath now. What it means, she doesn't know.

Then she remembers what she saw with that vision. What she saw in the Egrarian encampment from up on the dune. "There's another anchor witch in the ranks," she says. "Someone in the camp is an anchor witch."

Morvath furrows his brow. "How do you know?" he asks.

"I saw it during the spell. I could see all witches and elementals in that spell," she says. "I could see their energy, their power." Nadia shakes her head. "I didn't realize it at the time, but there was a bright spark in the camp. I could see it even from there."

There is a pause. "How could you see it with all the buildings in the way?" he asks.

She thinks for a moment, pulling the memory to the forefront and trying her best to remember the details. "I could see through the buildings," she says. "I could see through everything."

"Can you see that now?"

Nadia shakes her head. "No, but I think my vision isn't normal anymore. There's an odd halo around you," she answers.

Morvath looks confused and tilts his head to the right. He clasps his hands. "What do you see?"

"Just a slight halo," she says. "It's not even as bright as it was when I first woke up though. So maybe it's just my eyes being funny."

Morvath nods slowly. "I'd give it time," he says. "You might be right." He pauses, then he asks, "Do you need anything?"

Nadia shrugs but then thinks of something. "Have you heard from my father?"

"Not recently," he says. "I only heard from him

after you were injured that time a while ago."

"What did he say?"

"He sent me a witchwire asking me to look out for you."

Nadia smiles at him. "Well, you've been doing that," she says. And it's true he has. She wouldn't be alive right now if not for him.

"I'm trying," he says with a wan smile. "I'd say I'm not particularly succeeding though."

Nadia tries to sit up, but Morvath ends up helping her by adjusting her pillows. "When are Elise and Aidan coming back?"

"I'm not sure," he says. "I was just coming to check if you'd woken up. They're helping with the forward operations as far as I know."

Nadia nods and tilts her head, a wave of sad annoyance coming over her. Being stuck in the medical tent again is riding on her nerves. She wants to be out there, seeing that the fruits of their labors succeeded. "Did it work?" she asks Morvath.

He smiles a wicked smile and says, "All too well. You emptied the entire encampment. Only a few strong elementals were able to resist your power, and they were so subdued by the spell that they were easy to capture."

"They got the sand elemental?"

Morvath nods, that crooked smile showing his delight in the outcome. "I'm proud of you. I wish I could have helped."

"I wonder about that," she says. "I wonder if humans can contribute energy to spells, even if they don't have magic." A contemplative look crosses her face.

"A deep philosophical question if ever there was one."

"What happened to Elise's writer power?" she asks suddenly, the thought randomly coming into her mind.

"Conserved," he says. "Most of the witches within the diagram absorbed it. It was that taste of writer power that gave them the ability to trap the elementals."

A wry smile comes over her face. "Leave it to Elise to be completely knocked out and helping with the war effort anyway."

Morvath snorts a laugh. "She does seem the type," he remarks.

"She is. I'm not," Nadia says. "I'm the reluctant fighter."

"There's nothing wrong with that," Morvath says. "You're doing what you think is right."

Nadia makes a rueful face. "I don't know what is

right anymore," she says. "I just know I don't want to kill anyone. Ever."

"Have you killed anyone yet?"

She shakes her head. "I've seen too many people die. Too many close to me."

Morvath purses his lips in response to those words, a look of sad pity on his face. He reaches out and takes Nadia's folded hand.

A bell tolls within her.

A fleeting thought crosses her mind for a moment. Morvath lets go of her hand. The thought vanishes. She furrows her brow, trying to remember what just crossed her mind. It felt important. But the thought is gone. Maybe she'll remember later. Maybe it wasn't important after all.

"Why did you come down here?" Nadia asks him.

"I came because of the war effort," he says. "And you. I have a vested interest in you because of your father."

"Just because of my father?" she asks. Somehow that makes her feel like a commodity and not like a person.

"No," he says. "After meeting you, I found out you were being deployed the following day. When Shetler suggested that I join the party going to Rebluinia, I thought of you immediately. I thought about what you must be going through, and I made my choice."

"You don't have the same duty to do this as I do, as Aidan does," she remarks. Part of her respects him for his choice to come down.

A wry smile crosses his face. "I felt like I had no choice," he says. "It felt like the right thing to do."

"But you're not a witch."

"No, but humans enlist also," he says. "Humans are also called up to duty."

"That's true. But you're the Human Minister of People," she retorts. "You're like the head human."

Morvath laughs. "Not really," he says. "I'm important, sure. But I probably could have taken any other spot in the ministry and been just a regular minister."

Nadia smiles wryly. "Like my father being a regular minister," she says.

"I wouldn't describe him as regular," Morvath says, "but yes."

"He's definitely not regular."

Morvath smiles. "Well, I think I'll leave you to rest and recuperate," he says as he gets up from the cot. "I'm glad you're feeling much better."

"Thank you," she answers, sitting up taller in the bed so as not to feel like such a mouse next to Morvath's extra height.

He smiles down at her and says, "You're welcome. You really need to stop getting injured." The tease makes her smile.

She reaches up her right hand to shake his. He takes it. Her thumb hits his ring.

A bell tolls inside her again.

She blinks once, twice.

This time, the thought comes through clearly. This time she can see.

Morvath is the anchor witch.

Thirty-Nine

Morvath knows he made a mistake right away. Nadia's eyes glow with the power within her. They glow with the ability to see through walls and through spells and through seemingly everything. He knows the moment her thumb hit the ring the spell failed to work on her. He felt the spell flex and fail to work on her.

"You're an anchor," she whispers.

Morvath yanks his hand back, the ring ripping away from her thumb. "No," he whispers.

Her eyes widen. "But you are!"

"No one's supposed to know!" he hisses.

"Did someone attack you?" she asks, her eyes staring up at him plaintively.

It occurs to him he can lie here and cover his tracks nicely. "Yes," he whispers. Morvath takes a seat back on the cot next to her. "No one can know. I'm the Human Minister of People, for goodness's sake."

Nadia just stares at him in what he thinks is disbelief. Her glowing eyes have dimmed to their normal tone, not glowing but with that odd golden color to them now. "What happened?"

"I don't want to talk about it," he says, thinking that alluding to a trauma might help cover his tracks. If she thinks it was some horrible thing in his past, then she might not pursue it. He takes her hand again, her eyes flaring for a moment at the contact. "You can't tell anyone. Not Elise, not Aidan, not even your father."

Her face turns rueful. "I wouldn't tell *him* that," she says. After a long pause with her studying his expression, she finally says, "Alright. I'll protect your secret." For a moment, she doesn't say anything else. But then she asks, "How long have you been an anchor?"

He gives a rueful smile. "A while," he says, not giving specifics. She nods her head, seeming to mull over his situation. "I will lose my post if I'm found out as a witch," he says. "And I'll have a target on me like you have on your back."

She grimaces. "I can understand *that*," she says emphatically.

"Good," he says squeezing her hand before letting it go. "I'll protect you, Nadia. As best I can. My position is a good one to advocate for you," he explains. "I should be the Witch Minister of People, but that position is taken. I can help you from my current position though."

"Can you?" she asks, clearly doubtful. "With people like Colonel Ergamenes in charge, can you really help me?"

"I hope so," he says. "For your sake as well as mine."

A dark look passes over her face. "You mean because they would do to you what they've done to me," she says.

Morvath nods. He needs to sound reasonable here and like he's on her side. "I never felt it was right to force conscription for witches of certain power levels," he says. "I never thought forced conscription was the way to build loyalty to the Kingdom."

The tent flap opens and closes, and Elise and Aidan and John all come through.

"We'll talk about it later," she whispers. "I'll keep your secret," she promises.

Morvath smiles at her kindly and whispers, "Thank

you," before the other three come into earshot.

"You're awake!" Elise says, sitting down on the cot opposite the one Morvath sits on. Aidan and John simply stand at the foot of Nadia's bed.

"Yes," Nadia says. "Morvath was just catching me up on things." She glances over at Morvath but makes no indication that he is a witch.

Morvath stands up and says, "I was just about to leave. I'll let you four catch up." To Nadia he says, "Good to see you getting better. I'll check in on you again later." He flicks one eyebrow up and down at her, indicating the conversation they said they would have later.

"See you later," she says.

"How are you feeling?" Elise asks, taking Nadia's hand as Morvath walks away. He goes through the tent flap and out into the open air of the encampment.

He heads directly to his personal tent. Once inside, he wrings his hands in frustration. Stupid. It was *stupid*. He shouldn't have shaken her hand. Or else he should have been more careful about the spell. He should have known it wouldn't hold up against Nadia's phenomenally powerful anchor abilities. He should have known.

He did know, really. Maybe it was just self-sabotage.

Morvath sits on his cot, feeling rueful about the whole situation. He doesn't trust that she would keep it to herself. Not really. He doesn't think she would hide it well enough or at all from her girlfriend. Once again, he is faced with the same choice he has had twice now: kill her or let things be as they are.

He stares at the tent flap waving in the breeze. Morvath can't believe he's had two opportunities to take her anchor power, and both have gone wrong. The first time he only has himself to blame. Healing her really was the only course of action. But the second time . . . He can't really explain how she was able to defeat him. The killing spell should have worked on her. If not for the shield, it might have.

It comes down to two questions, really. First, does he really *need* her power? She outclasses him for sure, seemingly outclassing all witches. Her power, as Howells noted, is by far more powerful than the rest of the anchors. It's more powerful than Howells's own power that Morvath now carries. Having it for himself would ensure he would never be challenged. Jealousy swells in him. He desires that position above all else.

Second, is the power as strong as it is *because* it belongs to Nadia? Would it still be strong without her influence? This is the question he can't answer until he kills her and takes it from her. This is what he doesn't know and the risk he would have to take. And there's the added risk of his power not actually being weaker than hers. What if he goes to take hers and it just gets conserved? He has no answers to these questions.

The only real answer he has is his need for power. He has it now, has the kind of power only a handful of witches on Terra have. More than that, he has the most powerful weapon of all: knowledge. He knows who many of the anchor witches are. He is probably the only one to know about some of them. He wonders how closely guarded the secret of the Verhillian Princess is. She isn't the crown princess, but she is important, nonetheless.

Morvath rubs his face and lets out an emphatic sigh.

There is nothing he can do, and he knows it. Nadia will no doubt be regarded as a war hero after this, and his chances of getting close enough to kill her are getting slimmer and slimmer. After his last attempt, there had been a guard stationed outside the girls' tent every night. And they had been moved to a more secure area. So, any chance of anonymity is gone at this point. He would have to find a way to get close enough to do anything, and that seemed unlikely.

Morvath reflects on the past month or so since he first got Goliyant's power. He felt powerful, strong, and stable in ways he had never felt before. But his outward demeanor hadn't changed at all to protect his secret. Now that Nadia knows, he wonders what he should do. If she keeps her word and protects his secret, then maybe everything would be alright. He still feels stupid for letting his guard down. He feels stupid for making that mistake.

He stands back up and shakes out his hands. He calls on his power to steady himself again. Immediately, the calming influence of the anchor power flushes out the uncertainty. Steady again, he decides to go get food. Because that will solve all his problems.

Morvath leaves the tent.

Forty

The wind is blowing through the camp and Aidan is unamused by the weather. A sandstorm started blowing through about an hour ago and it shows no signs of letting up. He and John walk through the camp towards the infirmary.

Aidan catches stares everywhere he goes. His gently glowing form does nothing for his modesty, but he can't help that. The life he lived before is long gone, and he will never be that person again. He faces that kind of transition for the second time in a year. Only now, as a spirit of light, he doesn't feel dangerous. He feels safe and connected in ways he never thought possible. He feels like he belongs.

Next to him John is bundled up against the wind and sand. Aidan hadn't thought of it, but he extends his glow around his friend and the wind immediately drops off. John lowers his face cloth and says, "Thanks."

"Sorry I didn't think of it sooner," Aidan says regretfully. Truth be told, he just doesn't think about things like that anymore. Not in the past two days since he changed again.

"It's alright," John says. They walk in silence for a moment before John asks the question weighing on his mind. "Are you going to go back to the Waste again?"

Aidan smiles slightly, the expression bringing more light to his face. He doesn't answer at first. It is a question he has asked himself many times. "I don't think so right now," he says. "I think I might stay around and help Elise adjust and Nadia recover."

"I'm sure Elise will be fine," he answers. "I think she was probably better suited to being a writer witch, but she'll adjust and become even more of a prodigy."

"We can only hope," Aidan says.

Aidan knows right now Elise is on the edge of the camp, learning to burn with precision. A few of the soldiers they work with and Hughes are providing targets for her to aim at so she could be useful in a moment's notice. No, John is right. She's not the one to worry about.

Nadia didn't convert to spirit or elemental when Aidan worked on her injuries. That alone is enough of a mystery. She proved to be a violation of the Replacement Principle, a fact that unnerved those around her. She is as confused about it as everyone else. Only an expert in the Central Dogma might have any idea about why the magic enacted the way it did. And they wouldn't get to see one of them until they got back to Egraria.

That might be later than they all want. With Ecrium winding down for the moment, Rebluinia has the time needed to regroup and gather their forces for the inevitable push back. Aidan believes the changes will help alleviate the pressure put on them collectively to outperform themselves. Nadia showed the strength needed to turn the tide of the war. But it was temporary at best. He wonders if they can do anything permanent or if diplomacy is the name of the game in the end.

His thoughts stop long enough for him to realize they've made it to the infirmary. They duck inside and head down the hospital ward towards Nadia's bed. Nadia isn't there though.

John asks a passing nurse, "What happened to Oswald?"

"She was discharged this morning," the nurse

answers kindly.

"Of course, she was," Aidan says. "Did she say where she was going?"

"I'm not sure," she says. "She asked about Chulyin's practice though."

"She's probably there," John says. To the nurse, he adds, "Thank you."

They walk back up the hospital ward and through the tent flaps into the main corridor of the camp. For a moment, they just pause and wait as soldiers pass by, some of them staring at Aidan. Then Aidan begins to walk in the direction of the edge of camp where Elise presumably still is working. Smoke rises from the area, no doubt a sign she is managing just fine with her new elemental abilities.

"Are you sure we should interrupt while she's training?" John asks.

"I want to help," Aidan says. "I want to give her the help I didn't have."

"I understand," John says. "But she's probably focusing right now."

Aidan stops in his tracks, watching the smoke rise from the area where Elise practices. He tilts his head to the side and thinks about it. John is right and they probably shouldn't be interrupting her. On the other hand, he wants to make sure she really is alright after everything that happened.

He shakes his head. "I want to see Nadia too," he says.

Eventually John relents. He lets go of his reservations and follows Aidan through the somewhat haphazard spread of the tents out to the end of the camp. Here, on the edge of the city park that the camp occupies, he finds the open streets a prime area for elemental practice. Rubble lines the street from previous witch battles that took their toll on the infrastructure.

About three blocks down from the end of the buildings, Aidan can see several people throwing power around practicing. He can't quite see who all they are, but he can see fire produced from a smallish looking person and knows he probably just found Elise. He and John head in their direction, careful to dodge the rubble as they go.

As they draw closer, he can hear a soldier directing Elise's exercises. Before long, he can see Captain Dyrams working with Elise to produce controlled fire.

"Concentrate the line of flame down to a thin rope," he says.

A deep look of concentration on Elise's face shows she's attempting to do just that. The fire in front of her brightens as she concentrates it down to a thin line. The fire turns white hot and blinding as it goes. John shields his eyes against the brightness, but Aidan doesn't feel the need to do so. As they watch, she uses the line of fire to slice through a boulder as if it is a hot knife through butter. Then Elise lets go of the fire and the line of light dissipates.

Aidan is impressed. She clearly has the focus needed to be a fire elemental, but that shouldn't surprise anyone. She is the prodigy after all, and she always has been. The princess, talented mathematician, now-former writer witch turned fire elemental, and much else besides. Plus, she's just a genuinely good person. Nadia is lucky to have her.

"Aidan! John!" Elise exclaims, finally seeing them. She walks over and doesn't hesitate to give Aidan a hug, which only endears her to him more. The warmth of the fire within her tickles his arms around her, a feeling of familiarity mixed in with the light.

"How are you doing?" Aidan asks.

Elise gives a small smile and says modestly, "Alright I think."

"More than alright," Captain Dyrams says. "She's getting the hang of it better than most would."

"Well, that's our Elise for you," John remarks with amusement.

Elise blushes a fierce red.

"I've been working for hours on getting it right," she says. "I can access the fire just fine and control the flames, but Captain Dyrams thought it might be prudent to learn some precise control of the element given the close quarters of fighting in a city."

"Too true," Aidan says. He looks around at the somewhat ragged-looking soldiers and asks, "Can Elise take a break? Give your men time to rest?"

With a glance over his shoulder at the group, Captain Dyrams smiles wryly and says, "Probably a good idea." To Elise he adds, "Rest up. We should resume later."

She nods in agreement and then turns away from Captain Dyrams who begins the cleanup process with the rest of his men. "So, what should we do? I'm starving and could definitely eat."

Aidan shrugs. "I don't really need to eat anymore, but I still like it," he says. "Where's Nadia?" He asks the question realizing she is nowhere to be seen.

Confusion comes over Elise's face. "She's still in the

infirmary, isn't she?" she says. "That's where I left her this morning."

Aidan exchanges a look with John. "She was discharged this morning. The nurse said she asked about your practice area and sounded like she was heading here," Aidan says.

"I haven't seen her," Elise says, looking around as if Nadia would pop out at any moment. He can feel the anxiety beginning to creep up on her and see the edges of flames at her fingertips.

"Stay calm," Aidan says, gesturing to her hands.

"Right," Elise says. She turns to Captain Dyrams. "Captain, did Nadia come around while I was practicing?"

The Captain looks surprised. "I haven't seen Lieutenant Oswald in at least a day," he says. "She hasn't been by this morning. Why? What's going on?"

"The nurse at the infirmary says she was headed here after being discharged."

The Captain looks kindly at Elise's clearly anxious face and says, "She probably went back to your tent to rest some more. I would suggest looking for her there."

Elise nods and lets out a breath. She seems relieved.

"Let's head that way," she says. "It's on the way to

the mess tent and she's probably hungry, too."

The three of them turn and head back towards the camp. After a few blocks, they are among the tents housing the various Rebluinian and Egrarian soldiers. They pass row after row of canvas structures before coming to the more central section Elise and Nadia were moved to after the attack. They come along the line of tents to the one belonging to Elise and Nadia.

Immediately, Aidan knows something is wrong. No guard stands outside the tent and the flap waves in the wind. He can't quite see inside yet, but he can sense something is very wrong.

Elise darts into the tent ahead of them.

She screams.

Aidan and John follow, footsteps behind them suggesting soldiers were following as well.

The cobblestone street below the tent is pooled with blood. There, stained by the offensive color, lies the body of Nadia Oswald.

"She's not breathing!" Elise screams.

Aidan pushes Elise aside. He takes Nadia's body in his arms. She is lifeless. No heartbeat. No breathing. Nothing. Or . . . something?

Does he dare hope he can produce the same result

not just twice, but a third time?

Nadia's spark is waning. The last remnant of her life begins to dim and snuff out completely. He can feel it going. She must have just been killed a few minutes earlier. Or maybe she just held on long enough for them to get there. Maybe.

Fear courses through him. Fear fills Aidan's light-made body, turning the glow to a reddish orange. But fear can be a weapon. Fear can be channeled and changed. And he can do nothing more than try.

He has to try.

He *has* to.

So he does.

He lets his light seep into Nadia's body once again. He fills her lifeless form with the essence of his life, with the glowing power of his spirit self. He fights to keep her spirit in place long enough to draw her back into herself.

But she is dead. Nadia is good and properly dead this time.

Can he really call her back?

Fear tells him no.

Forty-One

It was so easy. Laughably easy, really. So simple and straightforward and Morvath can't believe it finally worked. He finally killed Nadia Oswald. He finally used the knife and slid the blade in her heart properly this time, the killing spell fighting with Nadia's natural defenses and winning.

She let her guard down. She let Morvath in and didn't seem to be threatened by his presence.

"What would I do without you?" she had asked kindly. "Who would have rescued me?"

And he hadn't answered. It was then that he noticed she was holding his hand and there was no barrier between them. So, he pulled her into an embrace, something that seemed natural and safe given their conversation. And he stabbed her as she stood there.

The look of surprise and shock in her face he'll never forget. He'll never forget the way the light went out of her eyes as death took hold of her. She slipped away out of the living world and her power—

Well, that's the problem of course. Her power wouldn't come loose. It wouldn't slip into him and displace Howells's anchor power. It wouldn't respond to him.

Now he stands in his tent with blood all over his hand and shirt and frantically changing his clothes. He can hear the screams from across the compound. It'll only be a matter of a few minutes before someone comes to find him to tell him what has happened. He slips into a new shirt and wipes his hands on the soiled one. Then he uses a bit of fast magic to clean the blood from the shirt and any remaining stains from his hands. He is getting all too good at covering his tracks.

Howells was right about one thing. Nadia's power far outclassed his own. The contact with her at her death made that starkly apparent. She outclassed every witch living. No wonder she was able to turn the tide of a war.

But Howells was also probably right that her power was so strong because it belonged to her. The theory that it wouldn't be as strong in someone else seemed to be accurate. And Morvath was not at all amused. As powerful as he had become, and as practiced as he was able to be in secret, he is still frustrated at not having her power. He would never possess it. And that reality sinks down on him.

In frustration, he shoves his soiled shirt into a bag with his other dirty clothes thankful he could spell the blood out of them. Footsteps alert him to the coming soldier. It is precisely what he expected.

"Sir," the soldier says, "Lieutenant Oswald has been attacked again."

Again, being the key word.

"Is she alive?"

"No, but I think the spirit is trying to heal her," the soldier says.

"Take me to them," Morvath says.

He follows the soldier through the maze of tents to the one surrounded by soldiers and glowing an angry red-orange light. He pushes through the crowd, many of whom draw back when they identify him, and shoves his way into the tent.

Aidan continues working on Nadia, keeping her from tipping all the way over into the land of the dead.

Elise is sobbing to one side, John holding on to her tightly. He surveys the area, knowing he hadn't left a trace but looking anyway.

"What's going on?" a voice asks from the door. It is none other than Colonel Ergamenes.

"*You*," Elise says accusingly. "None of this would have happened if she could have kept her bodyguard with her." The venom in her voice is so uncharacteristic of Elise. Fire burns in her eyes and at her fingertips. John holds her back.

The Colonel takes in what is happening in the tent and looks stunned. "Can you save her?" he asks Aidan.

Aidan looks up. Morvath didn't know spirits could cry. "I'm trying," is all he says.

Perhaps Morvath was successful this time. Perhaps he was able to pull off the murder on the third try. Isn't that what they always say? Third time's the charm?

A healer Morvath recognizes from his many trips to the infirmary pops into the tent followed by a pair of healer-nurses. They snap into action almost immediately. Morvath watches with mixed feelings as they heal the wound on Nadia's chest, the one he inflicted not even an hour earlier. He watches with morbid fascination as the wound closes and her body is unchanged by the healing.

Nadia's body glows still with the angry red-orange light pouring from Aidan. Light so thick and tangible it looks and moves like water. It pours into Nadia's heart, the source of her death. Morvath wonders if even a spirit clearly as powerful as Aidan can save someone who lay dead as long as Nadia has.

He hopes not.

He fears he will.

"Everyone clear out who doesn't need to be here," Colonel Ergamenes says gruffly. The various extra soldiers in the tent back out and clear the space. Not a soldier and therefore not under Ergamenes command, Morvath chooses to ignore the order. He will wait and see if Nadia wakes. He will wait and see if she remembers.

"Artificial respirator," the healer says to one of the nurses. The case she carried in with her she hands over to the healer. He opens it and pulls out a clockwork contraption that Morvath has only seen in hospitals. It partially runs on witchcraft, using the combined technology and magic to keep a heart beating and lungs breathing. They attach the collar to Nadia's neck with Aidan's assistance.

Slowly he can see the rise and fall of Nadia's chest as

the artificial breathing begins to kick in.

"We need to get her to the infirmary. We have a better set up there," the healer says to Aidan. The spirit nods and immediately picks up Nadia, clearly unwilling to break the connection.

Morvath steps back outside and waits as they come out. He follows them through the encampment to the infirmary where he and many others are told to wait outside. Only Elise and John go inside

Is she alive because she is breathing?

Can Aidan pull her spirit back to the land of the living?

Morvath doesn't have an answer to either question. He just fears she will come back. Again. He fears she will remember and know who did this. He fears he did not do a good enough job yet again.

But she is dead. Good and properly dead, he thought. Or else the device would not be needed. Or else Aidan's power would not be needed.

"Can I go in?" he asks a nurse. "I know her father."

The nurse studies him for a moment. His worry must show on his face, worry not for Nadia but for himself, though the nurse couldn't know that. Whatever the nurse saw must have convinced her. She waves him through.

Morvath hurries down the hospital ward and to the cot where Nadia lays and Aidan kneels next to her. Morvath thoughtfully pulls a chair over for Aidan to sit on. He won't let go of her hand.

"Anything?"

"She's there, but barely," Aidan says. "I'm scared to let go of her."

"Will she wake up?" Morvath asks the important question.

The grim look on Aidan's face says it before he does. "I don't know."

Elise sobs next to Morvath, still being comforted by John. She pushes John away. She kneels next to the bed and holds Nadia's free hand. "You better not leave me," she says roughly. "I need you. You can't leave like this."

Morvath feels embarrassed at witnessing such intimate words. He feels like he should leave the space and let them continue to work on Nadia. But he needs to be here.

He pulls another chair over and sits down.

"What are you doing?" Elise asks.

"Waiting," he says. "I can't tell her father what's happened if she's still in limbo."

Elise nods. She is still kneeling on the ground. Morvath pushes his chair towards her and fetches another for himself. John just sits on the adjacent cot on Aidan's side of the bed.

"All we can do is wait," John says.

So, wait is what they will do. Morvath will wait as long as needed to know if she is truly dead or if she wakes up. He would wait as long as it takes and as long as necessary.

And he will kill her again if he has to.

Forty-Two

Elise jolts awake having fallen asleep in her chair. Her hand is still in Nadia's. She looks up and around her. No one has stayed behind. They have all left her and Nadia alone. It is night and the whole hospital ward is deserted, empty even of patients.

"Elise?" Nadia calls out.

"Nadia! You're awake!" Elise whispers.

"You have to find him," Nadia says.

"Who?" Elise asks. "Who did this to you?"

"I don't remember," she says. "But you have to find him. You have to get him. He's killed before. That much I know."

Elise sobs and holds her girlfriend's hand. "Are you going to be ok?"

"No," Nadia whispers. "I'm not."

"But you're ok right now!" The tears just keep coming down Elise's cheeks. She can't control the flow, and she doesn't want to try. She just grips Nadia's hand as if she will at any moment float away.

"No, I'm not," Nadia says sadly. "This isn't real. Not in the way you're used to. I can't come back this time."

"Don't say that," Elise sobs. "Aidan brought you back. Of course you can come back."

"But I won't be the same if I do come back," Nadia says. "I can never be fully human or witch or even elemental or spirit after this. I will be a wraith, a half-living thing caught between two worlds if I come back."

Elise lays her forehead on Nadia's arm and sobs uncontrollably for a few minutes. Then she looks up and says, "But I need you."

Nadia smiles a glowing smile filled with love and pride. She puts her free hand on Elise's cheek. It's only then that Elise realizes the touch of Nadia's skin carries a faint buzz of energy, a power under the surface.

"Are you dead?" Elise asks.

"I died twice already," Nadia answers. She seems unbothered by this fact. "I will have to die a third time before I can fully leave this world."

"Can't you stay longer?"

"What do you feel is right?" Nadia asks. Elise has always been the analytical one. Her mind turns over everything she knows about the way witches and elementals and occasionally spirits die. She thinks about every angle and every truth there. Nadia watches steadily, seeming to trace Elise's thoughts, and nods.

"You can't stay even as a spirit? Like Aidan?" Elise asks.

"Aidan was always meant for that path," Nadia says. "I can see that now." A small smile comes over her face. "It's funny to me now that I can see the lines of destiny around us all. We were all always on this path. We just never knew it."

Elise bows her head again, the sobs taking over one more time. "But how can this be your destiny? To die like this?"

"My life is fading behind me," Nadia says. "I don't remember much from it now, but I remember you and I will always remember you." She strokes Elise's cheek and smiles again. "Where I am going, no mortal can follow. Where I am going, not even spirits can tread."

Elise shakes her head. "Can't I come with you?"

Nadia shakes her head. "No," she says. "But one

day you will follow me, and we'll meet again on the other side."

"Is there anything I can do?" Elise asks.

"Justice," she says. "Bring justice to the one who did this. He is a killer, and he has killed before. I don't know where or when; that's beyond my knowledge." She shakes her head as if in annoyance. "Just find him and bring him to justice."

"I'll kill him for this."

"No," she says. "You may have killed in war, but you are not a murderer. Do not become one because of grief over me."

"Why can't you stay and help me?"

"Because I have another path to walk now. One that will take me places far and abroad in times we don't yet see," Nadia answers. "I don't understand it yet, but I will have to walk that path." For a moment she just stares off into empty space, looking at something other than the shapes before her. Then she smiles again at Elise and says, "But I will visit you. That much I can promise."

"You really promise that?"

"I do."

"I would have stayed with you to the end of our lives." Elise squeezes Nadia's hand and kisses her arm.

"I would have been with you as long as we lived."

"I know," Nadia answers. "I would have to. But there are bigger plans here than just us. Bigger things in motion that we don't yet see. You have a part to play."

Confusion fills Elise's features. "What do you mean?"

"Bring justice to my killer. And then return to the north. Go back and finish what we started," Nadia says.

"Why does that matter now?" Elise asks in frustration. The tears just won't stop flowing.

"It doesn't matter now," Nadia says. "But it will."

Elise nods, crying still. She leans forward and kisses her girlfriend, feeling that tingling sensation on her lips. "Please," she says. "Don't go. I need you."

"You don't need me," Nadia says. "You are strong enough and always have been. You'll be strong enough on your own."

"But I don't want to have to be," she says.

"No one ever does," Nadia says. "But I believe in you, and I love you. You can hang on for me."

Elise kisses Nadia again. She feels the pain of the future she thought she was going to have slipping away in that moment.

"You have to wake up now," Nadia says. "It'll be

time soon."

"No," Elise whispers. "Please, not yet."

But Nadia fades away and the buzz from her touch leaves as well.

Elise blinks again, this time seeing Aidan sitting across from her and John asleep on the cot behind him. Morvath has gone, and so has the nurse and the healer.

"What happened?" Aidan whispers.

"What?" Elise asks.

"You were glowing in your sleep."

She looks down at her hands and looks at Nadia who is still breathing next to her. "She's still here?" she asks.

"Yes," Aidan says. He looks like he's holding back.

"It's ok," she says. "I know you're doing your best."

He makes eye contact with her, the glowing eyes showing more sorrow than all of humanity can hold. "I don't know how long we can keep her here."

Elise doesn't tell him about the vision or her conversation with Nadia. She doesn't say anything. That would be her sadness to bear. That would be a truth she holds in herself. She isn't even sure if it was real or just a dream or the product of her fears. She isn't sure that Nadia wouldn't wake up.

"Do you think we'll find who did this?" Elise asks,

remembering the request Nadia made in the dream. Maybe she felt the need to find the killer, and that's why she dreamt that.

"We better," he says. "After the last attack, I thought they would put more effort in. But they didn't," he says angrily.

"We'll find whoever did this."

"It's just us in this," Aidan says. "We can't trust anyone here."

"No," Elise says. "It could've been anyone in the camp."

He looks down at Nadia, his hands still on her arm. "I just don't understand why people would kill for her power."

"Can't you, though?" she asks. "After what happened to you?"

Aidan shakes his head. "This is so ruthless. You would think they would find another power source to steal," he says.

"It's the anchor power. It's so unique and unusual that it's coveted."

"Don't I know it." The rueful bite to his words colors his light deeper red. "I wish she could have been spared this."

"I feel the same."

"There's nothing we can do now but wait," he says. "And I'll wait as long as needed."

Elise nods. She still holds Nadia's hand, though it carries none of the energy she felt in her dream. Perhaps that dream was real, and Nadia really wouldn't be coming back this time. Perhaps Aidan could keep her here.

Rather than share her fears and tell Aidan what she saw, she sits back in her chair and waits. She waits and hopes with every fiber of her being that the dream was just a dream. They couldn't let go of hope so soon.

She would wait as long as it took for Nadia to wake up.

Epilogue

Kensa Chulyin-Siku sits at her desk, rereading the specs on their creation for what feels like the millionth time. She knows the specs inside and out, as if she wrote all of them herself. She didn't write all of them, but she certainly contributed to a significant portion of them. The rest of the team with her developed every aspect of the ship that now sits at the launch pad waiting to go up into orbit. She's just nervous about what will happen.

The first launch was a success. The test ship came back uncompromised and with an intact atmosphere reading in the tester dummies. By all accounts, the test run was a success. So why is she so nervous about the second launch? Perhaps because the next time this ship goes up it will have people inside? Perhaps.

"Are you still studying that?" a voice says from the

doorway to her office.

Kensa looks up to see Myrmen Pender waiting in the doorway, no doubt coming to fetch her for their weekly luncheon together.

"Always," she answers.

Myrmen steps into the office and smiles at Kensa. She sets down her pencil and shuffles the papers into a stack. Her witchglass still shows the launch and orbital diagram. Myrmen tilts his head and glances over it. He knows the diagram inside and out as he is on the team that wrote the orbital protocols.

"It's a thing of beauty," he remarks.

"What is?" she asks.

"The orbit. The ship," he says whimsically.

Kensa smiles at him. "The whole thing is beautiful," she says. "It's as if we took the work of the past four centuries and turned the dream into reality."

"It is indeed," Myrmen says. "Are you ready for lunch?"

Kensa laughs. "Always thinking with your stomach." But she gets up from her desk and grabs her coat, the day being bitter cold out there.

"Should we go to Ralph's?" Myrmen asks.

"What's the occasion?" Kensa asks. Ralph's is one

of her favorite places, but it's a touch fancy for a simple luncheon.

"Celebrating the conclusion of this phase of our project," Myrmen says. "And that the spring is coming at last."

"You wouldn't know it from today," she mutters. Ralph's might be too fancy for this, but why not? "Let's go to Ralph's then," she says.

They leave the building and head downstairs to the main vestibule of her office building. The hallways on the first floor are lined with classrooms and Kensa can hear the murmur of professors instructing their classes. A young student runs up the vestibule stairs, spots her, and makes a beeline for her. He hands her a gray witchwire envelope, which she accepts.

"Good news?" Myrmen asks.

She opens the envelope and reads the contents twice.

Nadia Oswald has been mortally injured in Rebluinia. Elise writes she was attacked.

— Carlotta Chulyin

A jolt of shock runs through her. Her niece's girlfriend, who was so helpful while she was here working on the ship, mortally wounded? The note is from Elise's mother.

"I think we have to skip lunch," Kensa says.

Myrmen looks over her shoulder at the note and draws breath. "'Mortally wounded'," he says. "But what does that mean?"

"I don't know," Kensa says, "but Carlotta would have had a witchwire from the main office if Elise was involved in any way. I should go see her."

"I'll take you," Myrmen says. "I have my carriage waiting."

Kensa looks gratefully at him and says, "Thank you." She didn't want to have to hail a taxi or call her own carriage. The delay would be unbearable.

"Let's go," Myrmen says, offering his arm to her.

A grim feeling of foreboding comes over her. Even with the steadying influence of Myrmen's arm, she feels shaky at how quickly things can change. This war of Ecrium's touches too many lives. And now it's creeping its long fingers into Umbra. The only escape would be to end this senseless war.

Kensa accepts Myrmen's hand as he helps her into his steam carriage. For a moment, he speaks to the driver. Then he climbs in next to her and his driver heads off in the direction of the Chulyin family home.

She isn't sure what awaits them or what would

happen next. But she is sure none of it is good. Whether Nadia is dead or dying, it isn't good.

The carriage speeds down the streets of Arcta.

Appendix

The Three Laws

<u>The Root Law</u>: Energy is the root of Magic. Magic is the root of Power.

<u>The Law of the Human Constant</u>: All species have Energy. Only humans do not have Magic.

<u>The Conservation Law</u>: All magic is conserved.

Consequences of the Laws

<u>The Witch's Constant</u>: Magic converts energy to power through the Witch's Constant.

<u>The Vacancy Principle</u>: If a witch is in contact with a human at death, the witch's magic will be conserved by the human. If no human is present, the magic will move to the witch population as a whole and be shared amongst them.

<u>The Replacement Principle</u>: An elemental's power is stronger overall than a witch's and thus will replace a witch's if released from an elemental, i.e., if an elemental dies in contact with a witch. The witch's power will also be conserved.

<u>The Rarity Conundrum</u>: The rarer a witch's power, the stronger it is and the higher in the power hierarchy it is.

Power Hierarchy

Anchor

Writer

Caster

Seer

Days of the Week

Solday

Anday

Tisday

Wodenday

Sammday

Vriday

Epday

Planet Names

	On Terra	On Yddril
Sun	Usil	Usil
1	Turms	Taira-t-il
2	Sethlans	Deyjil
3	Turan	Yddril
4	Terra	Anata-il
5	Uni	Zasil
6	Tinia	Imma-il
7	Nethuns	Oye-t-il
8/9	Aplu/Aritimi	Iedil/Avinil
10	Catha	Eiji-t-il
11	Laran	Iffta-il

ABOUT THE AUTHOR

Olivia "Lollie" Jones Black has been writing in some form or other since she was eleven. A background in science provides inspiration for her work. Her writing blends both science fiction and fantasy, epic and mundane, and leans on her science education to incorporate science fact into science fiction.

A cat who thinks she owns the computer occasionally helps with the writing. She lives on the east coast.

www.ingramcontent.com/pod-product-compliance
Lightning Source LLC
Chambersburg PA
CBHW021229190726
48289CB00005B/1231